The Rector's Daughter
Roberta Grieve

Print ISBNs
Amazon print9780228637547
Ingram Spark 9780228637554
Barnes & Noble 9780228637561
BWL Print 9780228637578

BWL Publishing Inc.

Books we love to write ...
Authors around the world.

http://bwlpublishing.ca

Table of Contents

Chapter 1

May 1940

A breeze stirred the long grass in the churchyard and Rosemary shivered, pleased she'd worn a cardigan over her blue summer dress. She pulled it closer around her and finished arranging the tulips in the vase on her mother's grave. Lois Turner's favourite - pale pink streaked with creamy white. Pleased that they had at last come into bloom after the late spring, Rosemary stood and brushed her skirt down, paused for a moment enjoying the sunshine. A blackbird began to sing and she thought that on a day like this it was hard to imagine that they were at war.

Until the retreat from Dunkirk a few weeks ago the war had made little impact on the quiet Norfolk village apart from the influx of evacuees from London in September last year. Most of them had gone back when the expected bombing didn't happen but a few of the children were still here.

Now, everyone listened avidly to the nightly news, dreading the threatened German invasion. Rosemary couldn't help worrying about her brother. Michael was serving with the Royal Norfolk Regiment and his unit had been caught up in the retreat to the French coast. But there had been no word. Had he been captured? She refused to contemplate his death.

She took one last glance at the grave and sighed. She should get home and start preparing lunch. Father would have finished writing his sermon and he liked his meals on time. But she lingered for a while, reluctant to return to the Rectory. The home she had loved was now a place of gloom in the shadow of her father's grief. She still missed her mother - even after three years she still sometimes thought she could smell Lois's rose perfume. But her father had never seemed to come to terms with the loss of his wife. Although Rosemary felt for him, she sometimes got impatient when he shut himself away in his study and then she would feel guilty. After all, he still cared for his parishioners, was a conscientious pastor to his flock, but he wasn't the same man he had been before her mother's illness.

Rosemary loved him, wished she could somehow make up for the gap his wife had left in both their lives. But beneath it all was a little core of resentment which she tried hard to suppress. She and her school friend Anne had been all set to go to university when her mother fell ill. Then the war started and Anne had joined the WAAFs but Rosemary had felt duty-bound to stay behind. Now her life was bound up with her father's parish work and the village community.

She sighed and, with one last glance at the grave, and its words, 'Beloved wife and mother', she turned away, gasping as a shadow fell over her.

'So sorry, I didn't mean to startle you.' The young man backed away, stumbling a little.

'Michael?' She stammered, then gave a small laugh. 'Sorry. I thought you were...'

His Royal Norfolk Regiment uniform was the same, even to the pips of a second lieutenant on his shoulder. But the stranger was taller than her brother with warm brown eyes and his hair was much darker, stray curls escaping from beneath his cap, despite the severe army haircut. He was also leaning heavily on a walking stick.

The soldier gave an embarrassed grin and scuffed his toe on the ground. 'I'm sorry I wasn't the person you were expecting.'

Rosemary coloured and put her hand to her face. 'No, no. Just for a moment I thought it was... Just hoping...'

He smiled. 'You must be Miss Turner – Rosemary,' he said. 'I recognised you from the photo Michael showed me.'

She gasped. 'You knew my brother?' Do you have news?'

'I'm sorry. I was hoping you might have heard.'

She sighed. 'We've heard nothing since Dunkirk. It was a shock seeing you standing there. The uniform...'

'I was going to say sorry again but it seems we've been apologising since I got here. Can we start again?'

Rosemary nodded.

'I can understand seeing me must have been a shock. My name's Simon Spencer – Lieutenant. I'm on sick leave.' He held out his hand and she shook it.

'You knew my brother well?'

'We were good friends.' He paused and sighed. 'He saved my life.'

'What happened?'

'I was wounded - Dunkirk.' He gestured to his leg with the stick. 'I was standing in water up to my waist. I slipped and fell and he grabbed me, helped me into one of the boats.'

'So, did he get in the boat too?' she interrupted, knowing in her heart what the answer would be.

Simon shook his head. 'He saw another man struggling and went to help him. When I turned back there was no sign of him. I hoped he'd managed to get on board but I couldn't find out. I was in the hospital for a long time. I'm still on sick leave so I came here hoping he'd made it home too.'

'Thank you for telling me. It's been hard, not knowing.' A tear escaped and rolled down her cheek. 'I must go and tell my father. He'll want to thank you. He's almost given up hope – but maybe...'

'I hope you get some definite news soon. It must be so hard for you and your father.' What else could he say? He shuffled his feet and almost turned away, then said. 'I was planning to call at the Rectory to see if you had news of Michael. I saw you laying the flowers and I didn't want to disturb you, so I waited.' He glanced back at the church. 'It's a beautiful old building — fifteenth century?'

Rosemary welcomed the change of subject. 'Mostly fourteenth, but some parts are even older. I love it.'

'I envy you - living in such a beautiful village,' he said.

She didn't reply, remembering how she had longed to get away, to travel, to see something of life. Then her mother had become ill and she'd stayed to look after her and Father.

He hesitated. 'Could you let me know if you hear anything of Michael? I know how lucky I was to get home.'

She glanced at the walking stick. Yes, he was lucky despite his injury. Suddenly, she didn't want to talk to him anymore. He was home, out of the war. But who knew what had happened to Michael? It was good to hear that he had been brave, helping his comrades — so like him - but it seemed she would have to accept that her brother was gone. Still, she wouldn't give up hope yet, would continue to pray for him. He *could* still be alive, a prisoner somewhere.

'I'm sorry, I must get home. Father's waiting,' she said abruptly.

'Could I call on him?' Simon asked tentatively.

'I'm afraid he isn't too well at the moment. He can't cope with visitors.' She hoped she didn't sound too unwelcoming. 'I'll tell him we met and he'll be grateful that you came to tell us about my brother.'

He shuffled his feet, gripped his stick and started to turn away. 'I'm so pleased I met you. I thought perhaps you might have already joined one of the women's forces.'

'I had hoped to join the WAAFs with one of my school friends but I was needed here.'

Simon glanced at the grave. 'I understand. I hated leaving my father on his own but felt I had to join up.' He sighed. 'He wanted me to go. Said he'd have plenty to keep him busy with his patients – he's a doctor in Bury St Edmunds.' He held out his hand and shook hers. 'Well, it was nice meeting you and visiting your lovely church. I'm staying at the *Four Bells* so perhaps we'll meet again.'

She summoned a smile. 'Perhaps.' She hurried away, skirting the graves and hopping over the low wall that separated her garden from the graveyard. They really should put a gate in, she thought, but ever since she'd been little, she had used this short cut to the church. As she neared the house, she spotted her father standing in the porch. As usual he seemed lost in thought and he started when she called out to him.

'Have you finished your sermon, Father? Lunch won't be long. I got waylaid in the churchyard.'

'I saw you talking to that young man,' Seth Turner said. 'I didn't recognise him.' As Rector for many years, he knew everyone in Oakleigh St James, had baptised many of those who were now old enough for military service.

'He's just visiting. Looking round the church, he said.' She didn't tell him they'd spoken about Michael. It would only upset him. Perhaps if he came back, she would introduce him to her father. He'd said he might and she hoped that he would, had enjoyed talking to him, liked his appreciation of the church she loved. And most of all she loved that he had spoken so warmly of her brother.

Father was looking better today but she hadn't wanted to raise his hopes and had thought it best not to mention that Lt Spencer had been a friend of Michael. If only he'd had been able to tell them something positive. It was comforting to know her brother had been such a hero though.

She followed her father into the house and hurried along the stone-flagged passageway towards the kitchen thinking that perhaps she should have told him about Michael's bravery. Of course, she would have spoken if Lt Spencer had had definite news but what was the point of getting Father's hopes up?

Seth went into his study. 'Just need to tidy up my notes. call me when lunch is ready.'

Thank goodness she didn't have to cook, Rosemary thought, as she laid a white cloth over the end of the scrubbed kitchen table and set out plates and cutlery. She had already washed and drained the lettuce and she added chopped celery and slices of a newly-ripened tomato from the greenhouse. Thick slices of ham and hard-boiled eggs completed the meal.

How lucky they were to have so much, she reflected, now that rationing was beginning to make itself felt.

Father came into the kitchen and stared down at the table, but sat down without comment. It had taken him some time to get used to eating in the kitchen but now that Mrs Norton, their former housekeeper, only came in to help on two days a week, and their one maid had left to join the ATS, it was more practical.

After Father had said Grace, Rosemary said, 'When I saw that soldier I thought at first it was Michael. It gave me quite a jolt.'

She changed her mind about telling him what Lt. Spencer had told her but, before she could say more, her father said, 'Oh, Rosie, dear, I think it's time you accepted that Michael will not be coming home. We would have heard by now.' He put down his knife and fork and murmured, 'It's God's will.' Then he pushed back his chair and left the room without giving her a chance to reply.

Rosemary was sorry she'd upset him. If only he would talk to her. She longed to share memories of her brother, to encourage her father to hold on to hope. But it seemed easier for Seth to keep it all inside.

She managed to finish her own meal and set about clearing the table and washing the dishes. Keeping busy helped.

Her thoughts strayed to Lt. Spencer - Simon. It was good of him to come all this way to tell her about Michael. She wished she hadn't dismissed him so abruptly. Perhaps she should have brought him to meet her father. It might have helped him to talk with someone who had known her brother. Too late now, she thought. She would probably never see him again, despite his saying he hoped they would meet again. She hoped his wound would heal – but not too soon. They would send him back into the fray once he was fit.

She swallowed a lump in her throat. Bloody war! She glanced around, realizing she'd said the words out loud. Father would reprimand her in his gentle way if he'd heard.

She bit back a smile. Poor Father. He would be so shocked if he realized how often she had such thoughts. Of course, she understood that the tyrant across the water had to be stopped but...

She put the crockery away and glanced at the clock. Time she was off to the Manor and the WVS meeting. Mrs Pargeter would be getting impatient.

****

Simon packed his kitbag and left the village pub, wishing he could stay longer. He would love to have spent more time in this pretty little village, maybe visit the church again. He looked up the village street past the church to the Rectory just beyond and had to admit it was the thought of seeing Rosemary Turner again that was uppermost in his mind.

He stood in the spring sunshine by the bus stop outside the *Four Bells* watching the comings and goings of the villagers. Several women carrying shopping baskets entered and left the village shop and across the road he could hear the ring of hammer on iron from blacksmith's forge and the baaing of sheep in a distant field. Such a peaceful scene. The war seemed far away and once he got the all clear from the Army hospital in Colchester, he would be back in the thick of it. But he made up his mind that before that he would find time to return to Oakleigh and see Rosemary again. He could not get her out of his head. His breath had caught when he spotted her kneeling by her mother's grave. He recognised her from the photo Michael had shown him but a monochrome snap had not prepared him for her beauty, the gleam of the sunlight on her fair hair, her eyes blue as a summer sky, matching the cotton dress she wore. He would carry that picture in his heart forever.

He sighed and picked up his kitbag as the bus appeared round the corner. He gazed out of the window as he passed the Rectory, hoping in vain for a glimpse of the girl he had fallen for on such meagre acquaintance.

***

The Rector stood in the church porch shaking hands and saying farewell to the congregation. Rosemary stood beside him until her friend Jenny Blackwell, the local school teacher, appeared, holding the hand of six-year-old Maisie, one of the evacuees from London. Three other children trailed behind her. Brian, eager to get outside in the sunshine, tried to push past.

Jenny grabbed his sleeve. 'Wait, Brian. There's plenty of time.'

Rosemary bent down to him and said, 'Where are you off to in such a hurry then?'

The boy scowled at her. 'Want go and play with me mates.'

A few of the London boys refused to attend church and spent Sunday mornings kicking a ball around on the village green. Brian would have been one of them if he could have got away with it.

He and his sister Maisie, along with two other evacuees, were billeted at the Manor with Colonel

Pargeter and his wife. Mrs Pargeter was a stickler for time-keeping and good manners and was doing her best to instill her standards into the children in her care.

Rosemary smiled. 'You can go in a minute but first, you must ask Mrs Pargeter for permission and ask her what time you have to be back for dinner.'

Brian scuffed the toe of his shoe against the step but he didn't protest. 'All right, miss,' he said.

'Good lad.'

The congregation had now dispersed and at last Mrs Pargeter bustled down the aisle, carrying a bunch of leaflets. 'Come along children,' she called, rounding them up like a collie with a flock of sheep.

Brian didn't move. The older woman tutted impatiently but relented. 'I suppose you want to play football with your friends.'

Brian nodded.

'Very well, Half an hour. And don't be late back.' She pointed to the church clock. 'You can tell the time, can't you.'

'Of course I can,' he scoffed.

'No excuse for lateness then,' she snapped and, gathering the other children around her, she set off down the path and through the lychgate. Maisie reluctantly let go of Jenny's hand and trailed behind them.

'I wish I could have taken one of them in,' Jenny said. 'I asked if I could have Maisie but they didn't want to split up brother and sister. Besides, my landlady doesn't really have room, although I'm sure we could have squeezed one of the evacuees in.'

Jenny's family lived in Somerset and she lodged with the widowed Mrs Kent in a tiny cottage on the edge of the village.

'Father didn't want children in the house, although we've plenty of room,' Rosemary said. 'He said it would make too much work for me.' She tutted. 'Ridiculous. I would love to have had some children to look after.'

'I think some of those whose parents took them home will send them back if the threatened bombing starts,' Jenny said.

'Or the invasion. We have to be prepared even here in the country.'

'Do you think they will invade?' Jenny asked with a shudder.

'Everyone thinks it's likely. Now we have the Home Guard to defend us but I can't see that they'll be much good.' Rosemary smiled wryly, picturing old Amos, the sexton, with his broomstick 'rifle' and those farm boys who hadn't been called up. Colonel Pargeter was in his element barking orders at them and organising training sessions in the woods around the village.

'We must pray it doesn't happen,' she said. 'But if they send us more evacuees, I'm going to insist we take one of them in. I will impress on Father it's his Christian duty.'

The friends parted and Rosemary took her usual short cut through the churchyard.

June 1940

Rosemary pushed open the west door and stepped down into the cool dimness of the church. She paused and glanced around with her usual feeling of peace and contentment, then entered the vestry. She laid the armful of flowers and greenery from the Rectory garden on the table just inside the door and went to the cupboard for a couple of vases.

She filled them at the sink in the corner of the room and set about arranging the few late tulips, love in the mist, early roses and tall alliums. Some stems of bracken, just unfurling, completed the arrangements. She stepped back to admire them, regretting that there were not more blooms to fill the vases. Usually, the church was filled with flowers but the Rectory garden, like most in the village had been turned over to vegetables. If she had more time, she would have gone into the woods and fields and gathered wild flowers but these would have to do.

She picked up the vases and stepped out into the nave, gasping as she saw a figure standing in the chancel beyond the rood screen. She hadn't heard anyone come in.

She recognised him straight away. It was the young man she had encountered recently in the churchyard – Lt Spencer. She placed one vase on the table by the entrance and walked down the aisle towards the altar.

'Good morning, Lt. Spencer,' she said as she approached.

Startled, he turned towards her. 'Oh, it's you, Miss Turner. I hoped I'd see you again. I went home to see my father but decided to come over in the bus before going on to the military hospital in Colchester.' He gestured to the stick leaning up against the pew.

'I hope they sign you off fit,' Rosemary replied, although privately she hated the thought of him going back to fight.

'I'm managing much better.' He paused, then said, 'I don't suppose you've had any news about your brother?'

She shook her head. 'I thought if he'd been taken prisoner we would have heard by now.'

Simon frowned. 'Don't give up hope yet. It was chaos over there.' He glanced at the vase in her hand. 'Beautiful flowers.'

She stepped up to the altar and put the vase on the end, tweaking some of the blooms to make the most of the budding roses.

'I thought you must have already left,' she said.

'I should really be on my way but I wanted to have another look at the church.' He pointed to the wall on the north aisle. 'This is so unusual. I haven't seen anything like it before.'

'Oh, the *Doom* – that's what it's called. fifteenth century – very rare.' She stepped closer and peered at the wall painting, part of it obscured by streaks of damp where the roof had leaked. She hadn't really taken much notice of it lately. Like the carved rood screen and stained-glass windows, the painting had been part of her life since she was a child. She'd been frightened of the images then. Now, it was just part of the familiar landscape of the church.

'Such a shame it's so damaged,' Lt. Spencer said. 'I would like to have seen it complete.'

'It's not just the damp from the leak in the roof. The whole thing was white-washed over during Puritan times, then the Victorians tried to clean it off to reveal the painting – not very successfully.'

'It would have been better to keep it painted over to preserve it until a proper restorer could have a go at it,' Lt Spencer said.

'You're probably right but the church couldn't afford it. We're lucky to have so much left.' She pointed. '*Doom* means Judgement. That section shows the weighing of souls – I think it was meant as a lesson to the parishioners in those days.' She pointed out the figure in a red cloak, holding a scale with two rather ugly impish figures sitting in the pan. 'That's St Michael.'

The left side of the panel was almost obliterated by the water damage, just faded streaks of colour remaining. At the top, barely visible streaks of a painted rainbow stretched above the faded figure of Christ.

'Are you interested in ecclesiastical art, Lt Spencer?' Rosemary asked.

'Please call me Simon.' He nodded. 'I studied it at university. It's such a treat for me to see something like this.' He rummaged in his pocket and pulled out a small sketchpad and pencil. 'Do you mind if I draw this?'

'Of course not. But wouldn't a photograph be better? I could go and fetch my camera. I'm sure I have some film left."

'Thank you but a sketch can show more detail – the light's not good in here.'

He perched on the edge of a pew and, holding the pad on his knee, sketched with lightning strokes.

Rosemary was impressed. She watched quietly, unwilling to break his concentration. When he had finished, she said, 'My father's feeling better today. Would you like to meet him? He can tell you so much more about the wall painting.'

He hesitated. 'If you're sure, Miss Turner.'

'It's Rosemary,' she said. 'Father will be delighted. He loves talking about the church and its history.' She hoped she wasn't being too optimistic and that Father was in a mood to welcome a guest.

'All right then.' He picked up his walking stick, swung his kitbag over his shoulder and followed her out of the church.

As she led him along the path through the churchyard, she said, 'I didn't tell Father you knew Michael. He gets so upset at any mention of my brother.'

'Don't you think I should tell him? Surely, he would like to know how brave he was.'

'Perhaps. Let's wait and see how he is.'

'All right. If you're sure.'

They reached the low wall leading into the Rectory garden and Rosemary paused. 'Sorry. I wasn't thinking. I always come this way.'

He grinned at her, putting one hand on the mossy wall, and throwing his stick and kitbag over onto the grass, vaulted across, stumbling a little as he landed.

Rosemary gasped. 'Are you all right?'

'Fine. The doc said I should get more exercise.' He laughed, picked up stick and bag and said, 'Perhaps you could give me your arm though.'

She took his arm and led him into the stone-flagged hallway. 'Just wait here a moment. Father's in his study. I'll tell him we have a visitor.'

'Don't let me disturb him,' Simon protested.

Just then a door opened and the Rector appeared. 'Ah, I thought I heard voices.' He peered over his glasses.

'This is Lt. Spencer who I met in the church the other day. He tells me he was in the same unit as Michael.' Rosemary said, tensing for his reaction.

'You knew my son?' the Rector's eyes lit up, then his face fell. 'He died you know – at Dunkirk.' The Rev Turner frowned.

Rosemary decided to change the subject. Father had given up hope but she still clung on.

'Simon's very interested in our church. I thought he'd like to see that old book with the picture of the *Doom*.'

'You're very welcome. Come on in.' The change of subject seemed to cheer him and he ushered Simon into the study. He turned to Rosemary. 'Can we rustle up some lunch for our guest?'

'Of course.' She turned to Simon. 'You will stay, won't you?'

'If it's not too much trouble,' he said.

'Not at all.' Her father led the visitor into the study and before she could say any more, he closed the door. She sighed. Banished to the kitchen as usual, she thought, and stomped down the passageway.

It would have to be salad again but there was no ham left. They had been lucky to get the last few slices the village shop had. Thank goodness they had the eggs from their own hens.

The table was laid and the lunch prepared and Rosemary sighed with impatience. Father was usually so strict about meal times. Still, she shouldn't really mind. It was so seldom that he had anyone interesting to talk to these days and talking about his favourite subject would help to take his mind off his grief.

She went along to the study, knocked tentatively on the door and then opened it. 'Lunch is ready,' she said.

Simon leapt up from his chair and apologised. 'I got so interested in the Rector's story. Sorry to have kept you waiting.'

Seth put down the book he was holding with seeming reluctance. 'It is good to see a young person taking an interest. Never mind, we can continue after lunch.'

Seated at the kitchen table, Simon tucked into the salad, hard boiled eggs and fresh crusty bread. 'This is good. I must make the most of it. I'll be back on army rations before long.'

'So soon?' Rosemary glanced at the walking stick leaning against the chair.

Simon grinned. 'Won't need that much longer. I'm due at Colchester army hospital next week. I'm hoping they'll sign me off fit for duty.'

The Rector laid down his fork. 'You young men! All so eager to go off and fight. My son...' His voice faded.

Simon said, 'It's our duty. I'm sure Michael felt the same.' He hesitated, then went on. 'You son was very brave. He saved my life.' He went on to tell the Rector what had happened.

Seth Turner smiled. 'That sounds like Michael. He would always help anyone in trouble.'

Simon leaned forward. 'Please, sir, don't give up hope. I'm sure he must be a prisoner. So many of my men were captured.'

The Rector nodded. 'Perhaps. I'll keep on praying. For you too, young man.'

Rosemary forced a smile, pleased that her father hadn't rejected Simon's optimistic words. But the thought of him going back to fight appalled her. Hadn't he done enough already?

They finished eating and Seth tried to persuade Simon to return to the study so that they could continue their discussion. But he declined, saying that he had to get the bus back to Bury St Edmunds and then travel on to Colchester. 'I need to get there today,' he said.

When he'd gone, Rosemary tried to stifle her disappointment. It had been so good to talk to someone interested in art and history. She must put him out of her mind though. Soon, he would be back to duty and she had no idea where he would be sent. Besides, she would probably never see or hear from him again, she thought. But she could not get his warm brown eyes and that endearing lock of blue-black hair that flopped over his forehead when he took his cap off, out of her head.

Chapter 2

July 1940

Rosemary was in the kitchen washing up the breakfast things. She couldn't believe how many dishes there were from just two people. She sighed. If she was on her own it would be one mug – not a cup and saucer – one cereal bowl. But Father had always insisted things were done properly – cups and saucers, side plates, milk in a jug. It all made extra work and with the fuel shortages there was never enough hot water.

She shouldn't complain, she knew, but she did get a bit fed up sometimes. It wasn't Father's fault. There had always been someone to look after him. Now that the only help they had was Mrs Norton, who only came in a couple of times a week, most of the housekeeping fell to her. This was one of those times when she wished she had insisted on following Anne into the WAAFs like most of her school friends.

The rattle of the letter box raised her spirits a little and she hastily dried her hands and rushed into the hall. There was always the chance of news. She hadn't given up hope of hearing from Michael. Her father still prayed for his safety but he seemed to have fallen into depression again.

There were two envelopes on the mat and she scooped them up, her heart sinking as she realised there was no official war office letter. They hadn't received the dreaded telegram after Dunkirk and continued to hope he was a prisoner but as Father had said, surely, they would have heard something by now. It had been weeks.

She glanced at the letters in her hand. Church stuff she guessed from the typed address on the top one. Father was out visiting parishioners but she would leave them on his desk. As she put them down, she glanced at the second envelope and her heart beat a little faster. It was so unusual for her to receive personal mail that she hadn't really looked at it. The writing was unfamiliar and the postmark said Bury St Edmunds. It could only be from the soldier she had met in the churchyard. It had been three weeks since their encounter and she had firmly told herself that she was unlikely to see Lt. Spencer ever again. Nevertheless, she had often thought of him and wished him well. She hoped he had been passed fit after his hospital appointment in Colchester although she hated the thought of him being returned to his unit. How could they send him back to fight after what he'd been through?

She put the letter for her father on the desk and returned to the kitchen, sitting at the table to read her letter. As she slit the envelope, she suddenly realised that if it had been sent from his home in Bury St Edmunds, he must still be on sick leave.

'Dear Miss Turner

Forgive me for not writing sooner to thank you for the excellent lunch and the interesting talk with you and your father. I have been taken up with visits to the hospital but I'm pleased to say everything is fine now. My father doesn't think so – being a doctor he thinks he knows best. However, I have been signed off fit for duty so by the time you receive this, I will have returned to my unit.

I really enjoyed meeting you and the Reverend Turner and visiting your beautiful and interesting little church. I hope to visit Oakleigh St James again in more peaceful times.

Yours sincerely
Simon Spencer.'

Rosemary folded the letter and put it back in its envelope, tucked it behind the clock on the mantelpiece. She would show it to Father when he came in for his lunch. It would have been more polite, she thought, if he had written to her father thanking him for showing him the book about the '*Doom*'. But he had written to her and the thought pleased her.

She would write back and say how happy she was that he was fit once more. If he had already gone back to his unit, surely his father would send it on. Not that it mattered, she told herself. She was only being polite. But why did she keep thinking of him? They'd only met twice, and she didn't really know him, apart from his interest in the church and its history. But he'd spoken warmly of her brother and she was grateful for that.

After lunch she washed up – again – and sat down to write to Simon. She didn't say that she hoped he had not yet gone back to his unit. It seemed too personal and she guessed also, that like most young men, he couldn't wait to get back to fighting the enemy.

She just said that she was pleased he had recovered from his injuries and wished him well in the future. She ended by saying that he would be welcome at the Rectory if he ever returned to Oakleigh St James. '*My father would love to meet you again as he so enjoyed talking to someone who shared his enthusiasm for the wall painting and our lovely church's architecture,*' she concluded.

She sealed and addressed the envelope, then put on her jacket and hat. She glanced at her watch. Just time to catch the post and then she would walk to the school and meet Jenny.

It was a lovely warm day and she enjoyed the short walk, stopping to chat to the verger, who was scything the long grass between the graves.

'Lovely day, Amos,' she said.

'We need some rain.' The old man frowned. 'Still, hope it keeps dry this evening. We've got a meeting of the Home Guard here. Colonel Pargeter wants to get more of the villagers involved. The farm boys aren't too keen – busy with hay-making.'

'We all have to do our bit,' Rosemary said.'

Amos stretched and rubbed his back, looking up at the church tower. 'Gotta get up there soon – them old pigeons are making a right mess of my bells.'

'I expect you miss your bell-ringing.'

'I rightly do. I was just getting some of the youngsters learning but they couldn't wait to get off to war.'

Rosemary sighed. Michael had been one of the village boys who were keen to learn campanology. She said goodbye to the verger and continued her walk through the churchyard, delighting in the wild flowers which grew in the older parts and listening with pleasure to the liquid notes of a blackbird perched on the church tower.

After two really bad winters and a late spring Rosemary dared to hope that at last, they were due a good summer. She reached the school gate just as the bell rang and the children streamed out laughing and shouting. She stood aside, smiling as they ran past, anxious to get home for their tea. Many of them had a long walk along the country lanes to the farms where they lived. Brian, the London evacuee, was the first out.

'Hello, Brian,' she said.

He barely stopped and, waving a hand, shouted, 'Hello, Miss Turner,' before rushing out of the gate and across the road to the village pond, where he was soon joined by several of the village boys.

She turned back to see Jenny coming out of the door marked 'Girls'. She was holding Maisie's hand and she shrugged when she saw Rosemary waiting.

'Looks like I'll be taking this one home,' she said.

'I thought Brian was supposed to look after her,' Rosemary said.

'He is but he rushed off before I could catch him.' Jenny grimaced. She glanced down at the little girl beside her. 'Can't let her walk back to the Manor on her own, although she should be safe enough but she hasn't got used to being in the country. She's scared of everything – cows, tractors...'

'Well, it's still strange for her. I guess being here after London is like being on another planet.' She pointed across the road. 'Anyway, Brian's over there by the pond.' She bent down to Maisie. 'Let's go and find your brother.'

Each holding a hand, they led Maisie over the road. The boys were leaning dangerously over the water peering down and exclaiming.

Brian looked up and saw them. 'Look, Miss. Frogs. They were still tadpoles last week, then they got legs and now – just look at them.'

'I should be cross with you, lad – running off and leaving your sister,' Jenny said with a mock frown.

'Sorry, Miss. We couldn't wait to see the frogs.' He glanced at Maisie who was still clinging on to Rosemary's hand. 'Come and have a look, Mais.'

She shook her head and backed away.

Rosemary encouraged her forward. 'They won't hurt you, love. It's one of nature's miracles.'

Brian scooped up one of the small frogs and held it towards his sister.

'Gently, Brian. Let her look but don't put it too close.' Jenny held her hand out and Brian put it into her palm. She turned to Maisie. 'See it's quite harmless.'

Rosemary grinned at her friend. She knew Jenny didn't really like slimy creatures and she admired her bravery. She turned to Brian. 'Get one for me, too,' she said.

They sat on the grass with Maisie between them and Jenny explained the life cycle to her. Eventually, the little girl was persuaded to stroke the creature with a tentative finger.

'Well done. Now, we'd better put them back in the water,' she said.

'There, Maisie. Nothing to be afraid of,' Jenny said as they watched the frogs swimming away from them. She turned to Rosemary with a shrug. 'The things we have to do,' she said.

'You could stick to the classroom like most teachers do.'

'I know, but I remember what it was like when I came to Oakleigh. I had a lot to learn - no knowledge of the countryside at all. I understand what it's like for these kiddies – everything so strange.'

'Brian seems to have taken to country life anyway.' Rosemary glanced at her watch. 'I must be getting home.'

'I'll make sure the children get back to the Manor all right,' Jenny said.

As she said goodbye, Rosemary looked up at the blue summer sky, gasping as she spotted several black spots on the horizon. Planes. Ours or theirs? She turned to Jenny. 'Quickly, better get the children home.'

Jenny grabbed Maisie's hand and called to Brian who was gazing up into the sky.

'Hurricanes,' he shouted with a grin, waving. 'It's all right.' His grin faltered as more planes appeared firing guns.

'Those are Germans,' Rosemary said as puffs of smoke appeared. Suddenly the sky was dark with aircraft wheeling and diving. Brian still stood transfixed, punching the air as if to encourage the fighters. Rosemary grabbed his hand and dragged him after Jenny across the road towards the church. They stood in the porch watching the aerial fight, gasping as one plane, then another plummeted to earth.

The battle seemed to go on for hours but finally the Hurricanes seemed to have got the upper hand and the enemy planes – 'Heinkels,' Brian declared – peeled away towards the coast.

Rosemary released the breath she had been holding and bent down to comfort Maisie who had hidden her face in Jenny's skirt.

Her friend sighed. 'I was so scared,' she whispered. 'I heard they were machine-gunning people in the streets over Yarmouth way.'

Rosemary had been scared too but she didn't admit it. 'Shh! Don't frighten the children,' she said. 'Let's get them home.' She stepped out of the porch and looked up at the sky, then across to the fields beyond the village. A pillar of smoke rose beyond the distant trees and she shuddered. Whether it was 'one of ours' or 'one of theirs' made no difference to her. They were all young men, sons, brothers, sweethearts. She would pray for them but she knew better than to voice her feelings to her friend. 'Bloody war,' she thought and for the first time the reality of it swept over her. She thought of Michael and Simon and all the young lads of the village who had joined up so enthusiastically almost a year ago.

In the days that followed, they got used to the overhead battles and didn't bother to take shelter when the fights took place over the village. By September the tide seemed to have turned. But then the bombing started.

Chapter 3

September 1940

Rosemary was preparing lunch when the siren sounded. She still couldn't get used to the alien sound which sent shivers down her back. It was the second raid in a week and so far, the village had escaped. She knew she should take shelter but it was hard to believe that the enemy would target them. Of course, Oakleigh wasn't their target at all. They were after the RAF station half a mile away but it was close enough to be a danger.

She dried her hands and hurried along the passage to her father's study. He was probably so immersed in writing next week's sermon that he hadn't heard the siren.

She went in without knocking and Seth glanced up in irritation. He hated to be disturbed. 'What is it?' he said.

'It's a raid, Father. Didn't you hear?'

He shook his head. 'I can't hear anything.'

Now Rosemary could hear the drone of enemy bombers passing overhead on their way from the coast to one of the many aerodromes in the surrounding countryside. A farm near Oakleigh St James had been badly damaged in the last raid and she feared the village might be next.

'Father, please. We must get down to the cellar. Bring your papers with you.'

He sighed. 'If you insist.' He gathered up his sheaf of notes and his Bible and reluctantly followed her down the stairs.

Rosemary had made the place as comfortable as she could with cushions on the two chairs, a small table with an oil lamp and a rag rug on the floor. It still smelled damp though but it would have to do. So far, the raids had been in the daytime but if they started bombing at night, she would have to fix up a bed of some sort for her father.

She lit the lamp and settled him in the most comfortable chair. 'There, you can carry on with your sermon,' she said, sitting down opposite him.

She picked up her knitting which she kept down here in a box to keep it dry. She wasn't particularly fond of knitting but it kept her hands busy. She should have brought her writing materials down with her, she thought. A letter to Simon would take her mind off what might be happening up above.

'I hope Jenny got the little ones to the shelter,' she said, as the sound of bombers overhead got louder.

'I'm sure they'll be all right. Such a pity those evacuees came back. They wouldn't have been any worse off in London and at least they'd be with their families.'

'Nonsense, Father. It's much worse in London and the big cities. When Jenny and I went to the cinema in Norwich last week we were shocked at what they were showing on the newsreel.'

Seth didn't appear to have heard, his head bent over the sheaf of papers in his hand. Rosemary was about to say something else when she realised his eyes were closed and he appeared to be praying. She felt she ought to join him in prayer but her heart wasn't in it. She wished she still had the faith she'd had when she was a child but it was hard with so much going on in the world.

Even down here in the cellar, she could hear the planes passing overhead and the noise of the anti-aircraft guns.

She glanced across at her father just as a loud thump and crash made him start up, his notes falling to the floor. Dust trickled down from the ceiling but then there was silence. 'It's all right,' she whispered, going over to him and clutching his hand.

A few minutes later the wail of the all clear sounded and they both sighed and stood up.

'We must go and make sure everyone's safe. That last one was a bit too close for comfort,' Seth said, stumbling towards the stairs, the notes for his sermon forgotten.

Rosemary gathered up the fallen papers, carried the lamp upstairs and turned it out.

They opened the front door and peered out. At first it looked as if the village had escaped any damage and Rosemary gave a relieved sigh. But then she glanced along the road, gasping and pointing to the row of cottages on the other side of the green. Smoke was rising from the end one and they both rushed across.

'It's Mrs Norton's house,' Rosemary gasped. She pushed open the front gate, her father close behind. As she reached the front of the cottage, Percy Fenton, the local blacksmith emerged, his ARP warden's helmet askew and his face streaked with dust.

'Don't come closer,' he said, holding out his hand. 'It's not safe.' He smiled, his teeth gleaming white through the grime. 'It's all right. She's not hurt. She was in the back garden cutting a lettuce. I've sat her down in the shed. She's a bit shaky.'

'Thank God,' Seth murmured.

'Is the cottage badly damaged? It looks dreadful from here,' Rosemary said.

'It's gone through the roof and the thatch caught fire,' Percy said. 'The Home Guard are on their way.'

'Well, Mrs Norton can't stay here.' Rosemary said. 'If she can manage it, we'll take her to the Rectory. We'll look after her, won't we Father.'

'Wait there then. I'll go and fetch her.' Percy walked down the side of the cottage and a few minutes later came back, supporting Mrs Norton with an arm around her shoulders.

As Rosemary comforted her, assuring her that she could stay at the Rectory until it was safe to return to her cottage, two Home Guard appeared, one carrying a stirrup pump. He proceeded to play water over the flames which soon died down.

'Think we were lucky this time,' Percy said. 'The rest of the village seems to have escaped.'

'Thank goodness,' Rosemary said. 'I was worried about the school.'

'So was I,' Percy said with a relieved sigh.

Rosemary laid a hand on his arm. 'Jenny would have looked after the children.'

Leaving the men to deal with the chaos, she and her father led Mrs Norton across the road and up the path to the Rectory.

When Mrs Norton was settled in a comfortable chair in the sitting room with a cup of tea, Rosemary said, 'You must stay with us until it's safe for you to move back in to the cottage. It might take some time to get the repairs done.'

'I don't want to be a bother,' she protested. 'I could go and stay with my son in Norwich.'

'Nonsense. Stay here until you've recovered from the shock at least.'

'I'm perfectly all right now. I was a bit shaken up I admit but...' She straightened her shoulders and shook her fist. 'Them jerries won't get the better of me.'

Rosemary smiled and nodded agreement but her thoughts were grim. The anti-aircraft guns on the coast were their only defence against the menace from the skies.

Mrs Norton finished her tea and stood up. 'I'll just wash up the cups and tidy the kitchen,' she said.

'No, you will not,' Rosemary said. 'You're a guest.'

'It's my job. So, while I'm here I'll get on with it. You know I'm not one for sitting about.' She grinned. 'I'll cook for you too.'

Rosemary smiled and gave in. She had to admit it would be good to have help in the kitchen. Having grown up with servants, she was beginning to find it hard to manage with Mrs Norton only working part-time. It would also give her more time for the parish duties which she had taken on after her mother died. Also, it would also be good for Mrs Norton to have something to occupy her and would help to take her mind off what had happened.

Leaving the older woman to her kitchen tidying, Rosemary went into her father's study. The Rev Turner sat at his desk, his head in his hands. 'Are you all right, Father?' Rosemary asked, putting her hand on his shoulder.

'I'm just thinking of what to say in my sermon on Sunday. It is so hard to preach love and forgiveness when we see what is happening all around us.'

'I'm sure the right words will come to you – as they always do,' Rosemary said.

Seth smiled. 'I'll pray on it,' he said.

'I must go over to the school to see if Jenny needs any help with the little ones. They must have been so scared by the raid.'

'Very well, my dear.'

'Mrs Norton will bring you a cup of tea.'

Seth nodded and Rosemary smiled. Already he had seized a pen and was scribbling on his notepad. He wasn't lost for words for long when it came to his sermons.

She left the room quietly and hurried across the churchyard, pausing at the church porch. On impulse she stepped inside, breathing in the familiar scent of old hymn books, flowers past their best and a slight tinge of dampness. She looked around thinking she should renew the flowers before Sunday. She murmured a quick prayer of thanks that no one had been hurt in the raid and turned to leave, catching a glimpse of the '*Doom*' on the north wall. Was it only a few months since she had met Simon, the young soldier, and enjoyed their conversation about the church and its history? Not just a soldier, she remembered – an artist. She pictured him sketching the '*Doom*', his face intent, his sure strokes on the paper.

She wondered where he was now. When she had answered his letter, she had hoped he would write back to her. A foolish hope, she knew. They had only met twice – casual meetings, she told herself. But he had said he hoped to return some day. She hoped he would and prayed he would be safe wherever he was.

She hurried across the road to the school, where she could hear laughter and shouts from the children in the playground.

The headmaster, Mr Davis, stood in the porch watching the older children rushing around. It seemed that they were not as traumatised by the air raid as Rosemary had feared.

'Miss Blackwell is in the hall,' he said as Rosemary approached. 'Some of the little ones are still a bit upset. She's trying to interest them in some games.'

'I'll go and give her a hand.'

She paused in the doorway of the school hall where Jenny was comforting one of the infants. She glanced around and spotted Maisie, the evacuee who was billeted at the Manor with her older brother. The little girl was sitting on the floor with her head bent over her knees.

Putting on a cheerful voice, Rosemary said, 'Hello Maisie. Would you like to play a game?'

Maisie shook her head. 'Want to go home, want my mum,' she whispered.

Rosemary didn't know how to answer but she lowered herself to the floor and took Maisie's hand. 'Your mum's very busy. You know she's doing important work now.' The girl nodded but her blue eyes were bright with unshed tears.

'You're being very brave.'

'I try to be but...' She shuddered and looked up at the ceiling. 'I didn't like those bangs and those noisy planes. They won't come back, will they?'

Rosemary couldn't bring herself to lie so she said, 'I don't think so. You're safe here. Miss Blackwell looked after you, didn't she?'

Maisie nodded. She scrambled to her feet. 'Mrs Pargeter gets cross if we're late for tea.'

'Don't worry. She'll understand.' Rosemary glanced to where Jenny was gathering the children to her, telling them it was time to go home.

She led Maisie over to the group. 'I'll walk the evacuees back to the Manor, 'she said.

'Thanks. Thank goodness there were no casualties. I heard the bomb drop.'

'It was Mrs Norton's cottage that was hit but she wasn't hurt. She's staying with us at the Rectory.'

'The children were very good, went to the shelter with no fuss. I think the older boys were more excited than scared.'

Rosemary managed a little laugh. 'I can imagine Brian...'

Jenny smiled too. 'Well, better get the children off home.'

Rosemary said goodbye to her friend and took Maisie's hand. She called to the other children who were billeted at the Manor. They stepped out into the sunshine, and Rosemary called to Brian to join them.

'Can't I stay and play a bit longer, Miss,' he asked.

'Not today, Brian. I think Mrs Pargeter will be worried about you all after the raid. She'll want you all back safe in time for tea.'

Brian pouted and kicked a stone across the playground but he followed his little sister, mumbling about not wanting to be with the 'babies'.

As they passed Mrs Norton's cottage, Brian hung back, staring at the hole in the thatched roof, from which a plume of smoke still emerged.

'Wow, look at that.' He spat on the ground. 'Bloody Jerries.'

'Brian. Mind your language. You're scaring the little ones. Besides, there's nothing to see.' She hurried the children past the row of cottages and turned in at the Manor gates.

Mrs Pargeter was standing in the doorway and she stepped forward, her hands outstretched. 'Oh, there you are children. Tea's ready. Go along in and wash your hands.' Her voice carried its usual bossy tone but Rosemary detected a slight tremor which betrayed her anxiety.

As she ushered them into the house and towards the cloakroom, Rosemary said quietly, 'They were all quite safe.'

'Thank goodness for the air raid shelter. It took a lot of persuading to convince the authorities that it was necessary out here in the country but it seems we were right.'

Rosemary told her about Mrs Norton's cottage and Mrs Pargeter nodded. 'My husband's gone along with two of the Home Guard to see if they can help,' she said.

They ushered the children into the dining room and seated them at the long table where they were soon tucking into mounds of sandwiches. Rosemary made sure the little ones got their share and then said, 'I must go. Father will be wanting his tea too, although Mrs Norton is staying with us for a while and she'll look after him. She'll probably go home if the damage isn't too great.

'If she stays at the Rectory, it will ease the burden on you, my dear,' Mrs Pargeter said.

'Father's not a burden,' Rosemary protested.

'But with your parish duties, the church...'

'I like to keep busy – and Father needs me.'

'I know, my dear, but women are being called up for war work and you may be forced to join one of the services. Or even go to work in a factory.'

Rosemary was a bit put out at what she saw as the older woman's interference. It was true she had been thinking about doing more for the war effort but she dreaded having to leave the village – and her father.

'I'm already registered but I'd like to stay in the village if possible. There's plenty of voluntary work I can do.'

'Of course there is. In fact, I need help with the Red Cross parcels for prisoners of war.'

The thought of working under the formidable lady of the manor didn't appeal but at least she wouldn't have to leave her father. 'I'll think about it,' she said.

When Rosemary returned home, she was still pondering on Mrs Pargeter's suggestion. Truthfully, she would love to have signed up for one of the forces. Since the start of the war, she had become increasingly discontented with what she felt was her rather humdrum life. Several of her friends were now in the WAAFs and Maggie, who helped her parents run the *Four Bells*, had talked about joining the ATS.

Over the next few days, there were several alarms but the planes had passed over the village towards the RAF station. Colonel Pargeter, who was in charge of the Home Guard, had told her their aim was to destroy the airfields and the planes still on the ground. She still made sure that the children were safely under cover and helped Jenny to calm the frightened little ones but most of the time she was bored.

Mrs Pargeter hadn't mentioned the Red Cross since their earlier conversation and with Mrs Norton still at the Rectory, there was little for her to do, since the older woman insisting on taking on most of the chores.

If she didn't find some local war work soon, she would be called up and have little say in where she was sent. Her father, as usual, was holed up in his study and had asked not to be disturbed. He was supposed to be working on Sunday's sermon but Rosemary was worried about him. He had begun to look quite frail and spent more time than usual in church. When she had gone in this morning to change the flowers, she had found him on his knees at the altar. He didn't seem to hear her when she entered, despite the sound of her shoes on the flagstones. She had crept out again, anxious not to disturb his prayers.

She found Mrs Norton in the kitchen preparing lunch. 'That was quick, Miss,' she said.

'I'll go over later and finish off,' Rosemary replied. 'Any post?' she asked without much hope in her voice. She had given up expecting news of her brother after so many months and she did not think she would hear from Lieutenant Spencer again.

'There was one for the Reverend. I took it in to him but when I went in to collect his cup, it was still on his desk.'

'It couldn't have been very important then.'

'Lunch is almost ready.'

'I'll fetch Father,' Rosemary said, although she was still unwilling to interrupt his prayers. But as she opened the kitchen door, she saw him in the hall, a brown envelope in his hand. She hadn't heard him come back to the house.

He was frowning and turning the envelope over in his hand as if unwilling to open it. Her stomach churned and she gasped. 'What is it, Father?' He looked up, his face pale and thrust the letter at her. 'You open it, please. I can't...'

'Come and sit down, dear. We'll look at it together.'

She took his arm and led him into the kitchen, easing hm down onto a chair at the scrubbed pine table. She turned to Mrs Norton who had paused in dishing out the soup, the ladle in her hand. 'A glass of water, please, Mrs Norton.'

She sat beside her father and opened the envelope, drawing out a single sheet of paper with an official looking heading.

'Is it...? The Rev Turner's voice shook.

Rosemary swiftly skimmed the page, a smile lighting up her face. 'It's Michael. He's a prisoner. Oh, Father...' A sob caught in her throat.

'Oh, Miss, Sir. Good news, praise the Lord. He's safe.' Mrs Norton clasped her hands together.

Rosemary hugged her father. 'I had almost given up hope,' she sobbed.

'Our prayers have been answered.' The Rector smiled, the colour had returned to his cheeks and he picked up his spoon. 'Now, Mrs Norton, I think I shall enjoy my lunch today.'

With a delighted smile, Mrs Norton proceeded to ladle out the soup.

Chapter 4

September 1940

The bombing of the airfield continued over the next few weeks but the village escaped serious damage, although a barn at Manor Farm with its store of hay was completely destroyed. Rosemary was relieved to hear that no animals or people had been hurt.

Now it seemed the enemy was turning its sights on Russia and raids on the airfields lessened. One evening after listening to Churchill's speech on the wireless, The Rev Turner turned to Rosemary with a smile. 'Our prayers are answered. This could be a turning point.'

She nodded but she could not feel the same optimism. Even if fears of an invasion had faded it could only be a temporary reprieve. She could not feel downcast for long though as, some time after the news of Michael's incarceration in the prison camp, they had received a letter from him. It was very short with much of it blacked out. There was no clue as to where he was, but he sounded cheerful and told his family that he was being treated well. He also mentioned his friend Lt Spencer and hoped he had got back safely.

Rosemary wasn't convinced and felt he had probably been coerced into sounding positive. Anything else was sure to have been censored. She didn't voice her concerns to her father though, worried that he would sink into depression once more. It was so good to see that news from Michael seemed to have restored him to his old self and even his sermons contained a more positive outlook.

The letter had given an official address to write to although she still wasn't sure where he was. After supper that evening, she sat down to write to him, pausing frequently to think what to write. It was hard to know how much to tell him – she certainly didn't mention the bombing of Mrs Norton's cottage but strove to sound cheerful and optimistic. She also didn't mention that she'd met Simon, anxious about giving too much away as she knew the letters would be read by their captors.

Despite the end of what they were beginning to call the Battle of Britain, there was no sign of an end to the war. The blitz on London continued and, although there were now fewer raids on the airfield, Rosemary was very conscious of what was happening in London and the big cities.

At church the next day, she couldn't wait for the service to end so she could tell Jenny she'd heard from Michael and to give her friend the address so she could write to him too.

'That's wonderful,' Jenny said, her face lighting up.

Before Rosemary could say more, Mrs Pargeter waylaid her in the porch. 'Are you free tomorrow?' she asked.

'Of course. What do you need?'

'There's a group of evacuees arriving at Diss station. Would you come with me to meet them?'

'How many are to be billeted in the village?'

'Just a few this time. I was hoping you could take one or two,' Mrs Pargeter said. 'I've already got the Cox children and two other boys.'

'I'd love to but I'll have to speak to Father. He hasn't been well and I worry children might be a bother for him.'

'Just one then. Perhaps a girl – less trouble than boys as I know too well,' Mrs Pargeter said with a smile.

At the station the next day Rosemary recognised several women from the village. Moira Thompson who ran the village shop with her husband came over to her and said, 'I want a girl but Alf is hoping for a boy, a strong lad who can help in the garden. He's out there in all weathers.' She sighed. 'Digging for victory he calls it. That's all very well, but I need him in the shop.'

'I suppose we'll have to take who we can. They all need homes, somewhere to feel safe,' Rosemary said.

At that moment the train steamed in to the station and disgorged a crowd of scruffy ill-clothed children. Tear-stained five-year-olds gazed around them in bewilderment while older boys tried to look brave, as if being shipped miles from the familiar streets of London was a big adventure.

The WVS women who accompanied them bustled about with their clipboards, deciding who would go with whom.

The Rev Turner had reluctantly agreed that Rosemary could take in one child, preferably a girl and she soon decided on the youngest looking girl who was clinging to the hand of one of the escorts and rubbing her other hand across her nose. Her blonde curls were an untamed tangle and she wore a too small coat over a dirty cotton dress.

Her heart went out to the child and she bent towards her and said 'What's your name, dear?'

'Lily', the child whispered.

The WVS woman ticked the name off her list. 'Lily Watson,' she said. 'And you are?'

She wrote Rosemary's name and address on her form and took some papers out of her satchel. 'Here's her ration book and the mother's address.' She bent down to Lily. 'Now, please be good for Miss Turner.'

'I want my mum,' Lily whispered.

'You'll see her soon,' Rosemary said hastily before the WVS escort could say anything. 'Come with me, love. We're going to have a ride in a motor car.' She took the little girl's hand and followed Mrs Pargeter to where she had parked the Daimler.

***

Rosemary leaned forward and switched the wireless off. Every night it was the same. Although fears of invasion had receded, it seemed that Hitler was still determined to beat them into submission with seemingly unending air raids on the big cities.

She sighed. 'Those poor little kiddies,' she said. 'I stood there on the railway station and I just wanted to give them all a hug.' She stood up and began to clear the table.

'I'll do that, miss,' Mrs Norton said. 'You go and see if the little one has settled.'

Rosemary nodded then turned to her father. 'Why don't you come up with me, Father, make sure she's all right.'

He nodded and, reluctantly, stood up and followed her upstairs.

Before entering the bedroom, she turned to him and said, 'Thank you for agreeing to take her in. I know you weren't in favour at first, but we must do our bit.'

'I know dear. I'm just relieved you didn't land us with a couple of rough boys.'

Rosemary didn't say anything. Yes, some of the London boys were a bit rough it was true, but surely they deserved to be safe as well.

'Most of the boys were taken in by the local farmers,' she said.

'Cheap labour,' the Rector muttered.

Rosemary did not answer. She had become used to keeping her opinions to herself.

She opened the bedroom door and peeped in. Five-year-old Lily was fast asleep, her faced streaked with tears, her fair hair matted on the pillow. She went across and straightened the eiderdown, ran her hand through the tangled curls.

'She seems to have settled all right,' her father said.

'I hope so. She looked so scared, poor little thing.'

As they went downstairs, Seth said, 'Just make sure she knows not to go into my study or disturb me when I'm working.'

'Yes, Father,' Rosemary said meekly, although she was finding it hard to hold her tongue. Still, she'd managed to overcome his objection to taking in an evacuee and she had to be content with that.

Having a child to take care of would take up more of her time but she still felt she should be doing more. She hadn't heard anything more from Mrs Pargeter about helping with the Red Cross parcels so she decided to go up to the Manor in the morning and ask her about it. It would count as war work and she would feel useful. She dreaded being called up into the services and having to leave the village. Before the war she had longed to get away, stifled by the predictability of village life and longing for adventure.

Now, she was beginning to enjoy helping Jenny with the evacuees and of course, Father needed her.

The next day, she went into the kitchen where Lily was sitting up at the table finishing her porridge and Mrs Norton was making toast.

'If you don't need my help today, I thought I'd take Lily up to the Manor to meet Maisie,' she said. 'It will help her if she already knows one of the other children when she starts school on Monday.'

'I can manage,' the housekeeper said. 'It's a nice day for a walk.' She nodded towards the little girl. 'Looks as if she could do with some fresh air. She's so pale.'

'All these London kiddies are. It's amazing the change in those who've been here longer.'

Rosemary poured tea and buttered a slice of toast. 'Father's settled in his study and doesn't want to be disturbed.'

'Writing another sermon?' Mrs Norton pursed her lips. 'Don't know what he manages to write about. He spends so much time cooped up in there.'

'I know. I worry about him but he gets cross if I nag him.' Rosemary frowned. When he wasn't in his study he was at prayer in church. The war preyed on his mind. It was as if he felt responsible for those young villagers who had so willingly marched off to war, including his son. She wished she could do something to help.

Thinking of Michael, she said, 'No letters today?'

He had written once from the prison camp since the initial note telling them where he was. At least he was safe, or so she hoped.

Lily finished her porridge and wriggled to get down from the table.

'Come on then,' Rosemary said, swallowing her last mouthful of toast. She lifted the little girl down from the table and took her hand. 'We're going for a walk.'

Lily's face lit up. 'See Mum?'

'Sorry, lovie. You can't see your mummy today. She's had to stay in London.' As Lily's face crumpled, Rosemary felt terrible but she managed to smile. 'Don't be sad. We're going to see a nice lady and a little girl who will be your friend.'

It was true. Mrs Pargeter *was* a nice lady – a kind soul who did much good work and was well respected in the village. But she was a large woman with a booming voice and to a tiny five-year-old she would probably appear terrifying.

As they walked up the lane to towards the Manor, Rosemary kept up a flow of chatter, pointing out the wild flowers in the grass verges, the sheep nibbling the grass on the green near the pond. Lily plodded along beside her, eyes fixed on the ground showing no interest. She didn't even look up at the group of children kicking a ball about on the green. Brian was among them and Rosemary was pleased that he wasn't at the Manor. She didn't feel that Lily was ready to meet Maisie's boisterous brother just yet.

At the Manor, Mrs Pargeter welcomed Lily and took her up to the old nursery. 'This is Maisie who is staying with me.'

Maisie looked up from where she was playing with the doll's house and smiled.

'This is Lily,' Rosemary said. 'Can you show her the doll's house, Maisie?'

Maisie nodded.

'Let's leave them to get acquainted,' the older woman said.

Reluctantly, Rosemary followed her downstairs.

'I hope they get on all right,' she said. 'Lily seems such a timid little thing.'

'Don't you worry. Everything's bound to seem strange for her. Remember how Maisie was when she first came.'

But Maisie had her big brother to look out for her and she had settled well, Rosemary thought. Poor Lily was so alone.

She wasn't allowed to brood though. Mrs Pargeter led her along a passage and out into a courtyard. 'To business,' she said. 'Red Cross parcels. I've been in touch with the Norwich people and they need all the help they can get.'

Rosemary's heart sank. 'I'm happy to do my bit,' she said. 'But I don't think I can go to Norwich every day. Father...'

'No need,' Mrs Pargeter interrupted. 'It's all organised. I've let them take over one of the outbuildings for storage. The stuff will be delivered here and we will be responsible for making up the parcels ready to be sent out to the various prison camps. We'll use the dining room to do the packing. The children can eat in the kitchen.'

In the Manor's large dining room several tables had been pushed together. Boxes were piled on them and a desk in the corner held stacks of forms.

'I've enlisted the help of some of the village women. I thought while the children are in school on Monday we could get the mothers together and explain what needs doing. There's no room here for them to all work at once. Perhaps you could set up a rota.'

Rosemary's head was spinning as Mrs Pargeter went through what needed to be done. It seemed a lot more complicated than she had anticipated. But she was pleased that, at last, she would be doing a worthwhile job. She thought how fortunate it was that Mrs Norton was staying with them and could keep an eye on Father, so she wouldn't have to worry about him. She hoped the repairs to the housekeeper's cottage would not be finished too soon so that she could stay longer at the Rectory. A stab of guilt pierced her and she hastily brushed the unworthy thought away.

Mrs Pargeter interrupted her thoughts. 'Well, that seems to be everything. We'll meet here at nine thirty on Monday then.'

Rosemary agreed and looked at her watch. 'I must go and see if Lily's all right,' she said. 'And then I have to get Father's lunch.'

To her relief Lily and Maisie were happily playing. As she entered the playroom, she heard Maisie say, 'We must be very careful with everything. This was Mrs Pargeter's dolly's house when she was at little girl. It's very old.'

'Have you had a nice time?' she asked Lily.

The little girl nodded. 'Can I stay a bit longer?'

'No, dear we must go back to the Rectory. Mrs Norton will have our lunch ready.' The little girl looked puzzled. 'Dinner,' Rosemary said. 'You'll see Maisie again at school on Monday.'

As they walked back through the village, Lily chattered away about the toys in the playroom. It was obvious she had never had anything like it at home.

There was a letter on the hall table. Rosemary recognised the handwriting and snatched it up, her heart racing. She hadn't expected to hear from Simon again and she was thrilled that he'd written. She was tempted to tear the envelope open at once but Lily pulled on her hand.

'Want dinner,' she said.

'All right, lovie. Run along to the kitchen. Mrs Norton will see to you.'

As Lily disappeared down the passage, Rosemary walked back outside and sat on a bench in the front garden.

She examined the envelope, hoping for some clue as to where he had written from but it had an ordinary Bury St Edmunds postmark. So, he still hadn't returned to his unit. She hoped his wound hadn't started giving him trouble again. As she tore the letter open and retrieved the sheet of writing paper, she felt something else inside, Intrigued, she pulled out a second sheet of thick paper.

She recognised it as a leaf torn from Simon's little sketchbook. She turned it over, a smile lighting up her face. It was a small watercolour painting of the church. What a talented artist he was, she thought as she turned to the letter.

'I promised I would keep in touch,' he'd written. *'I have been away training and had no chance to write.'* He sighed with relief that he was all right. *'I am home now but have to report for duty in a day or two. They haven't told us where we're bound for but from the kit we've been issued it seems likely to be somewhere hot.'*

Africa, she thought. She'd watched scenes of desert fighting on the newsreels last time she'd gone with Jenny to the cinema in Norwich.

The short letter said he would write when there was more news and finished with the promise that when he had leave, he would come and visit *'your lovely little church again, however far in the future it may be.'*

She read it again, then examined the little painting. They'd only met twice. She shouldn't read too much into his friendship, she told herself. She ran up to her room and tucked the painting into the edge of her dressing table mirror. She would have to find a frame for it. She put the letter into a drawer and hurried downstairs, apologising breathlessly for being late.

Father looked up from his plate and frowned but didn't say anything. Mrs Norton turned from the stove and Rosemary flushed as she detected a slight smirk on the housekeeper's face. 'You found your letter then?' she said.

Rosemary nodded and leaned towards Lily. 'Enjoying your soup, dear?' she asked.

Lily slurped another spoonful and Father tutted. Rosemary pretended not to notice but she decided that she would try to teach the little girl how to behave at table. It wasn't her fault she hadn't been taught at home.

Chapter 5

October 1940

Lily had settled in well, much to Rosemary's relief. She and Maisie had become firm friends and spent all their free time together. She was still nervous of the animals they encountered when Jenny and Rosemary took the children for country walks and held on tightly to the grown-ups' hands.

One day they were passing the entrance to Manor Farm when a gate opened and a flock of sheep swarmed through. She shrank back with a little cry.

Maisie laughed. 'They won't hurt you,' she said, putting out a hand and patting the nearest animal.

Lily wasn't convinced and hid her face in Rosemary's skirt. They waited until the flock had passed, watching as the collie dog herded them through a gate into another field. Only when the gate was closed did Lily calm down.

'I had hoped she would be over her fear by now,' Rosemary said. 'She seems to have grown used to living in the country – apart from the sheep and cows.'

Jenny looked up at the sky which had clouded over. 'We'd better get back. Looks like rain.'

Autumn had crept up on them and this was the first fine day for several weeks. 'We must make the most of the fine weather – if it lasts. It does the children good to get out in the fresh air,' said Rosemary.

'They'll soon be bringing the livestock in for the winter so Lily won't have to worry when we're out.'

'Perhaps we can take the girls to one of the farms to see the sheep and cows in their pens. They might not seem so scary if they're shut up. What do you think?'

'Good idea,' Jenny replied.

They reached the gate to the Manor and Rosemary said, 'I'll take Maisie home. I need to speak to Mrs Pargeter.'

'I'll see you in church on Sunday then.' Jenny set off down the village street to the cottage next door to the shop where she lodged with Mrs Kent, an elderly widow whose married daughter lived in Norwich.

She turned and waved to the children and they waved back, then they grabbed Rosemary's hands and skipped up the Manor drive swinging on her arms. Lily seemed to have recovered from her fright and Rosemary smiled. Perhaps in time she would come to love it here as Maisie and Brian and most of the other London children had.

'Can we play with the dolly's house?' Lily asked as they reached the house.

'We'll have to ask Mrs Pargeter, but we can't stay long anyway.'

'I love the dolly's house and all the furniture and stuff,' Lily said.

They walked round to the kitchen entrance where the housekeeper reminded the children to take their shoes off.

'Is Mrs P available?' Rosemary asked.

'In the dining room. '

'I'll go through.' She turned to the children. 'Go up to Maisie's room but don't touch the dolls' house. It's too near tea time to get it out now. I'll ask if you can play with it next time we come.'

Mrs Pargeter was surrounded by boxes, some piled up on the floor, more on the large dining table in the centre of the room. She looked up, a harassed frown on her face. 'Thank goodness you're here,' she said.

'I didn't realise they were being delivered today otherwise I'd have come earlier,' Rosemary said.

'They didn't tell me – said the telephone was out of order. There's more in the barn.' She waved a hand in front of her flushed face. 'My goodness, where do we start?'

Rosemary's heart sank. Surely the older woman didn't expect her to get stuck in now? She was about to apologise and say she needed to take Lily home when Mrs Pargeter laughed.

'Don't look so shocked – although I must admit it was a shock to me when Percy Fenton turned up and started unloading the van.' She waved a hand round the room. 'Anyway, I'm pleased you're here. I need you to help organise a rota.'

Before Rosemary could reply, she continued, 'Don't worry - I know you haven't got time now.'

'I only popped in to see if there was any news as to when we could start on the parcels,' Rosemary said.

'Will you have time tomorrow? I have a couple of WVS ladies coming too.'

'Of course. What time would you like me to come?'

***

There had been no more news from Michael but, since Rosemary had started working for the Red Cross, he was never far from her mind. With each parcel she packed, she pictured her brother opening it and enjoying its contents. Most of the items had been donated, small things which it was hoped would make prison life more bearable – toothpaste, soap, chocolate, hand-knitted socks and gloves.

Rosemary hoped and prayed that the parcels reached those they were intended for.

After the first few chaotic days when no one was sure what they were doing, Mrs Pargeter and Rosemary between them had worked out a system and everyone knew their job.

It was good to feel useful even if she was tired all the time, Rosemary reflected, straightening and rubbing her aching back.

Maggie from the *Four Bells,* who had been stacking the packed parcels on the sack barrow ready to take outside to the van, looked across at her and grinned.

'Time for a break,' she said.

'I'll make a cuppa,' Rosemary said. 'Then I'll have to go and fetch the children from school.'

'I can't stay too long either. Have to get ready for evening opening,' said Maggie.

'You must be exhausted, working all evening as well.'

'I'm used to it.' She gave the barrow a little push. 'This is just like helping Dad with the beer barrels – not that we have many deliveries nowadays.'

'Well, don't overdo it.'

'I'm all right. And at least living over the pub, I don't have to travel to work.'

Rosemary laughed. 'And there's the added bonus of all those RAF chaps from the aerodrome coming in.'

'They do brighten the place up,' Maggie agreed with a giggle. 'Why don't you pop in one evening?'

'I don't think Father would approve.'

'Well, he doesn't mind you going to the pictures in Norwich with me. I'll ask a couple of chaps to join us. He needn't know.'

Rosemary shook her head. She wasn't interested in meeting young men, not even for a brief flirtation as Maggie did. 'I'm too tired in the evenings, what with the war work and looking after Father and Lily.' She didn't tell her friend that since meeting Simon Spencer, the wasn't interested in meeting any young men.

'Suit yourself,' she said. 'But just because there's a war on, doesn't mean you can't have fun.'

'I'm happy enough,' Rosemary said. 'Besides, the buses to Norwich aren't very reliable these days.'

'Pity there's not a cinema in the village,' Maggie said. She pushed the barrow outside and Rosemary went to help her load the van.

Percy would drive it to the depot in Norwich in the morning and from there the parcels would be loaded on to a lorry and driven to the docks – Harwich or Felixstowe, Rosemary thought. From there it was a dangerous journey to a neutral country. It wasn't exactly secret but no one talked about the final destination.

Rosemary prayed fervently that after all their hard work, the prisoners actually received the parcels. She had been tempted to tuck a little note in one of them wishing the recipient well. She day-dreamed that Michael would find it and pictured his delight. A foolish dream, she knew, especially given the thousands of parcels the Red Cross dealt with and the many POW camps scattered around Europe.

***

Rosemary loved Harvest festival and particularly enjoyed decorating the church for the Sunday service. Mrs Norton had helped to bring in the sheaves of corn which had been left in the porch by a local farmer.

Fruit and vegetables donated by the villagers adorned the wide window ledges and Rosemary sniffed the appetising smell of ripe apples which filled the air. At the children's service on Sunday morning the little ones with their parents would bring produce from their gardens or from the village shop. Everyone joined in the celebration of thanks for the harvest, even those who were not regular church-goers. It was one of those events that brought the community together. After the festival most of the produce would be distributed to the poor and elderly of the village, with any leftover taken to the old people's home in the next town.

Several village women came in to help and soon the church was buzzing with activity and looking its best.

Mrs Norton put her hands on her hips and gazed round the church. 'Time for a break, ladies,' she said.

'Yes,' Rosemary agreed. 'Why don't you all come over to the Rectory for a cup of tea. I'll just tidy up and join you in a moment.' She gathered up the leftover

53

sprays of leaves and flowers. 'I'll put these in water in the vestry,' she said. 'We need them to fill in any gaps if the leaves start to drop.'

'I must get back to the shop,' Moira Thompson said. 'Can't leave Alf to manage on his own for too long.'

'Thanks for your help,' Rosemary said. 'See you on Sunday.'

The other two women followed Mrs Norton outside and Rosemary went into the vestry, filling two vases with water and popping the greenery in them. She looked around the cluttered space. Time we had a clear out, she thought.

Piles of old hymn books with tattered covers stood on top of a cupboard in the corner, choir boys' robes were piled up on a large chest instead of hanging neatly on their hooks behind the door. 'Have to have a word with those lads,' she muttered, scooping them up and draping them over a chair.

She didn't recognise the chest and wondered what was inside. She lifted the lid, releasing a cloud of dust. Stifling a sneeze, she peered inside, gasping in delight when she realised what the chest contained.

I must tell Jenny, she thought, as a childhood memory arose. Magic lantern shows had been part of their growing up. She recalled Maggie saying the other day that it was a pity there was no cinema in the village. Perhaps they could put on a magic lantern show some time, she thought. Better than nothing - that's if the thing still worked.

She lowered the lid of the chest and hurried to catch up with the housekeeper and her friends.

Chapter 6

December 1941

Time had flown with everyone busy with war work. The Red Cross parcels took up most of Rosemary's time and she had begun helping at the school as well. Jenny and Mr Davis were struggling to cope with the extra evacuee children and had been pleased when Rosemary offered to read to the younger ones or to take them on nature walks. When it was too wet or cold to take them outside, Mr Davis had offered the use of his sitting room in the small house attached to the school.

Rosemary had almost forgotten about the magic lantern which was still tucked away in a corner of the vestry until Jenny asked her about plans for the annual children's Christmas party.

'Usually it's all about the food,' she said. 'But with the rationing getting harder, it's going to be difficult to put on the sort of spread they're used to.'

'We'll have to put on some entertainment for them – not just the usual party games.'

Jenny thought for a moment. 'What about that old magic lantern you found in the vestry? We never did do anything with it.'

'I'm not sure if there are any slides. No good without pictures. I'll ask Father.'

The Rector couldn't remember ever seeing them although he recalled a former church warden giving a show to the Sunday School children some years ago.

'Yes, I remember,' Rosemary had said. 'They must still be around somewhere. '

Her father couldn't help but she determined to make a thorough search before giving up on the idea.

She hadn't found them in the vestry and turned her attention to the Rectory, waiting till Father was taking a service before venturing into his study. Her search had resulted in much a much tidier room although she had been careful not to disturb the Rector's many books and papers too much.

The cardboard box had been tucked away in a corner under a pile of books. Opening it, she had been disappointed at first, seeing only a layer of old newspapers. But as she lifted them out, she realised the paper was protecting the glass slides. These must be what she had been searching for.

She decided not to unpack them but carried the box over to the church, struggling to heave the box over the wall. 'Should have gone round by the gate,' she muttered.

She placed the box in the vestry. She'd spent so long searching there was no time to discover if the slides were indeed those which fitted the magic lantern. She would wait till Jenny was free to help her.

Now, they were in the vestry sorting them out, hoping that none were broken or damaged. They lifted each slide out carefully, wiping the dust off gently before holding them up to the light to see what was depicted. The labels on them were curling at the edges, the lettering faded.

'I can't make this one out,' Jenny said, squinting at one.

'We'll have to try them out in the machine,' Rosemary said. 'From what I remember they were mostly Bible stories and some nature pictures.'

Jenny held another one up. 'This looks interesting.'

Rosemary took it from her and peered at the rather blurred image. 'It looks like the *Doom.*' Are there any more in this set?'

Jenny scrabbled in the box and found five more. She set them to one side. 'I'm not sure the children will be interested in those.'

When the box was empty, they sorted the remaining slides into six sets. 'If they're not too faded, we should have enough for a good show.' Rosemary said.

'Where shall we hold it?'

'I thought of asking Mrs Pargeter – she has plenty of room.'

Jenny shook her head. 'She's already given up her dining room for the Red Cross parcels and, besides, I don't think she'd be happy having hordes of children trailing their muddy shoes and sticky fingers all over her drawing room.'

'You're probably right. What about the school rooms? The boys' classroom where you have assembly would do.'

'Good idea. I'll ask Mr Davis. I'm sure he'll agree.'

Rosemary carefully replaced the slides in the box, layering the different sets between sheets of paper on which she had written the subject matter of each. She wiped her hands on her apron and grinned. 'You do realise that all our hard work will be for nothing if the thing doesn't work.'

'Do you know how to work it then?'

'I've got a rough idea. Anyway, it might be broken. It's been tucked away in here for years, not been used since I was a child.' She thought for a moment. 'How about we ask Mr Davis to take a look at it – that's if he agrees we can hold the show in the school.'

'I'll speak to him tomorrow,' Jenny said.

'If he gets it working, we could put on the show at the end of term, just before the Christmas holidays,' Rosemary said.

'Maybe combine it with the Christmas party,' Jenny said.

***

Over the next few days Rosemary had no time to think about the magic lantern show as she was kept busy at the Manor packing and labelling Red Cross parcels. There was a lot of extra food to pack - Christmas puddings and tins of ham and other festive fare, all donated by the generous people of Norfolk. A lorry was due to pick them up and take them to the docks where they would be sent on to Portugal, a neutral country.

She tried not to think about the heavy loss of shipping in the Atlantic and prayed the precious goods would arrive safely at their destination.

Once the lorry was on its way, Rosemary decided to go and meet the evacuee children from school. If she was working, Lily usually accompanied Maisie and Brian back to the Manor to wait for her to finish work.

It was a grey wintry day, heavy clouds scudding across the sky, driven by the strong north wind. She put on her coat and wound a knitted scarf around her neck. December had ushered the winter in with a vengeance.

She reached the school gates as the bell rang and children surged out of the building. Most of them lived in the village and were able to make their way home safely but Rosemary worried about those who lived out in the countryside and had a long walk home, especially on winter days like today when it got dark so early.

She spotted Brian first, larking around with a couple of his friends. He was usually very good about seeing Maisie and Lily home but when he saw Rosemary, he grinned and ran up to her. 'Miss Turner, if you're seeing the girls home, can I go and have a kickabout on the green with my mates?'

'Just this once. But home before dark or Mrs Pargeter will be worried.'

'She don't need to worry about me. I can look after meself,' he scoffed.

'Maybe, but you know the rules,' Rosemary said.

'All right, miss.' He ran off join the other boys.

Jenny came out of the building holding Lily's hand followed by Maisie.

She waved and Rosemary quickly joined her. 'Have you had a chance to talk to Mr Davis?' she asked.

Jenny nodded. 'He's busy just now but he's agreed to come and look at the magic lantern tomorrow after school.'

'That's wonderful. Let's hope he can get it going.'

'He seemed confident. And also, he's agreed for us to have the show in the school.'

'Thanks, Jenny.' She bent to take Lily's hand. 'I'd better get these two back to the Manor.'

As they said goodbye and Rosemary turned to walk away, the door opened and Mr Davis appeared. His face was white and he had taken off his glasses and was polishing them with his handkerchief.

'What is it?' Jenny asked.

'I just turned my wireless on and heard the news...' He shook his head. 'They interrupted the programme. It's dreadful.'

He struggled to find the words and Rosemary thought, every day is dreadful news. What could it be this time? They were at war after all.

He took a deep breath. 'The Japanese – they've bombed Hawaii – Pearl Harbour. So many ships sunk...'

'Mr Davis – are you sure?' Jenny asked.

Rosemary was more worried about the children hearing, although they were probably too young to realise what it meant.

'I'm sorry. Didn't mean to upset you.,' Mr Davis replaced his glasses and took a deep breath. 'Well, children, time you were getting home,' he said, his voice almost steady.

'Yes, come along girls,' Rosemary said. 'Jenny, I'll talk to you later.'

Her friend nodded and gently took the head master's arm, leading him back inside.

As she walked back to the Manor, Rosemary hardly listened to the children's chatter about their school day. She was thankful that they didn't seem to have taken in the headmaster's distress or the import of his words. Her main thought was how the news would affect her own country and the progress of the war. People had been saying that America would surely come in on their side before long, but she couldn't see it happening now. Surely, they would declare war on Japan and would be too involved in defending their own country to help Britain.

***

A few days later the news broke that America had declared war on Japan and Germany. At first the news had little impact on the village and Rosemary continued with her plans to give a magic lantern show to the village children on the last day of term.

'We'll combine it with the Christmas Party,' she said as she met her friend after school and they walked the children home.

'Good idea,' Jenny agreed. 'I'm sure the parents will chip in with the food and we'll be able to put on a good spread for them.'

'It's a good job we have blackout curtains in the classrooms so we can put the show on in the afternoon.'

'Of course, I'd forgotten we need the room dark for the magic lantern.' Jenny paused. 'By the way, Mr Davis has checked it and tried out a couple of the slides.'

'I just hope the children will enjoy them,' Rosemary said. 'They might not appreciate the Bible stories and moral tales.'

'I think the novelty of it all will keep them entertained,' Jenny said. 'Will you show the ones of the wall paintings in the church?'

'I'm not sure. Some of the pictures are a bit grim – devils and imps and so on.'

Jenny laughed. 'You obviously don't know the boys I teach. They'll love it – little horrors.'

Rosemary grinned, thinking of Brian and his fascination with insects and slimy creatures. 'You're probably right,' she said.

60

They parted at the Manor gates and, as she followed the children up the drive, Rosemary thought about the pictures they would show and began to plan the programme for the afternoon's entertainment. Perhaps they would include the *Doom* paintings. The thought reminded her of her meetings with Simon Spencer and his interest in the church's wall paintings. Truthfully, he had never been far from her thoughts, especially since he had sent her the little painting of the church. She smiled. He was a very talented artist. Where was he now, she wondered. She had no idea where he had been sent but she remembered from his previous note that he had thought it would be somewhere hot. Maybe North Africa, she thought. Perhaps she would write to him again. She would tell him about the magic lantern show and the set of pictures of the *Doom*. He was sure to be interested. She'd have to send the letter to his home in Bury St Edmunds and trust that his father would send it on.

Lily wanted to stay and play with Maisie but Rosemary insisted on her coming home. 'You can help Mrs Norton to make some scones,' she said. 'She loves having you to help in the kitchen.'

'Scones with currants?' Lily asked, her little face lighting up.

'I expect so.' Rosemary mentally crossed her fingers, hoping they had some currants or sultanas in the pantry. Rationing was making it harder to find treats for the children. The thought brought her to the plans for the Christmas party to follow the magic lantern show.

Indoors, she settled Lily on a high stool in the kitchen where Mrs Norton was weighing out the ingredients for their baking session.

Rosemary went into the dining room and sat at the table with her notebook. She started to make a list but her mind wasn't on it. She couldn't wait to write to Simon and she got out her writing pad and started the letter, pausing frequently and chewing the end of her pen to try and find the right words.

She ought to write to Michael too, she thought as she finished the letter. But it was cold in the dining room and her fingers were starting to turn blue. She would write to her brother tomorrow.

She put her writing materials away and went along the passage to the kitchen where the warm aroma of baking welcomed her.

***

Rosemary looked around at the rows of expectant faces. The room was full, not just with the school children but parents and older brothers and sisters. She turned to Jenny and nodded. It was time to begin.

Mr Davis stood behind the table holding the magic lantern and the boxes of slides and held his hands up.

'Welcome everybody. I hope you enjoy the stories we will tell and the lovely pictures which go with them,' he said, pointing to the screen on the wall behind him. The blackout screens were in place and one of the older children turned out the lights.

Jenny stepped forward with the programme in her hands although she couldn't see to read it. She had memorised the order of the stories.

Mr Davis pressed a button and the screen lit up, showing a picture of camels in the desert with towering pyramids behind.

Rosemary began to speak, telling of Moses and the Israelites and their escape from Egypt, as Mr Davis turned the handle to reveal the pictures illustrating the story. When it came to the parting of the Red Sea, the children gasped in amazement at the colourful scene. Rosemary had seen it before but she had to admit the illustrations were very realistic.

After a short pause for Mr Davis to load the next set of slides, Jenny announced that they were now going to see scenes from Africa. There were 'oohs' and 'ahs' from the children as pictures of lions, elephants and crocodiles followed in quick succession.

Rosemary had deliberately broken the programme up so that there were not too many Bible stories. Next came photos of the Royal family and the Coronation of King George the sixth a few years ago, then more animal and nature pictures.

Finally, the Christmas story was projected on to the screen as a fitting end to the show.

The lights came on and people shifted in their seats. Rosemary was pleased to see smiles and nods of appreciation from the grown-ups as well as the children.

She clapped her hands to gain their attention. 'Please thank Mr Davis and Miss Blackwell for their hard work in putting the show together. I hope you all enjoyed it.' Then, when the applause had died down, she directed them to the next-door classroom where the party food had been laid out.

'When you've finished your tea, come back here for the party games,' she said, hoping some of the grown-ups would stay to help put the chairs away. Mr Davis and Jenny were carefully packing up the magic lantern and its slides.

'It went well, didn't it,' Jenny said.

'Perhaps we can do it again,' said Mr Davis.

'It certainly seemed to take their minds off the war and the air raids.'

'And the dreadful news from America,' said Mr Davis. 'I heard a rumour that they'll be coming here.'

'Here? To our village you mean?'

'Taking over the RAF station, they said.'

'Just a rumour, surely.' Rosemary dismissed the thought.

The children had finished their tea and were coming back to the hall. Rosemary and Jenny were kept busy organising the games.

It wasn't until she was on her way home after helping to clear up the debris from the party that she thought about the rumour. Even, if it was true, it would hardly impact the life of the village.

***

Christmas was not the joyful celebration that Rosemary remembered from her own childhood. Then it had been a magical time. But she and Mrs Norton did their best to make it so for Lily. In spite of the food shortages, they had managed to stretch the sugar ration to make cakes and puddings and Moira Thompson in the village shop had magically produced a pink sugar mouse from the storeroom in the back – 'to put in the little one's stocking,' she said.

Lily had seemed to enjoy herself though, and as Mrs Norton said, 'the poor thing would probably have had far less at home.'

The celebrations over, Rosemary was back at the Manor packing boxes for the Red Cross. She took Lily with her and the little girl was pleased to be back playing with Maisie and the doll's house.

Rosemary felt quite happy to leave her in the playroom with Maisie, confident that they would not get up to any mischief. Brian was a different story, always into scrapes. And if the weather was bad, as it seemed to be most days in January, he would spend his time teasing the girls and snatching at their toys.

Mrs Pargeter was at her wits' end. 'I don't know what to do with him,' she said.

'I don't think he means any harm,' Rosemary said, remembering her own tussles with her brother. When they were small, they were always arguing although fond of each other. Now, they were good friends and she missed him dreadfully, praying constantly for his safety.

'I think he's just bored and he resents having to look out for Maisie. And the other boys are too young,' Mrs Pargeter said. 'If only we could have some decent

64

weather so that he can get outside and work off some of that energy.'

Rosemary had an idea. 'Why don't we ask Percy Fenton if he can help in the forge. I'm sure he could do with some help.'

'I'm not sure. It could be dangerous. I wouldn't want the boy to get hurt.'

'I know Brian would like it. We stopped by the forge on the way home from school one day and he was fascinated. I'm sure Percy would make sure he was safe.'

The suggestion worked and Brian went to the forge every day after school, doing odd jobs for the blacksmith and running errands for him. Best of all he loved the big Suffolk Punches, patiently holding their heads while Percy fitted the horseshoes.

'He seems to have taken to country life,' Jenny said as they watched the boy racing out of the school gate one cold February day.

'I wonder if he'll want to go back to London when the war's over,' Rosemary said, taking Lily's hand.

'When!' Jenny exclaimed. 'It seems to be going on forever. I thought once the Americans came in it would be over soon.'

'Well, it seems the rumours were true. Colonel Pargeter told me they're moving in to the RAF station. A couple of farms up there have been taken over so they can extend the runways. It won't be for a while though. There's a lot of work to be done before the base becomes operational.'

'Yes, Percy said the American planes are huge bombers. They need a lot of room to take off and land.'

Rosemary shuddered. It was bad enough during the Battle of Britain when Spitfires and Hurricanes were swooping over the village firing at the enemy. She hoped that the village would be safer now.

Jenny changed the subject. 'Have you heard from Michael lately?'

Rosemary shook her head. 'I'm sure he writes but letters do go astray.' She didn't mention Simon, although she constantly hoped to hear from him. She had told her friend about meeting hm, nearly two years ago now, but didn't feel she could confide her growing feelings for him. Ridiculous, she told herself, when they had only had two brief meetings. She didn't even know where he was. But she still prayed for his safety and looked for the post every day. Rumours were rife that the Royal Norfolks were on their way to the Far East.

Chapter 7

January 1942

Simon clutched the ship's railing as another huge wave broke over the bows. He had never been seasick before, but then, until a year ago, he had only ever gone on boat trips off the pier at Great Yarmouth and never in storms like this.

At first, the voyage from Southampton hadn't been too bad despite the rough seas of the Bay of Biscay – just a little queasiness for a day or two.

After a brief stop in South Africa, he hadn't been too dismayed when they set off on another sea voyage. That was until they hit a tropical storm off Java. Thank goodness he hadn't joined the navy he thought as his stomach heaved and he leaned over the rail again. Second Lieutenant Ron Wells laughed. 'Not far to go now, mate,' he said.

'Optimist,' Simon scoffed. 'We don't even know where we're going.'

'Stands to reason – we've got tropical gear and this is tropical weather.'

'Well, wherever we end up, it can't be too soon for me,' Simon said. Despite having been quite good at Geography when at school, he had only a hazy idea of where they were. Rumours were rife and he'd heard Burma, Siam and India mentioned in the ward room. But the Japanese were the enemy now and it seemed they were intent on over-running the whole of Asia. In spite of the rumours he'd heard, it surely couldn't be as bad as this.

A few days later, the sea calmed and Simon began to feel a little more optimistic about their final destination. He was up on deck, his sketchbook open on his knee, trying to draw a school of flying fish which were following the ship. They were small, quite insignificant creatures, quite unlike those he'd imagined. It was hard to sketch them as they moved so quickly but he was determined to keep a record of the voyage. Before being overcome with seasickness he'd even captured the huge waves that crashed over the bow of the ship.

He was concentrating so hard he didn't hear Ron approach until he said. 'Got the word – it's Malaya, northern Malaya.'

'What?'

'Malaya – that's where we're going.'

'You sure? Someone said Burma.'

'I know it's supposed to be secret but everyone seems sure. Don't know why Malaya though. The north is all jungle.'

Simon knew from one of his old school friends whose father owned a rubber plantation that there were many Europeans living in Malaya who would need defending if the Japanese decided to invade.

Chapter 8

April 1942
The quiet of a Sunday morning in April was suddenly broken by the loud roar of engines as a stream of vehicles entered the village. Morning service had just finished and Rosemary was standing beside her father saying goodbye to the congregation.

Some of the older villagers looked alarmed and she heard one old lady say in a trembling voice, 'Is it the Germans?'

Before the Rector could reassure her, Brian pushed past and ran down the path to the gate. 'It's the Americans,' he shouted.

Several boys followed him, waving and cheering as jeeps and lorries passed by in a seemingly endless stream. Smartly uniformed men sat upright in the leading jeep, smiling and waving to the children.

Brian stopped suddenly, his face puzzled. 'Hang on – those aren't American airmen. Wrong uniform.' He grabbed his friend's arm and pointed to the line of open lorries following the jeep. 'Look at them. Never seen anyone like them before – 'cept at the pictures.' He ran across the road to the forge where Percy Fenton stood watching the procession of vehicles.

'What's going on, Mr Fenton? Who are they?'

'Those men are negroes – coloured men. They've come to get the airfield ready for the big bombers. They're actually soldiers – part of the US Army Air Force. It's not separate like ours.'

'But they've got runways and all that already – the RAF have been there for ages.'

Percy smiled down at the boy and answered patiently. 'They need more room. They've already bought up part of White's Farm so they can lengthen the runways. Those American bombers are huge – they need a lot of room.' He pointed across the road to where Mrs Pargeter stood with Rosemary and Jenny. 'Better not keep Mrs P waiting. Off you go.'

Brian ran back to where some of the villagers still stood at the roadside chattering excitedly among themselves. Mrs Pargeter grabbed him by the collar and marched him and his friend off towards the Manor.

The Rector had already gone home and Rosemary was about to follow him when she spotted Maggie the landlord's daughter outside the *Four Bells*. She was chatting to the men who'd gathered outside the pub clutching their tankards of ale, reluctant to go home to their Sunday dinner after the excitement.

'Perhaps she'll cheer up now the Americans are here,' she said.

'Well, she was a bit upset that the RAF boys had gone but I think she'll get over it,' Jenny said, chuckling.

Rosemary's face creased in a disapproving frown. 'I don't think so. They don't look like her sort.'

'That won't stop Maggie. Anything in trousers.'

'That's not very nice, Jenny. I know she's a bit of a flirt but there's no harm in it. Besides...' Rosemary didn't like to say what was in her mind. She'd seen a lot of American films and noticed how the coloured people were treated over there. She was sure those in charge at the air base would make sure their rules were followed over here as well.

'Besides what?' Jenny said. Her eyes widened as understanding dawned. 'Oh, I see.'

Rosemary shrugged. 'Well, I'd better get home. Father will be wanting his dinner.'

May 1942

Rosemary placed the bunch of cornflowers and ox-eye daisies on her mother's grave and sat back on her heels, holding her face up to the sun. It was so quiet here, just the sound of a blackbird singing his heart out in the nearby yew tree.

She pulled a few weeds from the area around the grave and sighed. She loved it here. A few years ago, she had longed to get away. Then, she had thought it was too quiet, nothing ever happened in this sleepy little village. Her school friends had gone away to work in the city or to do a university degree and she had been envious – guiltily so. Of course, she had been happy to give everything up to help nurse her mother. There would be plenty of time later. But as time went on and Mother didn't recover, she had begun to feel trapped. And after Mother's death, her father had needed her.

The war had changed her feelings and now, she loved being involved in village life, helping her father with his church duties, looking after the evacuee children. And her work for the Red Cross meant she could feel useful while still being able to care for her father.

Suddenly, the peace of the churchyard was rent with the raucous sound of heavy lorries trundling up the village street. It had been going on for weeks. First it had been steamrollers and tractors tearing up the ground around the old RAF base, adding more runways. Now it was lorries carrying prefabricated parts for the buildings which were now filling the spaces around the edge of the airfield. The original control tower had been demolished and a new larger one was in the process of being erected.

Rosemary stood up and brushed the grass from her skirt, her few precious moments of relaxation over. She looked down at the flowers she had placed on the grave, remembering her meeting with Simon Spencer two years ago. She still hadn't heard from him although he had promised to write.

She sighed. Why was she still thinking of him? What was it about him that had captured her heart?

She was still deep in thought when Brian came running up the path waving his arms around and making aeroplane noises. She stepped aside before he could bump into her.

'Watch out, Brian.'

'Sorry, Miss.' He grinned at her.

'What are you up to now?'

'I've just been up to the base. It all looks so different, Miss.'

'There's not much to see though, is there?'

Brian shook his head. 'I can't wait till the big bombers get here. I asked one of the men but the Sergeant chased me off. He was really nasty to the man I spoke to – told him to mind his manners. But I heard Maggie in the pub saying the coloured men were all very polite.'

'Well, Brian you shouldn't be hanging round the pub – or the air base. Mrs Pargeter would be very cross if she knew you were making a nuisance of yourself.'

'I'm not a nuisance – I'm just bored.' Brian kicked a stone in the road.

Rosemary sighed. 'Bored? I thought you were helping Mr Fenton in the forge.'

'He's got no jobs for me today.' Brian ran off before she could say more.

So, Maggie had been talking to the coloured men, Rosemary thought. That would give the old biddies something to gossip about. It was none of her business though and she made her way home deep in thought, hoping there would be a letter waiting for her.

Chapter 9

May 1942

When Rosemary went to get the week's groceries, the village shop was crowded and she stood in the queue, shifting her feet impatiently, list and ration book in her hand. She usually enjoyed chatting to the other villagers as she waited but today, she was keen to get on. She was late for her shift at the Manor and the Red Cross parcels were piling up. Mrs Norton had volunteered to do the shopping but Rosemary was reluctant to ask her to do too much. The older women looked tired, as they all were after nearly three years of war, and Rosemary reminded herself that she was a guest in the Turners' home, not a servant. She should not be doing such much of the cooking and cleaning. Lost in thought, she gradually became aware of the noisy chatter surrounding her.

'It's dreadful. They're saying hundreds killed,' someone said.

Rosemary tapped her neighbour on the arm. 'What's happened?'

'Haven't you heard. Tons of bombs dropped on Norwich. It was on the wireless.'
Rosemary gasped. 'I didn't have it on this morning. Hundreds? Are you sure?' She couldn't believe it. The blitz on London had been bad but there had only been a few raids here.

The other shoppers in the queue joined in with their thoughts on the raid. 'I hear they got the Caley's chocolate factory,' one said.

There were murmurs of shock and others had their impressions to add.

'What about the Cathedral?' Rosemary asked the woman who had spoken.

'I think it escaped serious damage but...' she sighed. 'St Benedict's – completely destroyed.'

She gasped, hoping the rector, a friend of her father's, was safe.

While the gossip and speculations flew, Moira carried on serving and at last it was Rosemary's turn. She handed Moira her list and ration book, hoping that they still had everything she needed.

'You're in luck today,' Moira said, piling the goods on the counter. 'We've had a delivery.'

Rosemary smiled and handed over her ration book, watching as Moira carefully clipped the coupons. But, as she packed the groceries into her shopping bag, she couldn't feel pleased about the supplies, her thoughts on the people of the nearby city.

She turned to leave, nodding at the shoppers still discussing the bombing raid. 'I hear the *Boar's Head* copped it,' she heard someone say.

'Oh, dear. My Bert won't be happy. He always enjoyed a pint in there after work.' It was the wife of a villager who worked in the Colman's mustard factory and was noted for his love of a pint.

A burst of laughter followed Rosemary out of the shop and she marvelled at people's ability to find humour in such a tragic situation.

***

Over the next few days there were more devastating bombing raids on Norwich and a few of the nearby villages. Rosemary rarely went into the city but she could imagine the devastation and breathed a prayer of thanks that so far, apart from the damage to Mrs Norton's cottage, their village had been spared.

The raids on Norwich had an effect on Oakleigh St James, however. In the next few weeks, the population of the village increased as friends and relatives from the town sought sanctuary with their families. They brought with them heart-rending tales of the destruction of their beloved city although the Cathedral had only suffered minor damage and the castle still stood unharmed.

'How are you coping?' Rosemary asked when she met Jenny from school on a sunny day in May.

'We're managing but with six extra children in our little classroom, it's not easy. We really do appreciate your help with the little ones.'

'I wish I had more time but we're so busy with the Red Cross work.'

Jenny sighed. 'Poor Mr Davis has seven extra boys - little horrors.'

Three of the 'little horrors' and their mother were staying with the Pargeters. Before her marriage, Betty Rook had been a maid at the Manor. She had now taken on the Manor cooking in addition to helping with the parcels. Rosemary had become quite fond of the children. 'They're not that bad surely,' she said.

'Not really. Mrs Rook's boys are quite well-behaved. Well, the oldest one, Ted, is a bit cheeky. He's made friends with Brian and the two of them get up to all sorts of mischief. The two younger ones are very quiet though, scared of everything. Poor lads. Billy's only five and John's still a toddler. They've suffered so much. We make allowances for them, what with losing their home and their father wounded and in hospital.'

'How long will they stay?'

'Until it's safe to go back, I suppose.'

When will that be, Rosemary asked herself. Suddenly the war seemed so much closer now she had seen the effects at first hand.

August 1942

The American soldiers were soon accepted in the village once the novelty of seeing black and brown faces wore off. Some of them came to church and the Rev Turner welcomed them.

A few of the older residents were a bit wary of them but the children were fascinated. Brian and Ted Rook came back to the Manor full of importance one day.

'We've been talking to the workmen,' he said. 'They've nearly finished the building work. Won't be long before the big bombers get here one of them told us.'

'You shouldn't be playing around up near the base,' Mrs Pargeter said. 'I told you not to go up there again. I don't want you boys getting into trouble.'

'Well, we ain't going up there anymore. That big bloke chased us off like before. Ted was scared.'

'I wasn't scared,' Ted protested.

'What big bloke?' Rosemary asked with a worried frown.

'He's a Sergeant in charge – not one of them darkies though. He shouts at them something awful.'

Rosemary knew which man he meant. A few days earlier she had been in the back room of the pub chatting to Maggie's mother after taking her some eggs from the Rectory hens when a commotion broke out in the public bar.

'They're not allowed in here,' the sergeant shouted. Rosemary peeped round the edge of the door to see a burly man waving his baton, the stick the men in charge carried to enforce their authority. Three coloured men cowered in a corner. Two farm workers sitting at the bar carried on drinking.

'Who says?' Ron the landlord growled.

'I do. It's against our rules for coloureds to mix with whites.'

'Your rules maybe, but they're off duty so...'

'That's right,' one of the farm workers muttered and got off his stool ready to back Ron up.

The sergeant ignored them and chivvied the soldiers outside, not giving them time to finish their beer. At the door, he paused and said to Ron. 'I'll be putting up a notice forbidding them to come in here on pain of punishment.'

'You can't do that,' Ron protested. But he was talking to empty air.

He stormed out the back, slamming the door. 'Bloody cheek, telling me who I can and can't serve.'

'Can he do that?' Rosemary asked.

'We'll see. Any notice he puts up on my pub will be torn down, just you see.'

Just then Maggie came downstairs, hair done and fresh makeup on. 'What's all the row about?'

When her father told her, she said, 'I don't understand. They seem such nice boys, always polite.' She giggled. 'One of them called me, mam.'

Maggie's mum, Dot, said, 'You're right, love but perhaps you shouldn't get too friendly with them. We don't want any trouble.'

Rosemary agreed but she didn't think Maggie would take any notice. Thank goodness when the work on the airfield was done the men would be moving on.

Chapter 10

November 1942

Rosemary was worried about Percy's mother. He had told her she was feeling under the weather. 'She don't like the cold, says it gets into her bones,' he'd said.

'I'll go and see her when I have time, see if she needs anything,' she said.

'I get the shopping for us. She don't go short. It's company she needs so if you could pop in when you've got a minute, she'd be grateful.'

Although she was very busy, she determined to make time for a quick visit to the old lady and the day after talking to Percy she walked up to the Fentons' cottage and knocked on the back door.

Although he had said not to take her anything, Rosemary felt she couldn't call empty-handed and she had scrounged a couple of Mrs Norton's famous cheese scones already spread with a scrape of precious butter.

Mrs Fenton was, as usual, sitting in her chair by the fire, the woollen shawl over her knees and another draped round her shoulders. Her eyes lit up when Rosemary unwrapped the treat. 'Your Mrs Norton's a grand cook,' she said, biting into one of the scones. 'I don't know how she does it with the rationing as bad as it's got lately.'

'She certainly has got a magic touch,' Rosemary agreed, filling the kettle and putting it on the hob.

'How are you getting on with the evacuees?' Mrs Fenton asked. 'My Percy tells me that young Brian is a real help in the forge.'

'It keeps him out of mischief,' Rosemary said with a laugh. She filled the teapot and brought the tray over, set it on the little table by Mrs Fenton's chair. 'He certainly seems to enjoy helping. Maybe he'll be a blacksmith when he grows up,' she said.

Mrs Fenton sighed. 'I think Percy would like a son to follow on but it don't look likely. I know he's sweet on that Maggie from the *Four Bells* but she won't give him the time of day. Not that I'm sorry – a barmaid's not the right sort of wife for a man like my Percy.'

'Maggie's not just a barmaid, she helps with the Red Cross parcels when she has time. Besides, I think she's too young to be thinking of settling down,' Rosemary said, handing Mrs Fenton her cup of tea.

'Not a question of too young – too flighty more like.' The old lady pursed her lips. 'I hear things you know. Always flirting with those RAF boys, going dancing in Norwich.'

Rosemary leapt to defend her friend. 'I think most young people feel like that – with the war and all. They want to have fun. Who knows what tomorrow will bring. Besides, the RAF have left the airfield. There's soldiers up there now, getting it ready for the big American bombers.'

Mrs Fenton leaned forward. 'Coloured men,' she whispered. 'Let's hope young Maggie don't get mixed up with them.'

'I'm sure she won't.' Rosemary tried to change the subject. She didn't like talking about her friend behind her back. She stood up and picked up the teapot. 'More tea?' she asked.

'No thanks, love. But I'll have that other scone if you don't mind.'

'You're welcome,' Rosemary said, placing it on the plate. 'I'll just wash up the tea things, then I must be off to meet Lily from school.'

As she hurried down the village street past the pub, she saw Ron nailing a sheet of paper to the public bar door. She crossed over and said, 'What's this in aid of then?'

Ron showed her the poster. '*All American soldiers welcome. Anyone not wishing to mix with the coloured men are welcome to use the saloon bar next door.*'

A big red arrow pointed towards the other bar and the word 'ALL' was heavily underlined. 'That's put that big sergeant in his place,' Ron said with a satisfied grin.

'Good for you.' Rosemary hurried on to the school, hoping that Ron's gesture wouldn't lead to any trouble. She also agreed with Mrs Fenton's hope that Maggie would steer clear of the controversial visitors to the village.

Fortunately, the work at the base was almost finished and the soldiers would soon be gone.

December 1942

Christmas had come round again all too quickly. Rosemary and Jenny were determined to give the children as good a time as possible despite the shortage of festive fare in the village shop. They put a notice up in the church porch asking for donations of toys and games which the older children no longer played with.

'People are so kind,' Rosemary said, adding a doll and a wooden train to the box in the vestry. 'We'll have something for every child in the village, not just the evacuees.'

'Yes, it's a good idea to include the village children so they don't feel left out,' Jenny agreed.

'I was wondering if we could give them another magic lantern show. There's still some slides they haven't seen,' Rosemary suggested.

'They seemed to enjoy the last one.,' Jenny said. 'Besides some of the more recent evacuees haven't seen it.'

They decided to ask Mr Davis if they could use the school again.

Preparing for Christmas helped to take their minds off the news of the RAF's recent heavy losses. It wasn't so much due to the enemy as the really bad weather which seemed to have gone on for weeks.

'I can't believe we're still at war after all this time – the fourth Christmas. When will it all end?' Rosemary sighed.

'There seems to be better news from the Far East – the Americans are making progress.'

Rosemary didn't believe it. Why hadn't they had any real news? Why hadn't anyone heard from the prisoners captured by the Japanese more than a year ago? She worried about Simon, sure that he must have been captured. She wondered whether she should write to Dr Spencer again and ask if he'd heard from his son. Perhaps she would send him a Christmas card.

Chapter 11

February 1943

One cold grey day in February the quiet of the little village was once again broken by a roaring overhead, accompanied by the trundling of vehicles entering the main street.

People rushed out of their houses and the children abandoned their lessons, ignoring Jenny and the headmaster's protests. They thronged the playground, looking up at the huge aircraft darkening the sky.

'They're here – the Americans are really here at last,' Brian shouted, jumping up and down in excitement.

The older people weren't quite so excited at the invasion of their village, albeit a friendly invasion.

'About time,' Ron muttered, standing outside the *Four Bells* with Percy and Amos.

'Let's hope they do some good now they are here,' Amos said. 'We've struggled on alone for too long.'

They stood in silence as a long line of jeeps and lorries snaked through the narrow main street.

'Your Maggie will be happy,' Amos said. 'She was missing those RAF chaps buying her drinks and taking her dancing.'

'Don't talk about my daughter like that,' Ron snapped.

'Just joking, bor. Didn't mean anything by it.'

Percy just scowled and didn't comment. Just because she was a pretty lass who enjoyed a bit of a giggle with the boys didn't mean anything. When the war was over and the lads had all gone home, he'd still be here.

The newcomers made little impact at first, although there was a lot more traffic through the village. The Americans soon settled in and by the end of the first week the sound of the big bombers roaring overhead filled the air. It was hard not to flinch and duck when they passed over but after a while everyone in the village got used to it as the presence of the men and their aircraft became part of daily life.

Brian was fascinated by the huge American planes and, whenever Percy Fenton didn't need him in the forge, he and his friends would walk up to the airfield after school and watch the aircraft landing and taking off. Soon he knew all the names of the different planes, the size of the bombs and how many crew they carried.

Most of the airmen tolerated the children hanging around the perimeter fence and offered them chewing gum and chocolate. Some of the senior officers chased them off but the lure of sweets for children deprived of treats due to rationing proved irresistible and Brian and his friends crept back whenever they got the chance.

One spring day Brian, bored with lessons, hid away when the bell rang after dinner break and when all was quiet, ran across the fields to the American base. He ducked at the sound of a roar overhead, clinging on to the chain link fence as a B17 came in to land. The plane taxied to the end of the runway and the crew leapt out.

Engrossed in the activity around the plane, Brian jumped as a hand landed on his shoulder. 'What are you up to, sonny?' a gruff voice said. 'And what's your name?'

'Brian, sir. I'm not up to anything - just watching.'

'A spy, eh?' the American said.

Brian shook his head.' No, sir. I just like planes. I'm going to fly when I'm old enough.'

'OK. I believe you, sonny. Now tell me, why aren't you in school?'

'I don't like sums, so I ran away.'

'Now you listen to me, young Brian. Your schooling, especially if you want to fly some day, is very important, especially sums. So don't let me see you hanging around here again on a school day.'

'Me and my mates come here most days after school. The other airmen don't mind.'

'Well, I'm not an airman, I'm chief of the ground crew. If it wasn't for me and my crew, those planes would never get off the ground.' He tousled Brian's hair and grinned. 'Ok, coming here after school is OK, and at weekends. I'll look out for you. If I'm not around, just ask for Master Sergeant Floyd Bowman.'

'Thank you, sir.' Brian saluted and ran off.

As he approached the school, the bell for end of classes rang and, as his classmates poured out of the building, he tried to slip in among them, hoping he wouldn't be noticed. But to no avail and he cringed as Mr Davis called, 'Brian Cox, where have you been?'

Brian sidled over to the headmaster thinking furiously. If he said he'd been helping Mr Fenton, he might get away with it. But he was sure to be found out in a lie. He had learned early on that nothing escaped the notice of the villagers.

'Well, Cox. What have you been up to?'

'I went to look at the planes, sir.'

Mr Davis sighed. The presence of these Americans had brought much excitement to the village, especially the boys. He couldn't blame them. Even the grown-ups seemed to be fascinated by these exotic seeming foreigners in their midst. The novelty would soon die down, he hoped.

He glanced down at the boy, who was studiously examining his shoes as he waited for his punishment. He sighed again. 'All right, Cox. I won't cane you this time. But you will stay behind after school tomorrow and do some sums. And you must promise me not to play truant again.'

Brian let out the breath he had been holding. 'I won't, sir, I promise. Can I go now, please?'

Mr Davis nodded and Brian ran off. He didn't fancy the prospect of doing sums after school tomorrow but it was better than getting the cane. The master at his London school had got the cane out on the slightest provocation and he'd been on the receiving end more than once. He paused by the pond but none of his mates were there. He couldn't wait to tell them that he'd actually spoken to a Yank and had been invited up to the airfield to look at the planes again. He pictured their disbelieving looks when he got to school the next day. But Mr Fenton would be waiting so he ran across to the forge.

***

The colt reared and whinnied and Percy Fenton held on to his halter. Where was Brian? he thought with a twinge of irritation. He had begun to rely on the lad coming after school to help in the forge. The other children had already run past, chattering like a flock of sparrows but there was no sign of Brian.

He could have done with the lad holding the feisty colt's head to keep him steady. H finished fitting the horse's shoe and patted the animal's neck, leading him over to the railing, tying him securely. One of Farmer Hubbard's men would come and fetch him later on.

As he started to tidy his tools away, Brian almost fell in the doorway, panting.

'So, what've you been up to boy? I thought you'd be here when school let out.'

Brian caught his breath. 'Sorry I'm late. I was kept in,' he said.

'Been up to mischief, eh?'

Brian hung his head, reluctant to admit he'd been playing truant for the afternoon. 'I've got to stay behind tomorrow too but I'll come after,' he said.

Percy's annoyance faded. He had some sympathy with the lad. 'Not to worry. I was young once, you know. Always sloping off – I preferred the horses to lessons.'

'I like horses but planes are more interesting,' Brian said.

Percy guessed where the boy had been but he didn't say anything, just handed him a bucket and shovel and directed him to clean up the droppings in the yard.

When he'd finished the job, Percy told him to be off home. 'Don't want to be late for your tea,' he said, 'otherwise Mrs P will be on my back for making you work too hard.'

Brian grinned and ran off.

Two hours later, Percy was sitting in the *Four Bells*, a foaming tankard in front of him. He was making his pint last – eking it out until Maggie came on duty. Why did he bother though? She'd let him take her to the pictures in Norwich a couple of times but the RAF lads in their smart uniforms were more to her liking. When they'd left, his hopes had risen – and then the yanks had arrived.

They'd be here soon, filling the pub with their loud jokes and laughter, throwing their money around. He took a swig of his beer and another. Might as well finish it and go home. As he drained his tankard, the curtain behind the bar was swept aside and there she was.

Her blonde curls framed her pink and white complexion, her blue eyes sparkled and without conscious thought, he picked up his tankard and went to the bar. He'd take a chance while the yanks weren't here to cramp his style.

'Evening Percy – another pint is it,' she said, her fingers brushing his as she took his empty glass. His heart beat faster as he smiled back at her.

She pulled a pint and pushed it across the bar. 'Been working hard?' she asked.

'Quite busy,' he said. Then, taking a deep breath, he said, 'I was wondering...'

Before he could finish speaking, the door opened and a noisy group of American airmen pushed their way in.

Maggie's eyes lit up and she quickly deposited Percy's money in the till and turned to the newcomers. 'Evening boys, what can I get you?'

A chorus of calls for drinks the pub didn't have and Maggie's attempts to explain about rationing and shortages, kept her busy and Percy watched, his mouth turned down in a frown. Who did they think they were, coming over here, throwing their weight about and eyeing up the girls? Not that there were many girls left in the village, apart from the land girls on the surrounding farms. Most had joined the forces, lured by the glamour of a uniform, or gone to work in factories. But Maggie was still here, though what chance did he have – with his blackened fingernails, dirty leather apron and the constant smoky smell of the forge lingering in his clothing?

He downed his pint and slammed the glass down, pushed his way through the crowded bar. Outside, he breathed in the scent of hawthorn blossom and tried to forget Maggie. She was known for her flirtatious ways and he knew deep down she wasn't for him. He prayed the war would soon be over and the village would be left in peace again. Maybe he'd have a chance with her then.

Chapter 12

April 1943

Rosemary sat in the family pew at the front of the church gazing up at her father. He looked so tired and his sermon today lacked his usual enthusiasm and vigour. She was quite worried about him. Even after all these years, he was still grieving for his wife and she knew his faith was being tested. She often heard him pacing his room, muttering prayers. He was worried about Michael too and also concerned that she might leave home to join one of the forces although she had repeatedly tried to reassure him.

The church was full today, the usual congregation filled out by the newcomers to the village. The rear pews were crowded with men in uniform and there were several Land Girls present. They were not regular churchgoers and Rosemary thought they had been drawn in by curiosity about the strangers in their midst. The Rector had welcomed the Americans warmly and thanked them for being here, expressing hope that their presence would help to shorten the war.

At last, the service ended and Rosemary was glad to get out in the fresh air. Most of the congregation lingered outside, many eager to make the acquaintance of the Americans. She didn't linger, making the excuse that she had to get home to see to the dinner. She hoped Father would not be detained too long. She really was worried about him. He had brightened up after getting the news that Michael was a prisoner and receiving a letter from him. But there had been no further news. Why didn't her brother write and set their minds at rest, she wondered.

Jenny caught up with her as she stepped over the churchyard wall into the Rectory grounds. 'What's the hurry?' she asked.

'Sorry, Jen. I just couldn't stand everyone fawning over the Yanks. It's as if they've forgotten about our boys and what they've been through.'

'No news from Michael then?'

Rosemary shook her head. 'Father's worried. He convinced he's not being treated well – or worse.'

'I keep hoping for a letter too. When he went away, he promised to write but I suppose it's not easy for him.' Jenny took her friend's arm. 'What about you? Have you heard from Simon?'

'Why do you think I might have. I wasn't expecting him to write. I don't even know where he is now.'

Jenny gave her arm a little shake. 'You can't fool me. I know he made quite an impression on you. Why don't you write to him.'

'I can't – I don't have an address.' She couldn't admit to her friend how much she longed for a letter. Truthfully, she was more worried about him than she was about her brother. At first, she had imagined him in North Africa which was bad enough but, since the fall of Singapore she couldn't help feeling that he had been sent out there. The news from Malaya wasn't good and no letters were getting through.

At least she knew where Michael was and that he was safe – that was, as far as they knew, given that she knew very little about conditions in the POW camps.

They stopped at the entrance to the Rectory and Rosemary said, 'I must go – Mrs Norton will need help with the dinner.'

'I haven't seen much of you lately – you're always so busy.'

'I don't have much time to myself these days what with the Red Cross parcels and helping with the children. Not to mention parish duties.'

'You must have some time off. It's a lovely day. Why not join me for a walk this afternoon?'

'All right, but I'll have to bring Lily. Where shall we go?'

'Nowhere near the airbase, that's for sure. They must get fed up with the boys hanging around, not to mention the land girls.'

Rosemary laughed. 'We'll go across the stream to the copse. The bluebells might be out now.'

'A bit early,' Jenny said.

'Primroses then.

Rosemary laughed and they agreed to meet later.

***

A few days later, Rosemary had packed the last box ready for collection and she and Betty Rook were on their way to the kitchen for a welcome break and a cup of tea.

Mrs Norton, who was helping out at the Manor today, was making pastry and she thumped the rolling pin down as they entered. 'Have you heard the latest?' she asked, her face red with indignation.

Before they could ask, the housekeeper said, 'That Maggie from the *Four Bells*. She's been seen up in Carter's wood with one of them yanks. Disgusting I call it, when that RAF boy she was sweet on is flying into danger every day.

Betty raised her eyebrows and Rosemary shrugged. She couldn't help thinking that the American lads were also flying into danger every day. It wasn't as if Maggie had been engaged to the British airman. She didn't get a chance to comment as Mrs Norton was in full flow, condemning the local girls who were 'throwing themselves at the yanks' as she put it.

Rosemary busied herself making tea while Betty made spam sandwiches for their lunch. Mrs Norton gave a final thump to the pastry and began to line a dish. She glanced over at the girls and shrugged her shoulders. 'Don't mind me. I just get so cross thinking

90

about our poor lads away fighting and they're here with their smart uniforms and plenty of money.'

'And my Bill lying in a military hospital wondering if he'll ever walk again,' Betty said.

'Well, you see what I mean then?' Mrs Norton pursed her lips and carried the pie dish to the big oven, slamming the door and then noisily clearing up the debris from her baking.

The girls ate their lunch in silence and hurried back to work. Out in the corridor, Rosemary said, 'I do understand how she feels although I wanted to remind her that the Americans have left their loved ones behind too. It's just as hard for them. Who can blame them for wanting to have a bit of fun?'

They worked for a couple of hours and then it was time to go and meet the children from school.

They were standing by the school gate with the other mothers and carers when a huge army truck pulled up with four American airmen in it. A tall man with flaming red hair got out and strolled over to where the women stood.

'Is one of you ladies Brian's mom?' he asked.

They shook their heads. Rosemary said, 'He's an evacuee. His mother lives in London. He's staying at the Manor.' Her curiosity roused, she asked. 'What do you want with him?'

'I met him the other day. He snuck onto the base, looking at the planes. I just wanted to make sure he wasn't in trouble.'

'I believe the headmaster was cross with him for truanting. He should have been in school that afternoon.'

He glanced across at the school building. 'I guess he'll be out soon. Would it be OK to talk to him?'

'Why?' Rosemary asked sharply.

'Well, the lad seemed so interested in the planes and my buddies and me – we thought it would be nice to invite him and his friends to look over the base. We've got permission from the CO.'

'You'd have to get permission from the headmaster too.'

The American nodded. 'I'll do that. Nice to talk to you ladies.' He stuck his hand out. 'Master Sergeant Floyd Bowman at your service.'

Before any of them could reply, the bell rang and children poured out of the building. They swarmed around the American truck but Brian ran up to Rosemary, closely followed by the Rook brothers.

He grinned at the American. 'Hello, Mr Bowman,' he said and turned to his friends. 'He's my friend.'

'Hello, Brian. And it's Master Sergeant – not Mister.'

'Yes, sir – Master Sergeant.' He glanced over at the truck. 'Can we have a ride?'

The American shook his head. 'We're not allowed to carry civilians.'

Brian looked disappointed but Floyd said, 'I have to see your headmaster. '

The boy looked alarmed for a moment until he spotted the American's grin. He said a polite goodbye and raced off with the other boys.

'Nice kid,' Floyd said, turning to Rosemary. 'I hope we meet again,' he said and walked across the playground to where Mr Davis was talking to some of the older boys.

Rosemary gazed after him, wondering if he was the 'yank' Maggie had been seen with. She gave a mental shrug. It was none of her business anyway.

Jenny came towards her holding hands with Lily and Maisie. 'I saw you talking to that American,' Jenny said with a grin.'

Rosemary felt a blush creeping up her cheeks. 'He wanted to see the headmaster,' she said with an effort at nonchalance, unwilling to admit how attractive she thought Floyd Bowman was, despite his ginger hair.

'You seemed to be getting on well,' Jenny teased.

'I was only being polite. Anyway, he's the one who caught Brian sneaking into the base. He wanted to make sure the boy wasn't in trouble.'

Chapter 13

May 1943

Rosemary finished praying, sat back on the seat and picked up her hymn book. Before she could open it, Jenny gave her a nudge. 'Look who's here,' she whispered. 'They've just come in.'

A few of the Americans had become regular worshippers at morning service and had ceased to be objects of interest but Rosemary could not help turning round and having a peek. She turned back quickly when she spotted Floyd Bowman with a group of his fellow airmen seated in the rear pews.

The organ started up and she dug her elbow into her friend's side. 'Shh. Behave yourself,' she whispered.

As the service progressed, she tried to concentrate on the familiar words. But her thoughts kept returning to the group of young men seated at the rear of the church. Some of the older villagers resented the newcomers with their smart uniforms, brash voices and plenty of money. She couldn't blame them when so many of their own menfolk were away fighting. But the children and, especially, some of the young women, had made them welcome, to the dismay of those like Mrs Norton who could not accept the strangers in their midst,

Master Sergeant Bowman, however, seemed different, very polite and respectful and he had seemed genuinely concerned about Brian.

As they stood for the last hymn she looked up at the wall painting. It was such a familiar sight that she hardly noticed it anymore but since her encounter with Simon Spencer all those months ago it had gained more significance for her. If only he would write to her, she thought. His safety was far more important to her than a good-looking American, however nice he seemed to be.

At the close of service, she stood beside her father in the porch, shaking hands and smiling as the congregation filed out. Jenny gathered the children and led them out into the spring sunshine saying she would wait for her friend outside.

The Americans waited politely for the villagers to leave and then approached the Rector, thanking him for the service and smiling at Rosemary.

'Good to see you again, Miss Turner,' Floyd said.

'You know my daughter?' Seth interrupted.

'We met at the school, Father. Master Sergeant Bowman was calling on Mr Davis.'

'Yes, sir,' said Floyd. 'I wanted to get his permission to show the boys around the airfield. They seem so interested in our aircraft.'

Seth nodded. 'Good to see you boys getting involved in village life. And attending church,' he said.

'It reminds me of home.'

'Me too,' said another.

'We're country boys, see,' Floyd said. 'Oklahoma. Farming country.'

Seth smiled and shook hands with Floyd, who started to walk away with his buddies. At the lychgate he said hello to Jenny who was waiting there. As Rosemary caught up with her, Floyd called out, 'Miss Turner, would you and your friend like to come to the movies in Norwich one evening?'

'The movies?' Rosemary frowned.

'He means the pictures,' Jenny said with a laugh. 'We'd love to, wouldn't we, Rosie?'

'I'm not sure. I don't think...'

'You must come,' Jenny said.

'Please do. We've got the use of a truck, plenty of room. Just a few of us and we've asked a couple of the land girls to join us, haven't we, Will,' Floyd said, turning to his friend.

Will nodded. 'And Maggie from the pub is coming, isn't she, Hank?'

Faced with their enthusiasm, Rosemary couldn't say no. After all, she'd be with a crowd. It wasn't as if she was going on a date with just one of them.

'OK. We'll pick you up outside the *Four Bells* tomorrow evening,' said Floyd.

***

Rosemary shivered and pulled her jacket closer around her, wishing she'd worn her winter coat. It had been a warm sunny day and she hadn't realised how chilly it could still get in the evenings. She was starting to have second thoughts about the outing, especially as she was worried about Lily who still often woke up crying for her mum. Betty Rook had offered to keep an eye on her but she had three children of her own to look after. Rosemary felt a little guilty. She had taken on responsibility for the little girl who was still missing her mother and felt she should not be going out enjoying herself.

She was about to say to Jenny that she wouldn't come after all, when her friend linked arms with her, saying. 'Hope they won't be too long.'

'Perhaps something's happened on the base. I know they're supposed to be off duty tonight but you never know....'

'It's all right. They're here,' Jenny said as an American jeep roared up the village street.

'I thought they weren't allowed to carry civilians,' Rosemary said but Jenny just shrugged and laughed.

The jeep stopped outside the pub and Hank leaned out of the driving seat. 'Where's Maggie?' he asked.

'Here I am.' Maggie came out of the pub, stumbling in her high heels. She was wearing a flowery summer dress, a lacy stole around her shoulders.

Jenny nudged Rosemary. 'I bet she'll feel cold in that,' she said.

Floyd jumped down and took Rosemary's hand. 'Come along, girls. Up you get.' He helped her up into the rear of the jeep where two land girls were already sitting. He turned to Jenny. 'A bit of a squeeze but we'll be OK.'

The two other airmen shifted to make room and Jenny said, 'What about Maggie?' But as she looked round for the other girl, she saw that she had already got into the front seat beside Hank and was snuggled up beside him.

Rosemary felt a bit uncomfortable, remembering Mrs Norton's remarks about the 'flighty' barmaid. She hoped the other young men wouldn't get too familiar. She knew her father disapproved but she had persuaded him that Floyd and his friends were decent church-going young men and he had reluctantly agreed to the trip. She sat stiffly between Floyd and Will and tried to enjoy the unaccustomed treat of a night out at the cinema.

It was getting dark and Hank switched on the jeep's lights, showing only the tiny glimmer that was allowed in blacked-out Britain. She glanced nervously over the side of the open vehicle as Hank confidently navigated the dark country lanes.

She was surprised when Floyd said, 'Nearly there,' and she became aware of buildings looming up out of the darkness. She hadn't been to Norwich at night since the start of the war and had almost forgotten that there would be no street lights or lit-up shopfronts.

They pulled up outside the cinema and climbed out, stiff with cold. Rosemary was glad she'd worn a jacket and envied the land girls in their jumpers and dungarees.

The group hurried inside where, after a brief argument as to who was to pay for the tickets, which was won by the Americans, they were ushered to their seats.

The lights dimmed and the curtains opened on the screen. A short public information film reminding patrons to carry their gasmasks at all times had Maggie giggling. 'I've got make-up in mine,' she whispered.

Rosemary smiled. Hardly anyone in the village carried theirs but she supposed it was more important in the city in case of attacks. She sat up and paid attention when the newsreel came on, anxious to find out what was happening in other parts of the world. The film didn't reveal much that she hadn't already read about in the papers but there was a clip of the King's visit to Norfolk and a short piece about the arrival of the American Air Force in East Anglia which brought cheers from the girls' companions.

Rosemary felt embarrassed as people around them expressed disapproval of the Americans' behaviour, but Maggie turned round and told them sharply that they should remember why the lads were here.

'Shh, the film's starting,' Jenny said.

Rosemary wished she'd asked what film they were going to see and hoped it wasn't a war film or anything too romantic. She seldom went to the pictures and hadn't even seen *Gone with the Wind* which all her friends had raved about.

She was quite a fan of Judy Garland and began to enjoy *Easter Parade*, especially the music. She was so absorbed she didn't react to Jenny's nudge until a sharper dig made her look up.

'Look at those two,' her friend whispered, nodding her head to where, further along the row, Maggie and Hank were locked in an embrace.

'Leave them alone,' she replied and returned her attention to the film. But she couldn't get the image of those two out of her head. Unbidden, the thought came of that last meeting with Simon Spencer and the little thrill when he had taken her hand to say goodbye with the hope that they would meet again. Had she read too much into it? Sometimes she wished she wasn't so prim and proper – a product of her strict upbringing. Not that she would be as free and easy as Maggie of course. But she was nearly twenty-one, not a shy school girl. What was it about Simon that had attracted her when no other man had had such an effect on her?

Their first meeting had been so ordinary – just a conversation about the church and its treasures, something she could relate to. Of course, her constant thoughts of him had nothing to do with his dark wavy hair and warm brown eyes, or his lovely smile, she told herself.

Lost in thought, she didn't realise the film was ending until Jenny nudged her. She followed her friends out of the cinema where they stood on the pavement trying to decide what to do next.

Rosemary was all for going straight home but it was clear Maggie didn't want the evening to end.

'Let's go for a drink,' she said.

The Americans agreed and they left the jeep where it was and walked down a side street where Maggie knew of a pub.

When they'd arrived at the cinema there hadn't been time to notice the ruined buildings and piles of rubble around. Now, they walked cautiously, arms linked, stumbling over the uneven path. Most of the rubble had been cleared away from the main streets but silhouettes of damaged buildings loomed up around them out of the darkness.

'I hope she knows where we're going,' Jenny said, just as Maggie stopped in front of a small timbered building.

'Here we are,' she announced, pushing open the door and sweeping aside the blackout curtain.

'Put that light out,' a loud voice shouted and the group hastily pushed their way into the pub.

'Welcome to the '*Crown*', my favourite pub,' Maggie said. 'It's a miracle it's still here.'

The Americans crowded up to the bar telling the girls to find a table. A few of the patrons looked askance at the group but soon went back to their drinking when the girls and their escorts settled quietly at a table in the corner.

Rosemary sipped her shandy slowly, conscious of her father's disapproval if he discovered she'd even been in a pub, let alone drinking.

Her friends were talking animatedly to the Americans and seemed to be enjoying themselves. But she just wanted to go home. She took another cautious sip of the shandy, not really liking the taste.

'You're very quiet. Did you enjoy the movie?' Floyd asked, leaning towards her.

She nodded. 'I liked the music.'

'Good, wasn't it?'

She nodded, wishing she could say something positive about it. The truth was, she'd hardly concentrated on the film, her thoughts on the devastation of the city. It was far worse than she'd imagined. She'd also been thinking about her brother, wondering why she hadn't heard from him lately.

"You seem a bit sad. Are you thinking of your sweetheart.' Floyd asked.

Rosemary felt herself flushing but she answered honestly. 'I don't have a boyfriend. I'm worried about my brother. He's a prisoner in Germany.'

'Aw shucks, sorry. Is he OK, do you hear from him.'

'Not recently.'

'Miss Turner – Rosemary – I don't want to upset you but...' he hesitated. 'I'm really sorry about your brother and I hope you get news soon. But the reason I mentioned a sweetheart is – well, I like you and I wouldn't want to step on anyone's toes.'

If only she had mentioned Simon, she thought. But that was silly. She didn't even know him that well, couldn't even say they were friends. And Floyd was a nice young man, had been kind to Brian – and he was a churchgoer which would please her father.

She smiled at him. 'There's no one special,' she said.

He grinned. 'So, you'll let me take you out some time – just us two not...' he waved his glass at his friends and the girls who were laughing and chatting. It was as if the two of them were alone.

'Maybe,' she said, looking across the table at Jenny who seemed to be enjoying Will's company. Where was the harm, she thought. Then she saw that Maggie, as usual was draped all over Hank and the two land girls were chatting up a couple of RAF airmen who had joined them.

Will stood up and rapped on the table, shouting, 'More drinks anyone?'

At that moment the landlord rang the bell over the bar and called out 'Time, please. Drink up.'

There were simultaneous groans from the Americans but the RAF airmen drained their glasses. 'Got to get back to camp anyway – early start tomorrow.'

With a noisy scraping of chairs, the group dispersed. Stumbling through the dark streets they found their way back to where the jeep was parked.

***

Rosemary's father was already in bed when she got home so she was spared any questioning about the friends she'd gone out with. She made herself a mug of cocoa and took it upstairs, looking in on Lily, who was fast asleep, before going to her room. Once in bed she couldn't sleep, confused thoughts of Floyd Bowman and Simon Spencer vying for attention in her head.

She liked Floyd, had enjoyed listening to his tales of life on the farm in Oklahoma where he'd grown up. A country person, like herself. But she couldn't imagine leaving her home and family to go and live so far away. And Rosemary was not the sort of girl to indulge in a casual relationship. She sat up and threw back the covers, laughing quietly at herself.

What was she thinking of? Floyd had said he liked her, would like to take her out. And he had held her hand in the back of the jeep, pecked her on the cheek when she'd been dropped off at the Rectory gate. It didn't really mean anything though.

She reached out to her dressing table for the little drawing of the church Simon had sent her which she had tucked into the edge of the mirror. She looked at it every day, remembering his intense concentration as he had sketched the *Doom*. She held the drawing close to the bedside lamp. She might never see him again but she would always treasure it. She switched the lamp off and fell asleep, still clutching the picture. If only she knew where he was and if he was safe.

Chapter 14

May 1943

'Speedo, speedo.' Simon winced at the harsh voice and staggered under his heavy load but managed to stay on his feet. There was no let-up as the Japanese guards screamed and shoved at the line of men carrying boxes of grenades. That morning, the prisoners had been marched out of the camp to a British ammunition dump that had been captured by the enemy.

His friend Ron stumbled and Simon tried to help him up, only to receive a blow from a rifle butt across his shoulders accompanied by a stream of curses. He tried to ignore the pain – truthfully, he hurt all over, especially the leg which had been wounded at Dunkirk. It had never really recovered although he had been passed fit before embarking for Malaya.

'I'm OK,' Ron muttered and managed to get to his feet, still holding the heavy box.

By the end of the day, the dump was clear and the loaded lories drove away. Seven men in the working party did not return to the camp, having fallen and not been able to get up.

'Bastards,' Ron muttered as they began the weary march back to camp. 'I can't believe we're actually helping the enemy.'

'No choice,' Simon said. 'We shouldn't have left all this stuff behind for them. We should have blown up the dumps before they caught up with us.' He felt sick at the thought that the grenades and ammunition they had loaded on to the lorries would be used against their own troops.

'No time though. Who would have thought they'd overrun us so quickly?'

They trudged on, slipping in the mud, slapping at the flies and midges that swarmed around them.

Back at camp they queued for their rations – the usual small bowl of rice.

Conditions were dreadful for them all, even the officers, despite the Geneva Convention on the treatment of prisoners.

'No work, no food,' was the enemy's oft-repeated mantra.

Simon tried to eat his portion slowly but Ron shovelled his down in seconds. He didn't say anything to his friend, knowing it would do no good. Sure enough, minutes afterwards, Ron made a dash for the latrine.

'Hey, my rice is alive.'

Simon turned at the cry.

Hugh Wilson, a fellow lieutenant in the Royal Norfolks, was spitting the rice on to the ground.'

'Don't waste it. It's only some sort of grub - protein anyway. I've eaten mine.'

The other inmates of the hut nodded agreement. In the weeks since their captivity they had learned to cope with anything that was thrown at them. How long had it been – and how long would it go on for?

So far, Simon had managed to hide the sketchpad and pencil and now, he got them out of his haversack and sat with his back against one of the hut's supporting poles. He looked out between the fronds of the attap screen to the jungle beyond the camp, forcing himself to see past the muddy compound where emaciated prisoners lay exhausted. Bamboo and tangled vines crowded up close to the wire and Simon quickly sketched some of the plants. He was determined to survive and show those at home that despite what he and his fellow prisoners were going through, there was a kind of savage beauty in their surroundings.

He bit the end of his pencil, frowning. What was he thinking of? He tore the page out, almost screwed it up but hesitated. He turned it over and took a deep breath, filling the sheet with lightning sketches of the hut and its occupants. Hugh doubled over clutching his stomach, Ron asleep on what passed for a bed, Bill sitting on the steps, chin in hand, lost in some world of his own, all of them skeleton-like ghosts of the strong young men they had been only short weeks ago.

This is what those at home should see – if he ever managed to send his sketches. They had received no mail since landing on the Malay peninsula. He wasn't even sure if his father knew he was a prisoner. His thoughts turned to home and the beautiful town he had grown up in. He pictured the Abbey gardens and the romantic ruins where he had played as a boy. And that pretty little church deep in the Norfolk countryside where he had met the Rector's daughter. Rosemary. He sighed. Would he ever see her again?

June 1943

Percy Fenton was fed up. He wished he hadn't agreed to help with the children's visit to the base. Most of the villagers had accepted the Americans, but he resented their presence and the disruption to village life. Most of them were all right, he supposed but he couldn't stand the sight of that Hank who was always smarming around Maggie. And his mates were just as bad, couldn't leave the village girls alone. Percy had sat in the pub the other evening watching Maggie flitting between the tables serving them, smiling and flirting.

He knew he didn't stand a chance with her but he didn't have to watch the yanks making up to her. He didn't blame *her*. She'd grown up in the pub helping her parents from a young age. Until the arrival of the RAF lads, and now the Americans, she'd served farm lads, plough boys and shepherds, always with the same smile and cheeky repartee. He couldn't blame her for wanting a bit of glamour in her life.

As he walked up to the airbase he muttered to himself. 'Hope *he* ain't there today.' If he saw him, he'd have to say something, warn him off.

Two of the children ran up to him, Brian red-faced with excitement. 'They're going to let us get right up close to the planes. Exciting isn't it, Mr Fenton.'

Percy forced a smile. 'Yeah. Lucky lads. Mind you behave yourselves though.'

Mr Davis was waiting by the gate talking to the guard. He counted heads as the boys arrived and, when he was sure they were all present he gestured to the guard to open the gate.

As the boys poured through, running and whooping with excitement, he called out, 'Now, boys. Line up. Wait for our escort. And no running off.'

He turned to Percy. 'Just keep an eye on them. And remember, this is a privilege. We don't want to take advantage of their good will.'

Percy pursed his lips. He didn't need to be told. Talking to him like one of his pupils – the cheek!

Master Sergeant Floyd Bowman appeared round the side of the Guard Room and welcomed the visitors. 'Right. First off, I'm going to show you round the buildings where I do most of my work.' He led them off towards a huge hangar saying, 'When the planes get back from a mission, some of them are in a bad way. We need to get them fixed as soon as possible to get them back in the air for the next mission.'

Outside on the tarmac, the men were working on two huge bombers. 'Sometimes we have to work on them out here,' Floyd said. 'They need to be airborne in double quick time.'

He led them inside the hangar where spare parts were scattered around two scarcely recognizable bombers looking more like heaps of tangled metal. Maintenance men darted around, selecting pieces to replace the damaged parts. The noise was deafening.

Some of boys covered their ears but Brian laughed. 'Don't bother me,' he said, turning to Percy. 'We're used to all that hammering in the forge, aren't we, Mr Fenton.'

Percy's mood lightened. He enjoyed having Brian helping him after school. It was good to see the lad's enthusiasm. He looked around, pleased there was no sign of the pilot he had come to dislike – hate was too strong a word, he thought. He didn't wish harm to any of those brave pilots despite his resentment at their taking over his village.

Floyd seemed all right and Percy found himself listening with interest to the American's description of his work. At the end of his spiel Floyd asked if anyone had any questions. Percy was about to ask for information about the tools they used but Brian butted in with his own enthusiastic comments. Percy couldn't help grinning at the lad, his own question forgotten. He glanced at the American who was bending to talk to the boy, pleased that he was taking Brian seriously. For all his cheekiness and mischief making, Percy had become fond of the lad and realised that Brian was genuinely interested and enthusiastic – not just about planes but black-smithing too. He pictured taking him on as an apprentice when he was old enough. He brushed the thought away. When the war was over the lad would go back to London and forget about him and the forge.

When the boys had seen enough, Floyd said, 'Now to see one of the aircraft we've just finished patching up. *Oklahoma Belle* got back yesterday in a fine old state. Great holes all over her. We worked on her all night. Now she's ready for her next mission.'

'Why's she called *Oklahoma Belle*?' Brian asked.

'Her crew's all from Oklahoma – like me. That's why she's so special to me. The boys all choose the name for their own aircraft;' Floyd explained.

They followed him outside. Seen close up, even Percy was awed by the size of the bomber and the boys gazed wide-eyed as Floyd pointed out the features of the plane.

They vied for attention, all talking at once, asking questions. Floyd answered patiently. When they'd seen enough, he said, 'I expect you're ready for some chow now.'

'What's chow?' one of the boys asked.

'Food,' Brian shouted before Floyd had a chance to answer. 'That's' right, isn't it Floyd?'

'Manners, Brian,' Mr Davis said, 'And it's Master Sergeant.'

Percy grinned. Like Mr Davis, he approved of the boys being taught respect.

They all trooped over to the mess hall where a table had been laid with sandwiches and lemonade. The boys fell on the food as if they hadn't been fed for days.

Percy and Mr Davis stood on the sidelines with the American, watching indulgently. Percy looked round the mess hall at the crowds of pilots eating and relaxing.

They had just returned from a mission over Germany, he guessed. They looked tired and most of them still wore their flying jackets, their helmets on the table beside them.

At a nearby table three pilots were laughing and Percy frowned as he recognized Hank.

He moved closer as he heard one of them saying, 'Can't keep out of the *Four Bells,* can you, Hank?'

'Do you blame me? I'm on to a good thing with that lovely barmaid,' Hank replied.

Percy clenched his fists at his sides and took a step forward, stopping as he felt Mr Davis's grip on his arm. 'No trouble, please, Percy.'

Floyd spoke softly. 'Take no notice. He doesn't mean anything by it.'

Percy wasn't so sure but he couldn't do anything about it at the moment. His suspicions were right though. Hank wasn't serious about Maggie; he was just playing around. He hoped that the girl he loved wouldn't do anything silly.

***

Rosemary and Jenny sat on a hay bale watching the little girls in their care playing in the dirt. Two ducks swam across the pond and Maisie ran around the side laughing. Lily still seemed a little nervous of the animals but, encouraged by Maisie, she went over to the fence where a flock of sheep crowded up to the wire. She knelt down and tentatively stroked one of them.

She smiled and looked up at her teacher, 'Soft,' she said.

Jenny nodded. 'Very soft. You like it?'

Lily nodded. 'Maisie said these are the mummy sheep. Where are the babies?'

'They're all grown up now. There'll be some more babies in the spring.'

Lily's face clouded. 'Do the sheep miss their babies?' Before Rosemary could speak, she added, 'I miss my mummy.'

'I know you do, dear. I hope you'll see her soon.' Rosemary mentally crossed her fingers. Surely the war couldn't go on much longer. She was saved from having to say more when Maisie ran up to them and said, 'Can I take one of the piggy babies home?'

'No, love,' Jenny said. And managed to persuade her that baby pigs were happier on the farm with their mummies.

Soon it was time to go. They didn't want to leave but Farmer White said the animals needed to be fed and they reluctantly followed him out into the sunshine.

'You can feed the hens before you go,' Farm White suggested.

'I do that at home,' Lily said.

Rosemary smiled, pleased that the child was beginning to think of the Rectory as home. They crossed the farmyard and the farmer's wife met them carrying bowls of corn. She showed the children how to scatter it around so that all the hens got a share.

When the feed was all gone, Mrs White invited them into the farmhouse kitchen where she gave the children scones warm from the oven and glasses of milk.

Jenny thanked the Whites and the little girls all chorused a thank you before setting off down the lane back to the village.

'A good afternoon,' she said.

Rosemary agreed. 'It's good that the London children have learned a bit about life in the country.'

'I'll get them to write thank you letters when we're back in school on Monday,' Jenny said. 'The boys too. I hope they enjoyed their visit to the base.'

***

A week later, Rosemary still hadn't written to Simon although she had composed a letter many times in her head. Suppose he had forgotten her? Suppose he had met another girl – one of those smartly uniformed ATS girls? Worse, suppose he really was a prisoner in the Far East. And where would she send the letter anyway?

And then there was Floyd. The American seemed to pop up everywhere – at the school, in church. When did he ever work on the planes? she wondered.

Every time they met, he asked her to go out with him and she was running out of excuses. She liked him and, if she had never met Simon, she would have been only too willing to get to know him better. But she couldn't get Simon out of her head.

She was thinking about him yet again when she bumped into Floyd as she was coming out of the village shop.

'Hi, Rosemary, glad I've seen you. Some of the boys are going to a dance in Norwich on Saturday night. How about you and your friends come too. We had such a good time at the movies didn't we.'

Rosemary hesitated. She hadn't been dancing since before the start of the war. And she did love to dance.

'Please come,' Floyd said. 'I'd love to dance with you.'

The look in his eyes melted her heart. Why not? It was just a dance, and it would be fun. 'I'll ask Jenny,' she said.

'And Maggie – Hank's coming and I know he's keen on Maggie.'

Rosemary couldn't help smiling. Everyone in the village knew that Hank was keen on Maggie – and she was keen on him. It was the talk of the older women, especially the church ladies who disapproved of her relationship with the 'Yank'.

They arranged to meet outside the pub as before and said goodbye. Rosemary walked away, wondering if she had done the right thing. She didn't want Floyd to get the wrong idea about her. And on top of that was the worrying thought of her father's disapproval. He had welcomed the Americans, especially those who attended church, but he didn't like the way the village girls fawned over them.

As usual when she got home, she looked on the hall table in the vain hope there was mail for her. Swallowing her disappointment, she ran up to her room to change out of her work clothes.

She picked up Simon's little painting and smiled, then reached into the bedside drawer for his letters. She had kept both of them, re-reading them so often that she knew them by heart. She read again the final sentence in his second letter: *I promise to come and visit your lovely little church again, however far in the future that may be.'*

She sighed. She had to face the fact that she had read too much into it. He was interested in the church – not her. Perhaps she should try to forget him.

But she couldn't. She went over to her little writing table under the window and got out paper and envelopes. Thank goodness she had kept the letter with his home address on it. She quickly wrote a short note to his father, reminding him that she had met his son in the church and that he'd told her that Michael had saved his life. She said she was pleased Simon's wound had healed and he had rejoined his unit. She went on to say that her father, the Rector, had enjoyed Simon's visit and looked forward to him being able to visit the church again. She ended by asking him to send the enclosed note to his son.

She read it through, not sure whether to send it. What would Dr Spencer think of a strange girl writing to his son? She sighed, hoping he wouldn't think she was too cheeky.

She sat for several minutes, pen in hand, trying to decide what to say to Simon. She gazed at the little painting. Of course. She had never thanked him for it. That was a start. From then the words flowed and she filled both sides of the sheet of notepaper, first saying how much she and her father had enjoyed talking to him about the church and its architecture. She went on to tell him about the children who were staying in the village and how they were adapting to country life and how much they had enjoyed the magic lantern show. She couldn't mention the air base and the arrival of the Americans in their midst, or talk about the air raids and the bombing. Everyone had been warned about giving information away - who knew who might get hold of the letter?

She ended - *'I do hope this letter reaches you, wherever you are, and that you will write back and let me know how you are.*

Yours sincerely, Rosemary Turner.

She read it through, satisfied that she had struck the right note of friendly interest and prayed he would write back.

***

Saturday came all too soon and Rosemary was still undecided about going to the dance. Father had warned her about the dangers of going into Norwich in the blackout. 'It's far too dangerous with all the bombed-out buildings,' he'd said.

But there had been fewer raids lately and she had persuaded him that she would be quite safe in company with her friends. Rosemary knew that he was genuinely worried for her safety but she couldn't help thinking that he wasn't happy about her riding in the back of a jeep with a group of American airmen either, although he didn't say so.

Trying to set his mind at rest, she said, 'Master Sergeant Bowman and Pilot Officer Ridley will look after us. You know them from church.' And with a sigh he had succumbed, telling her not to be too late home and hoping she would have a nice time.

Now, Rosemary and Jenny waited outside the *Four Bells* for the truck which was to take them to the city. Jenny was excited. 'I can't wait to be whizzing round the floor doing the quickstep and the foxtrot,' she said. 'It's so long since we had any real fun.'

When they reached the locally famous Samson and Hercules Ballroom, they got a surprise. Instead of the usual band the stage held a group of Americans, smart in their uniforms, playing the sort of music they had only heard in films.

The floor was crammed with dancers, mostly uniformed airmen, whirling young women around the large room. Most of the girls were in brightly-coloured dresses but there were a few in uniform – WAAFs and ATS from nearby military establishments, land girls in their green jumpers and dungarees as if they'd come straight from work.

Rosemary had been looking forward to dancing the old-time waltzes and quicksteps familiar to her from countless church socials. But she realised the music wasn't right. She looked on in amazement as the men picked the girls up, swinging them around while doing what, to her, seemed like complicated steps.

Floyd and Will had gone to get drinks after showing them to a table. Maggie and Hank were already on the floor, both joining in with enthusiasm.

'Not my idea of dancing,' Rosemary said. She couldn't imagine herself allowing anyone to pick her up and throw her about like that.

'I don't know. It looks like fun,' Jenny said, smiling up at Will as he deposited their drinks on the table and held out a hand to her. She followed him on to the dance floor and was soon swallowed up in the crowd.

'Would you like to dance?' Floyd asked.

'I don't know how,' Rosemary said.

'Nothing to it.' He grinned at her. 'Not what you're used to, eh?'

She shook her head and took a sip of her lemonade.

'We can watch for a bit if you like.' He nodded at the dancers as Maggie and Hank swept past them. 'Your friend seems to be enjoying herself.'

She finished her drink and took a deep breath. 'It does look like fun. If you show me the steps, I'll have a go.'

Floyd grinned and seized her hand. 'Come on then, before you change your mind.' Out on the dance floor, he took both her hands and pulled her towards him. 'Don't worry about the steps, just move in time to the music.'

She looked round at the other dancers. It all looked a bit chaotic to her, everyone doing their own thing. 'Watch me, not them,' Floyd said.' Just do what I do.'

She let him lead and gradually began to relax. I'm enjoying this - so long as he doesn't try to pick me up or throw me about, she thought.

Before long she was out of breath and longing to sit down and have another drink but then the music changed to a slow waltz. The bandleader started to sing and the room quieted as his mellow voice filled the room. Floyd pulled Rosemary towards him and they moved slowly round the room. Oblivious to the other dancers, she realised she was enjoying the feeling of his arms around her. She leaned her head on his shoulder and his arms tightened around her.

Startled, she pulled away. This wasn't what she had expected and, trying to keep her voice normal, she said, 'I know this music – *Sleepy Lagoon*, I heard it on the wireless.'

Floyd didn't reply but he must have sensed she wasn't ready to become closer and he led her back to their table.

Without asking her, he went to the bar and got more drinks. She hoped she hadn't hurt his feelings but she could tell by his expression that she had. While they were dancing, he had let himself go, showing a lighter-hearted side of himself. He had always seemed so serious, except when he was teasing Brian and the other boys. She suspected that he was quite shy and that, together with his strict Baptist upbringing, made him seem quieter than his buddies.

The music, the dancing and the atmosphere had loosened him up and she had liked seeing the more carefree Floyd.

All too soon the evening ended, the lights dimmed and there was a rush to find their coats.

As they left the ballroom, their ears were assaulted by the wail of the air raid siren. Floyd grabbed Rosemary's hand. 'Come on, let's make a dash for it. Get out of town – we'll be safer in the countryside.'

She pulled away. 'We need to get to a shelter.'

Hank and Betty were already huddled in the covered entrance to the ballroom, wrapped in each other's arms, apparently oblivious to the air raid warning.

Jenny tugged at her hand. 'Come on, we need to get to the truck.'

'Too late.' Will pushed Jenny further into the shelter of the entranceway and called to the others. 'Better stay here until the all clear,' he said.

The girls had never been outside during a raid and Maggie clung to Hank, burying her face in his shoulder. 'Get us out of here,' she moaned.

The men, stoical after living through the bombardment of the airfield and from countless sorties over enemy territory, were anxious to get back to their base. But Floyd, protective of the girls, insisted they stay under cover.

'We ought to make a dash for it - we'll be needed back there,' Will said.

The decision was made for them when someone shouted. 'You can't stay there. Get to the shelter.'

The ARP man hustled them out of the covered entrance and pointed along the road, where they joined the stream of dance-goers. They huddled together in the crowded brick-built shelter, all eyes turned up to the ceiling as the bombers droned overhead.

The girls trembled at each whistle and crump, followed by the sound of falling masonry. The Americans fidgeted impatiently. 'We need to be out there,' muttered Hank, his fists clenched.

'Nothing we can do, bud,' said Will, putting his arms round Jenny and pulling her close. 'We have to look after the girls.'

Rosemary understood their frustration but he was right, except that she didn't need looking after. There would be plenty for them to do when the raid ended.

After what seemed like hours, the all clear sounded and everyone moved towards the doorway.

The sight that met them looked like an illustration from Dante's *'Inferno'*. Flames leapt high in the air, lighting up the ruined buildings around them, while ARP men and fire fighters rushed around, trying to quell the fires, shouting orders and urging people out of the way.

'Oh, God,' Hank gasped. 'The bastards, how could they?'

Rosemary wanted to stay and try to help the injured but Floyd pulled her away. 'Nothing we can do.' Let's get out of here.'

'That's if the jeep's still in one piece,' Hank said.

They stumbled over heaps of rubble to where they had left the vehicle. To their relief it seemed intact and they piled in. Hank wrenched the wheel round and turned towards the main road.

As they left the city behind them, Rosemary looked back at the blazing buildings which were visible even from miles away. Tears ran down her cheeks and she prayed for the poor folk caught up in the devastation. Now she understood what Be tty and her three little boys had gone through.

Turning off the main road into the narrow lane that led to the village, all seemed quiet after the horrors they had left behind. Rosemary hoped that the noise of the bombers and their cargo had not reached the village or disturbed the children. The villagers would hear about it the next day.

Chapter 15

August 1943

Simon and Hugh sat apart from the other prisoners, leaning against the back wall of their hut where there was a little shade.

'How far do you think they've got?' Hugh asked in a low voice.

'It's been two days. Let's hope they've made it.' Simon bent his head over his sketch book, clutching the tiny stub of pencil which was all he now had. He was determined to keep a record of the camp and the enemy's treatment of their prisoners. He marvelled at how he had managed to hide his activity from them for so long despite the frequent searches. But the Japanese guards were only intent on finding stolen food and cigarettes, shaking the rice sacks the prisoners stored their meagre possessions in, pouncing with glee on anything that fell out. Savage beatings followed and Simon knew what was in store for him if they ever discovered his hidden treasure.

A sudden clamour from the guardhouse brought Simon's head up and he hastily stowed his drawing things into the pouch he had sewn to the inside of the sack which never left his side. 'What's going on?' he muttered.

'Sounds like they've been caught,' Hugh said, getting painfully to his feet as angry shouts echoed round the camp. 'Better get over to the parade ground.' He took Simon's arm and Ron took the other, helping Simon to hobble over the rough baked earth where they joined the other prisoners.

Of the six men who had escaped, only four had been caught. They could barely stand and from where he stood, Simon could see how badly beaten and bloodied they were. Had the other two got away?

Captain Jones had wanted Simon to join the escape attempt but he had refused, knowing that in his present weakened state he would be a hindrance to his friends. Now, he was glad of the decision as he waited to see their fate.

Hugh touched Simon's arm giving a slight nod in the direction of Captain Jones who stood to the right of the other captives. Jones had raised his arm and drew his hand across his throat, a sign that the other two had been killed. A Japanese guard saw the movement and clubbed him to the ground.

After their years of captivity, torture, disease and death had become a daily part of their life. Simon thought he had become inured to it all, passing each day in a kind of fugue state, except for the rare moments he could escape into his art. But Captain Jones was a friend; they had gone through so much together. Knowing the imminent fate of his friend and the other escapees, he hung his head, biting down hard on the inside of his cheek, concentrating on the pain.

He opened his eyes briefly as sunlight flashed on a raised sword, closing them again at once. He swayed and Hugh gripped his arm. Beheading was the enemy's favourite punishment.

There was a sudden hush, followed almost immediately by a burst of muttered oaths and some of the foulest language Simon had ever heard. The men were hustled back to their huts, prodded and beaten with rifle butts, accompanied by screams of abuse – 'no food, no food.'

This was nothing new. The daily ration of a handful of bug-infested, mouldy rice was all too often withheld for the slightest reason – or no reason at all.

Sometimes one of the prisoners managed to trade food with the natives, but they had little left to bargain with. Hunger was something they had learned to live with.

A few days later a rumour flew round the camp. A ship had docked in the harbour laden with Red Cross parcels. But as they waited in vain for their arrival it was gradually accepted that it must have been just a rumour.

Simon had almost filled his sketchpad and his worry that it would be discovered and confiscated increased with each day that passed. When he was engrossed in his drawing, even though the subject matter was so distressing, Simon could disappear into a world of his imagination. He was back in that little Norfolk church talking to Rosemary. It was only the thought of one day being reunited with her that kept him going. If only he could write to her - but letters were forbidden. Some months ago, the prisoners had been allowed to send a brief note to their families. Only twenty-five words saying they were fine and being treated well. He had written to his father, managing to include a greeting to 'Cousin' Rosemary and hoping his father would understand. He had received nothing back but he lived in hope. Maybe one day he would be able to write to both of them. He would try to send one or two of his sketches. Hugh shook his arm. 'Something's up,' he whispered.

Simon hurriedly hid his sketchbook and pencil in the pocket he'd made in the lining of his sack of belongings and scrambled into line. The men in the next hut had already been shipped off a few weeks ago – God knew where, although the rumours didn't bode well.

Forty men were hustled into line and told to bring their belongings – meagre as they were each man held on to anything scrounged or stolen. Anything to make life more bearable.

They were marched out of camp and down to the railway siding, then herded into cattle trucks. Simon stumbled as he climbed up and Ron grabbed his arm. 'Don't let them see how weak you are,' Hugh said.

'I'll be OK,' Simon whispered. 'At least we're not walking this time.'

Over the next few days as the train trundled through virgin forest, twigs and leaves brushing the sides of the wagons, Simon began to wish they could get out of the wagons just to escape the heat. The metal walls were red hot and many of the men were burnt as the train swayed around bends throwing them against the side. They took turns changing places so that they occasionally had a little respite from the hot metal.

When the train finally stopped and they were let out they had no idea where they were. Simon gazed around at the jungle closing in on all sides with just a narrow track leading into it. Then he heard the sound of pickaxes and shovels ringing against the rock-hard earth and murmured to Hugh, 'So the rumours are true. They're building a railway.'

'I wouldn't have thought it possible,' Hugh replied.

But moments later their guards started screaming at them, the familiar cry of 'Speedo, speedo,' accompanied by thrusts from rifle butts urging them up the track into a clearing.

They were given no time to get their bearings as each man was handed an axe. Their job was to clear the forest for the next section of the railway which they could see was already well under way.

'No use protesting that officers don't work,' Hugh muttered. They'd learned that lesson back in Changi.

Simon nodded. No chance of escape out here in this wilderness either, that's if any of them even survived, he thought, looking around at the stick-thin men their legs and arms covered in sores and infected insect bites.

So began months of hard labour. Many fell and were left to die, instantly replaced by more of the thousands of prisoners who filled the camps. If it hadn't been for Ron and Hugh's unfailing support, Simon would have given up. That and the determination that one day he would get home to Rosemary.

Chapter 16

December 1943

Rosemary added another parcel to the packing case, stretched and rubbed her back. She glanced at her watch. 'Nearly time to meet the children,' she said.

Betty looked out of the window. 'Still raining,' she said.

'I'm fed up with all this cold sleety weather – especially the wind. I hate the wind.' Rosemary waved a hand at the piles of goods waiting to be packed. 'There's so much to do still. I had hoped we'd fill another crate today.'

'Why don't you carry on then? I don't mind walking up to the school. It will do me good to get out in the fresh air. I've been cooped up indoors so long.'

'Your boys are old enough to come home on their own, but I'm responsible for Lily and Maisie,' Rosemary protested.

'I'll go – no argument,' Betty said. 'And I'll make you a cup of tea when I get back.'

Rosemary gave in. She had much rather be getting on with work than fighting her way through the wind and rain even though it was only a short distance to the school. She was grateful not to have to brave the cold.

She hated the winter evenings when it got dark so early. She would have to call in to the shop on her way home to collect the week's rations. Thank goodness she wouldn't have to get a meal ready as Mrs Norton was at the Rectory today and would have something warming ready when she got home with Lily.

She fetched another box from the pile in the corner and began to fill it, blessing the kind people who had donated so much. She packed a pair of hand-knitted socks, a tube of toothpaste, chocolate, a writing pad and pencil, and several other items which she hoped would make the prisoner's lives easier. She never knew where the parcels would end up and often imagined that they were destined for the camp in Germany where her brother was incarcerated. She pictured Michael's smile as he opened his parcel. If only she could let him know that she might have packed it. But they had been warned repeatedly against including notes of any kind in case they revealed any secret information.

She sighed. Perhaps there would be a letter from Michael waiting for her when she got home. She stifled a hope that Simon might have written too. There had been no reply to the note she'd sent to Doctor Spencer and she wondered if he had even received it.

Hearing noisy footsteps in the hall, she quickly labelled the last parcel and stepped out of the room. She was nearly bowled over as Lily and Maisie rushed towards her throwing their arms around her legs.

'We nearly got blown away,' Maisie said, giggling.

Rosemary hugged the little girls, inhaling the frosty scent which clung to their hair. Betty was hanging their coats up and she grinned. 'I thought we were never getting home.'

'Where are the boys?' Rosemary always worried about them getting into mischief.

'In the kitchen already – starving as usual. I think they'd forgotten Mrs Norton isn't here today. They'll have to wait for me to get their tea ready.'

'I'll help.'

'No, you won't. You need to get home before this weather turns worse.'

Rosemary reluctantly agreed and went to get her coat. As she took Lily's hand and turned to open the door, Betty said, 'Oh, before I forget, I saw Jenny – she wants to talk to you about the children's Christmas party.'

Leaving the shelter of the porch, Rosemary clutched Lily's hand and, head down into the wind, hurried as best they could towards the Rectory. She would leave the shopping till the next day.

She bent down to listen as Lily spoke, the wind almost tearing her words away.

'What was that, love?'

'Mrs Rook said there's going to be a party.'

'Yes – soon – for Christmas.'

'I like parties,' Lily said. 'Lemonade and cake – yummy.'

Rosemary almost groaned. Where would they get lemonade and cake? Rationing had hit harder this year and even necessities were getting harder to find. The villagers would rally round, she knew but...

A wry smile twisted her lips. If she mentioned it to Father, he was sure to quote the Bible story of the loaves and fishes.

***

The next day was cold and frosty but at least it was dry and the wind had died down. Rosemary decided to get her shopping done early before going up to the Manor.

As she passed the pub, Maggie came round the side of the building and Rosemary called out to her. But the other girl turned and went inside. Perhaps she didn't see me, Rosemary thought. She shrugged. I don't think she really likes me anyway. But since their outings to Norwich with the Americans she had thought they were becoming more friendly.

Father wouldn't approve, of course. But Rosemary had enjoyed her company, admiring her carefree attitude and her gift of making them all laugh. She had been looking forward to another trip to the cinema or dance hall but so far it hadn't happened.

As she reached the door of the village shop a stomach-churning roar rent the air and she looked up to see the sky black with aircraft as a huge formation flew over the village towards the coast. Another German city in for a pasting, she thought. After seeing what the enemy had done to Norwich, she felt they deserved it.

She entered the shop and greeted Moira who was weighing out meagre amounts of sugar and pouring it into blue paper bags.

'Morning, Rosemary. Come for your rations? I won't be a minute.'

'I've remembered my ration book this time,' Rosemary said with a little laugh.

'Well, you've got a lot on your mind, what with your work up at the Manor and looking after little Lily, not to mention helping out with the other evacuees.'

'I enjoy it,' Rosemary said. And it was true. Over the last few years, her resentment at not being able to go to university or join the WAAFs like her friend Anne had gradually faded and she had found contentment in doing what she had come to realise was just as worthwhile a job as her friend's.

Moira filled the last sugar bag and said, 'Now, what can I get you – that's if we've got it of course.'

Rosemary handed over her list and waited while Moira scanned the shelves, placing items down on the counter.

Another wave of bombers passed over the village, making the tins stacked on the shelf behind the counter rattle.

'What a racket – can't hear myself think,' Moira said. 'Can't complain, I suppose. They're doing a grand job.'

Rosemary agreed with a smile. But she couldn't help feeling a pang of sympathy for the ordinary people in the targeted cities across the Channel. It wasn't a sentiment that would go down well with her neighbours, she knew, and she kept her feelings to herself.

Moira frowned. 'I must admit I wasn't too keen on the yanks at first. You hear such stories...'

'The ones I've met in church are very polite.' Rosemary felt bound to defend the young men she'd become friendly with.

'Polite, yes I suppose.' Moira was about to say more but the shop bell jangled and two older women came in. 'Well, that's the lot – most of what's on your list, anyway.' She clipped the coupons out of the ration book and handed it to Rosemary, turned to the new customers with a smile.

Rosemary picked up her shopping bag, smiled at the newcomers and hurried outside. No doubt they were pleased she'd gone, leaving them to enjoy a gossip about the Americans and the girls who were making the most of their generosity.

She had a feeling that Maggie and her friendship with Hank would be on the receiving end of their disapproval.

***

Rosemary didn't see Jenny for the next few days. As well as her work for the Red Cross she was kept busy with Christmas preparations. The church decorations, especially the Nativity scene, were looking very shabby and she had decided to make new ones or try to refurbish the old. She had scoured the Rectory attics for bits and pieces and had already cut out some stars from a tattered gold satin curtain. She had painted the cardboard stable in some glossy brown paint she'd found in the garden shed and her next task was to make a thatch for the roof.

There was nothing for her to do at the Manor today as they were waiting for a delivery of goods for the Red Cross parcels so she decided to walk up to White's farm and scrounge some straw or hay. She had become quite friendly with Farmer White and his wife after the children's visit back in the summer.

It was a fine but cold day and she enjoyed the walk. She never minded the cold so long as it was dry. She passed the entrance to the air base, smiling in response to the salute from the guards. She hadn't seen Floyd lately and she dreaded meeting him since the group had suffered many heavy losses and several of his friends had not returned from recent raids. She just didn't know what to say to him.

She opened the farm gate to be greeted by a furiously barking collie. She stood still for a moment, let him sniff her hand. After a moment, tail wagging, he followed her up to the barn and she called out, 'Anyone about?'

Old Ray, who had been a shepherd here since he was a boy, came round the side of the barn and greeted her with a smile. 'What you doin' up here, lass?' he asked with a toothless grin.

'I'm on the scrounge, Ray.' She explained about the Nativity scene she was making for the church.

'I remember that from years ago,' he said. 'I daresay you need a new one after all this time.'

'Well, not exactly new. Just tidying it up, painting and such. I've mended the stable and now I need some straw for the roof.'

'I can let you have some hay. Will that do?'

'Super. You sure Mr White won't mind?'

'Course he won't,' Ray assured her.

'Thanks. I'll need a bit for the manger too.'

Ray went to where the hay was stacked in the corner of the barn and pulled out a handful from one of the bales. 'Enough?' he asked.

'Could I have a bit more, please?'

'As much as you like, lass. The sheep won't go short,' he said with a laugh.

Rosemary had brought an old shopping bag with her and together they stuffed it with the sweet-smelling hay. She thanked him and hurried away.

As she reached the school, the children were just coming out and she saw Betty chatting to a group of parents and carers.

'You didn't need to come. I said I'd pick the girls up,' Betty said.

'I know.' Rosemary explained where she'd been. 'I want to speak to Jenny while I'm here.'

'I'll take the girls back to the Manor and look after Lily then.'

'I won't be long.' She saw Jenny across the playground and waved to her. Lily ran up to her and she gently explained that Betty would look after her. 'I'll be along very soon,' she said.

Lily said goodbye and ran off with Maisie quite happily. Rosemary was pleased that the little girl was not quite so clingy now and seemed to be happier. At least she no longer cried for her mother.

She greeted Jenny and said, 'Have you got time to chat about the party?'

'I must tidy the classroom but come inside. We can talk while I do that.'

Rosemary followed her friend into the classroom and said, 'Can I help?'

'I can manage. I know where everything goes. I can't believe the chaos just from an art lesson. Paint and paper everywhere.'

Rosemary sat down in one of the child size chairs and watched as Jenny darted around, picking things up and in minutes the room was straight.

'Now - the party. You look worried.'

'I was thinking about the food – what are we going to give them? Lily was asking if we're going to have cake – and lemonade.' She sighed. 'No chance. There's nothing in the shop.'

Jenny smiled. 'No need to worry. It's all arranged. I thought Floyd would have told you.'

'I haven't seen him. They're so busy up at the base.'

'Well, here's the good news. The lads are giving the party. They've got permission to hold it on the base and they'll be supplying everything.'

'Really? You're kidding.'

'No. Will and Floyd have arranged it with Mr Davis.'

'That's wonderful. A weight off my mind. I've been racking my brains for ideas. Mrs Norton's made a cake – she's been hoarding ingredients for months, but...'

'You can keep the cake for Christmas day. The yanks have so much and they're happy to share.'

'We'll have to meet up with them and make the arrangements. Have they said what day?'

'Mr Davis said the last day of term. It's only a few days before Christmas. The boys said they'll arrange transport for the children who live further away.'

'Seems I've been worrying about nothing,' Rosemary said. She showed Jenny the contents of the bag. 'Now I can get on with the nativity scene. I've been working on it in the vestry. It would be good to have it finished for Advent Sunday.'

'What else do you need?'

'Lots. Poor Mary's robe is looking very shabby.'

'I could help. I'm sure I've got some scraps in my sewing bag – I could make a new robe for her – and for Joseph too.'

'That would be lovely. You're so much better at sewing than I am.'

'I'll come along tomorrow after school then.'

When Jenny turned up the next day she was accompanied by Floyd, who hovered in the vestry doorway, clutching his cap.

'Didn't want to disturb you as you're busy,' he said. 'My CO needs to know how many children will be coming to the party.'

'Come in and sit down,' Rosemary said. 'It's good to see you. I know things have been difficult.' That was an understatement but she was reluctant to mention the heavy losses both in aircraft and men.

Floyd perched on a rather dilapidated chair, placed his cap on his knee and ran his hands through his hair. 'I've been wanting to see you but it's been a bit frantic up at the base. So many planes damaged. We're working flat out to keep as many as possible in the air.'

'I understand.' She couldn't say any more for the lump in her throat, thinking of the many planes and their crews who had not returned. She turned to Jenny, forcing a bright tone to her voice. 'Have we any idea of numbers? Will it be just your pupils or all the village children?' A few of the older children now travelled to the big school in the nearby town.

'All of them, I think. It wouldn't be fair to leave them out.' Jenny thought for a moment. 'So, about thirty-five.'

'Sounds about right.' Rosemary agreed, turning to Floyd. 'We'll let you know the exact numbers. Is there anything we can help with?'

'You just leave it all to us. The guys are dead keen. We're all missing our families back home and this will be a way of celebrating Christmas for us all.' Floyd stood up. 'I need to get back.' At the door he paused. 'We must arrange another outing to the movies, perhaps when things quieten down a bit.'

'That would be nice.' 'Yes, I'd like that.' Jenny and Rosemary spoke in unison. Floyd sketched a quick salute and was gone.

Jenny sighed. 'Will things ever quieten down. It seems like this war is going to last forever.'

'I was a bit more hopeful last year, after hearing about El Alamein, but then things got worse again.'

'Well, Churchill did say it was the end of the beginning.'

'Let's not talk about the war. We've got Christmas to look forward to – and we'd better get on with the nativity or the church will look a bit bare.' Rosemary rummaged in the box at her feet and pulled out a square of blue material. She held it up. 'Mary's robe?'

The last day of term dawned crisp and cold after several wet days. Thank goodness the muddy lanes had dried out, Rosemary thought smiling at the sight of the children assembled in the playground for the walk up to the base. The boys were neat and tidy, with slicked back hair and shiny shoes and the girls all wore pretty frocks and had ribbons in their hair.

Jenny and Mr Davis insisted on them walking sedately in line two by two and walked alongside, making sure they behaved.

Rosemary could sense their suppressed excitement. She followed with Percy Fenton in his ARP uniform and a couple of the church ladies who had come to help.

As they neared the base, Brian shouted, 'There's Floyd,' and he and his friend Ted Rook, broke ranks and ran ahead, ignoring the headmaster's calls for them to keep in line.

The boys clung to the wire fence calling out to the American, who strolled over and said, 'Better do as the teacher says, boys. Otherwise, you'll be sent home and no party.'

Rosemary caught up with them. 'Floyd's right. Off you go.' She pointed to the gate which the guard had just opened. 'Wait for everyone to go in before you – no pushing in,' she said, trying to keep her voice stern.

Floyd grinned at her. 'Can't blame them for being excited. There's not much fun for them these days.' He walked along on the other side of the fence towards the gate, keeping pace with Rosemary. Will was ushering the children through the gate and Floyd hurried away with a wave of his hand.

Two trucks drove up and Will and his mates helped the children up into their rear cargo space. 'Hang on tight, kids,' he shouted, banging on the cab roof as the vehicles moved off.

The Nissen hut where the party was to be held was on the far side of the air field and the boys waved and shouted excitedly as the truck passed ranks of B17 and B52 bombers lined up on the runways.

Inside the hut, the children stared open-mouthed at the two long rows of tables, almost groaning under the plates and dishes of food. Brian and his friends rushed forward but Mr Davis put on his stern voice and ordered them to wait. 'Ladies first,' he said, gesturing for the girls to take their places. Rosemary smiled, noticing the twinkle in his eye. She, Jenny and Mrs Davis made sure the smallest children were seated before letting the older ones sit down.

The children gazed at the heaped tables. They had never seen so much food, even before the war and rationing, fancy food had been in short supply for most of them.

'I hope they're not kept waiting long,' Jenny whispered. 'They look as if they can't wait to start.'

Rosemary agreed and nudged her friend. Several officers had entered through the far door and Will banged on the end table for silence.

The chief officer in command of the base, Colonel Hamilton, stepped up and said, 'Welcome to Oakleigh St James Bomb Group. We are delighted to lay on this party for the children of Oakleigh in appreciation of the welcome we have all received from the people of the village. Now, before we begin, I will ask Master Sergeant Bowman to say grace.

Floyd had scarcely uttered the 'amen' when the children fell on the food and the helpers were kept busy making sure the smaller boys and girls got their fair share. Air base personnel hurried to and fro, pouring lemonade and Coca Cola, bringing out more plates of cake and sandwiches.

Rosemary was sure that some of the children were going to be sick from eating so much rich food. 'Oh, let them enjoy it,' Jenny said. 'It'll be a long time before they get anything like this again.'

At last, the tables were almost bare except for a few sandwich crusts, cake crumbs and spilled drinks.

Mr Davis stood up from his place with the officers and was about to bring the party to a close when Colonel Hamilton interrupted. 'The party's not over yet,' he said. He raised his voice and the chatter died down. 'Please welcome our music men.'

Floyd and two other Americans, who had been helping with clearing the tables, had come back in. They waved to the children and climbed on to a raised dais at the end of the room. One of them proceeded to set up a drum kit while Floyd and the other man started to strum guitars. They were about to start playing when Floyd stood up and called out to Percy. 'Did you remember your squeeze box?'

'You really want me to play?' he asked.

'Come on up. Let's make some music.'

The children clapped enthusiastically and Floyd started to strum his guitar. The music grew louder and the Americans began to sing. To Rosemary's surprise some of the tunes were familiar and she hummed along. Then Percy played an old English folk song and before long everyone was joining in.

When the song finished, Jenny tapped Rosemary on the arm and indicated that some of the younger children were starting to nod off. 'Time to get them home,' she whispered.

But Mr Davis said, 'There's another treat to come.' The men were putting their instruments away and he tapped on the table.

'Children, would you like some ice cream?'

There was a chorus of 'yes' and nodding heads.

Surely, they couldn't manage to eat any more, Rosemary thought.

Heads turned towards the door as several airmen came in, carrying two huge metal containers and piles of plates. 'What is it?' one of the boys asked, craning his neck.

Some of the children had never had ice cream but it didn't take them long to taste and then start enjoying scoops of the vanilla and strawberry-flavoured treat.

The room fell silent broken only by the scraping of spoons on china and in only a few minutes the dishes were empty.

Now, the party was well and truly over and, as the children left, some of the Americans stood by the door handing out paper bags to them.

'Save the candies for later,' Floyd advised as Brian poked a finger into his bag.

'Candies – what's them?' Brian asked.

'We call them sweets,' Rosemary said. 'And as Floyd said, save them for tomorrow. You've had far too much to eat already.'

Brian laughed and he and Ted ran off in the darkness towards the gate.

'He's bound to eat them now,' Rosemary said. 'And I shall blame you and your friends if he's sick.'

Floyd laughed but his face changed when Rosemary said, 'I noticed Hank wasn't here. Is he flying?'

She had been apprehensive about asking, fearing the worst. But Floyd shook his head. 'He's been posted to another base.'

'Does Maggie know?'

'It was quite sudden. I expect he'll write to her.'

'So that's why Maggie's been looking so miserable lately. She must be missing him.'

'She'll find someone else to take her to the movies I expect,' Floyd said carelessly.

'I thought they were serious – at least that's the impression Maggie gave everyone.'

'Stupid to get serious in wartime,' Floyd snapped. 'And Hank – well, Maggie's not the only one he's been seeing.'

Rosemary was embarrassed. It wasn't her business anyway. She turned her attention to the children who, were scrambling up into the lorries for the ride home in the dark. She climbed up with them, cautioning them to sit down.

As they were about to drive off, Floyd reached up and grabbed her hand. 'I shouldn't be telling you this, but you might warn your friend before she gets too fond of Will. He has a wife and child back in the States.'

Rosemary gasped and Floyd said, 'I'm sorry to have upset you. We're not all like that, you know.'

The lorry pulled away and Rosemary pulled Lily on to her lap. She couldn't think about what Floyd had said. Besides, the children needed her attention. 'Did you have fun?' she asked and smiled at the clamour of enthusiastic chatter in reply.

But she couldn't concentrate on them. Floyd's revelations ran around in her head. She didn't think Jenny had really fallen for Will but she seemed to enjoy his company. She would have to warn her friend before it was too late. As for Maggie, she had given up flirting with every male in sight once she'd met Hank. Perhaps the silly girl had really fallen in love.

Rosemary bit her lip. Perhaps I'm the silly one, she thought. She liked Floyd and sensed he wanted more than friendship but Simon was the one she thought about constantly, worried and prayed for his safety. They'd only met twice and she didn't even know where he was. Could you fall in love on such meagre acquaintance?

Chapter 17

February 1944

Rosemary looked at her watch and stretched. It had been a long morning. Another hour till she could take a break. Time seemed to pass more slowly when she was working alone. What had happened to Maggie today? She was usually so punctual.

Perhaps her mother was unwell and she'd had to help in the bar. She should have sent word though, Rosemary thought. There was so much to do and Mrs Pargeter would be cross if the boxes weren't ready for the van.

She crossed the room to the box of knitted goods that had been donated by the church ladies. She would pack these and then go and get some lunch. She laid out the assortment of items on the big table, deciding which should go in each of the parcels. As well as the hand-knitted socks, gloves and scarves there were the usual cigarettes, matches, razor blades and bars of chocolate, writing pads and pencils.

She picked up a pair of mittens and put them in one of the boxes. She smiled, wondering who might end up wearing them. She still dreamed that one of her parcels might reach Michael, although she had no idea where he was. Wherever in Germany or elsewhere on the continent it might be, it was sure to be cold – colder even than here, she guessed. The knitted garments would be most welcome.

As usual she couldn't help thinking of Simon as well as her brother. Perhaps he was a prisoner too. She was sure now that he must be somewhere in the Far East. Mrs Pargeter had told her that the Colonel had connections to the military and had learned that several units of the Royal Norfolks had been in Malaya and no news of them had been received since the fall of Singapore. 'They are probably prisoners of war – or worse,' she'd said.

Rosemary sighed. Wherever he was there would be no need for gloves or scarves. She was still day-dreaming when the door opened and Mrs Pargeter entered. She hastily put another pair of gloves into the box and looked up.

'How are you coping all alone today?' the older woman asked.

'Still lots to do, but...' Rosemary said.

'Don't worry. I'm sure you've done your best. Mrs Rook will be here this afternoon. She's been visiting her husband in the nursing home.'

'No news of Maggie then. I thought she was supposed to be working today.'

Mrs Pargeter pursed her lips. 'Not a word. I telephoned the pub but got no reply.'

'Perhaps she's not well,' Rosemary said.

'More likely out with that American.' Mrs Pargeter sniffed. 'She's making a name for herself, that one.'

Rosemary ignored the last remark and leapt to her friend's defence. 'Oh, no. Hank's not here. He's been posted to another squadron'.

'Really – and how would you know that?' Mrs Pargeter sniffed. 'Of course – you're friendly with the yanks too.'

A couple of years ago, Rosemary would have coloured and hung her head at the implied criticism but she had grown a thicker skin lately. 'They've been very helpful, entertaining the children, giving the Christmas party. I was happy to help. They're just young men away from home, missing their families...'

'You're right, of course. It's just – some of the young women are making fools of themselves over them.'

Rosemary was pleased Mrs Pargeter appeared to have backed down but secretly she thought the older woman might be right about Maggie.

She decided that before meeting the children from school she would pop into the pub and see her. She knew Maggie was unhappy that Hank had left the village, seemingly without letting her know, but she would try to comfort her and convince her that she had read too much into Hank's attention. After all, there were plenty more fish in the sea as Maggie herself had often said when a brief fling came to an end.

***

After making herself a quick sandwich for lunch, Rosemary put on her raincoat and hurried down the lane to the *Four Bells*. The pub was closed after the morning session and she guessed the family were resting in the living room at the back before opening for the evening.

She was about to rap on the back door when she heard a sound from the lean-to where the empty barrels were stacked. She walked round the side of the building and saw Maggie sitting on one of the barrels smoking a cigarette.

'What are you doing out here in the rain – and why didn't you come to work this morning?' she asked.

Maggie shook her head and took a drag of her cigarette.

Stepping closer Rosemary realised the other girl had been crying. Her hair was a tangled mess and her eyes were red and swollen.

'What is it, Mags? Are you missing Hank?'

'He doesn't care about me. Floyd told me he actually asked to be transferred.'

Rosemary sighed. 'Oh, dear. You mustn't cry over him. He's not worth it.'

'I thought he loved me.' Maggie wailed.

Rosemary remembered what Floyd had said about Hank – that he was just playing around and had been dating other girls. She wished now that she had warned her friend. But would Maggie have listened? Probably not.

'I didn't realise you were serious about him,' she said now.

'It's not just that.' She swept her hair off her face and stubbed out the cigarette. 'Oh, I can't tell anyone.'

Rosemary sucked in a breath as realization dawned. Poor Maggie. Silly Maggie. 'You can tell me,' she said. 'It won't go any further.'

She touched her stomach. 'Never mind – soon everyone will know.'

'You mean - you're expecting?'

Maggie nodded.

What about your parents? Do they know?'

'I think Mum's guessed.'

'Will they stand by you?'

'Mum might – but not Dad – especially...' She swallowed. 'If it was a nice local lad, it would be different, but... He hasn't got much time for the Americans, except when they're spending money in the pub.'

'What will you do?'

'I don't know.' Maggie started to sob again.

Rosemary put her arms around her friend and patted her back. She was about to reassure her that she would help if she possibly could but just then the back door to the pub flew open and Ron Newman stepped out, shouting, 'Maggie, get in here – now.'

Maggie pushed Rosemary away. 'Better go. Don't worry. I'll be all right.'

Ron shouted again and after a brief hesitation Rosemary walked away.

It was still raining and freezing drops crept down her neck. She tied her scarf more tightly over her head and hurried up to the school, her thoughts still with Maggie. Soon it would be all round the village.

She was tempted to tell Jenny but their friendship
had cooled a little since she had spoken to her about
the possibility of Will being married. When Floyd had
told her, she didn't want to believe it but she had felt
bound to warn her friend. Jenny had flared up, telling
her to mind her own business.

'Besides, I already knew. He's always talking about
his family back home, showing me pictures,' she'd said.

'I thought you were falling for him. I didn't want you
to get hurt.'

'I thought you knew me better than that. I'm not like
Maggie, you know.'

Rosemary had apologized but she knew Jenny was
still smarting from their quarrel.

Now, she decided not to mention Maggie's problem.
As Maggie had said, soon everyone in the village would
know.

Chapter 18

April 1944

Rosemary was in the village shop getting their weekly rations and wished those in the queue a cheerful good morning. Only one neighbour responded but the other villagers looked away. Had something awful happened, one of them received bad news perhaps?

She ignored them and concentrated on her shopping list. She'd hear soon enough. When it was her turn to be served, she leaned over the counter and whispered, 'What's happened?'

Moira shook her head. 'Usual gossip. Take no notice.' She took Rosemary's list and ration book and proceeded to pile goods on the counter.

Behind her the gossip had started up once more. She heard one of the women say, 'I heard she'd been called up. War work, her mother said.'

Her companion nodded her head. 'Hmph. We know what war work she's been up to, don't we.'

Rosemary bit her lip. So, it had started. Nothing in this village was secret for long.

She turned round and faced the gossips. 'Are you talking about Maggie from the pub?' And, without giving them a chance to answer, she continued, 'She's gone to Ipswich - working in a factory making stuff for the navy, so her mother told me. She didn't want to go but you don't have any choice, do you?'

'How come she's been called up?' another neighbour asked. 'I thought she was helping out up at the manor with those Red Cross parcels – like you are,'

'Well, it's not a paid job - she was just volunteering when she had time. Her job in the pub could hardly be called war work, could it.'

Rosemary packed her shopping into her bag and Moira clipped the coupons from the ration book. She leaned forward to hand her the change and said quietly. 'That's shut them up.' She smiled and said loudly, 'Thank you, Miss Turner. Now ladies, who's next.'

Outside, Rosemary took a deep breath of the fresh spring air and started back towards the rectory. Why did those old gossips have to be so horrible? It was none of their business what Maggie got up to. She hoped her father wouldn't hear about it. He didn't like her being friends with 'that barmaid' as he called her.

She hadn't managed to see Maggie before her sudden departure from the village and she decided to call at the pub and ask for her address. A letter would reassure her that not all her friends thought badly of her.

The pub was closed but she went round the back, pleased to see Dot Newman hanging washing on the line. She didn't want to encounter Maggie's father.

Dot bent to pick up another towel from the basket at her feet, straightening with a smile as he spotted Rosemary.

'I wondered if you'd heard from Maggie. How's she getting on?'

Dot frowned. 'You know what those old biddies are saying, don't you. It's not true of course...'

Rosemary stretched out a hand. 'Mrs Newman – I'm sorry. Maggie told me...'

Dot's face fell. 'Oh. You know then. You haven't told anyone, have you?'

'No. I wouldn't. It's nothing to do with me. I'm just so sorry. I do know Maggie's heartbroken. She really hoped Hank would marry her.'

'Foolish girl.' Dot jammed a peg savagely onto the washing line. 'I didn't know what to do. Her father has forbidden me to have anything to do with her but...'

'I wanted to write to her. Is she really working in a factory?'

'She was but...' Dot hesitated. 'She's had the baby – a girl.'

'What's she going to do now?'

She wants to keep the baby. She's staying with my sister. They're telling people she's been widowed.'

'Will she come back to the village...?'

'I doubt it. Her father...' Dot sighed. 'I can't believe I'm a grandmother.' Her face crumpled. 'I don't suppose I'll ever get to see the little thing.'

'Perhaps her father will come round in time.' Rosemary tried to comfort the older woman.

'She's always been a bit flighty. I did hope she'd settle down but then the yanks came. That Hank - she was dazzled by him – good looking, plenty of money.'

Rosemary didn't know what to say. She made a note of the address Dot gave her and said goodbye.

As she passed the forge, Percy waved to her but she hurried past, not wanting to confront him. She hoped he didn't know the real reason Maggie had left the village. Everyone knew how he felt about Maggie.

***

Rosemary switched off the wireless and sighed. The news was so depressing. She still hadn't heard from Simon or his father and now, after what Mrs Pargeter had told her, she felt sure he had been taken prisoner in the Far East. Still no one had heard anything since the fall of Singapore but she still clung to the hope that he would write. After all, he had promised. But that was months ago – years. She was starting to give up hope. Perhaps she would write to Dr Spencer again asking for news. But would he even remember who she was?

She went upstairs to her room and got out a clean blouse and skirt to wear to church tomorrow. She wished she wasn't obliged to attend but unless she had a valid excuse her father would not hide his displeasure. She hated to upset him but it was becoming harder to keep silent when he insisted on trying to convince her that God was on their side.

She feared she was beginning to lose her faith – a faith that had been part of her life since she was a child. Witnessing what had happened in Norwich and hearing the nightly news on the wireless was hard to bear. Not to mention the huge loss of aircraft from the base. If only she could confide in someone but she didn't think even Jenny, her closest friend, would not understand.

The thoughts that had kept her sleepless still churned in her head during the service and she found it hard to concentrate. When the service was over, she glanced across to the side aisle where Lily was sitting with the other children in the care of Jenny and Mrs Filby the church organist. She didn't feel like chatting today and took Lily's hand, saying she had to get the dinner ready as Mrs Norton was helping out at the Manor today.

As she stepped off the path to take the shortcut through the churchyard, Mrs Pargeter called to her. 'So nice to hear good news at last,' she said.

Rosemary forced a smile. 'News?'

'Didn't you hear? Mrs Filby has news of her son at last. He's a prisoner of war – in Malaya. She got an official letter from the war office.'

'I'm so happy for her. Is he all right?'

'They haven't told her much. Just where he is. Shocking though, isn't it – all these months and nothing at all heard from our men.'

Rosemary could hardly take it in but she murmured appropriate responses and managed to get away. As she stumbled along the uneven path towards the Rectory, her thoughts were not on the meal she should be preparing for Lily and her father, but on Simon.

Malaya – no wonder she hadn't heard anything. She hoped his father had heard. And alongside that hope was the wish that Dr Spencer would remember her and pass on any news. She decided to write to the doctor straight away.

Surely the authorities must have known what had happened, she thought, but since the fall of Singapore over two years ago there had been no real news. For all anyone knew, the whole of the British army, as well as troops of Australians and Canadians, had been wiped out or lost in the impenetrable jungles of the Malayan peninsula.

She glanced in the oven where she had left a small joint of beef cooking before leaving for church. Then she peeled potatoes and chopped carrots, barely aware of what she was doing, her thoughts in chaos. Now she *would* write to Dr Spencer – she had put it off till now. Or should she? Suppose he had received bad news – or even worse, no news at all. But she had to know.

A tap at the kitchen door startled her and she almost cut her finger. Opening the door, she was surprised to see Floyd standing there, twisting his cap in his hands, an anxious frown on his face.

'Floyd, how nice to see you,' she stammered.

'Really? I thought I had upset you when you didn't speak to me after church.'

Rosemary gasped. How could she have ignored him? 'Of course you haven't. I just didn't see you, and I was in a hurry,' she said.

'You did look a little pre-occupied. Is something wrong?'

'No. I just needed to get home.' She gestured behind her at the kitchen table with its pile of vegetables, realizing she still had the knife in her hand. 'I'm cooking today. Father will be back soon and expecting a meal on the table.'

'I'm sorry to have disturbed you – I was just worried.'

'I'm sorry too. I didn't mean to ignore you. I have a lot on my mind lately.'

'I wondered if you would join me for a drink this evening. We haven't met up for a while.'

'That would be lovely.' She answered impulsively, wishing she hadn't agreed when Floyd's face lit up.

'You sure?' he asked

'I'll have to go to evensong first – Father expects me to be there.'

'Of course. I'll see you in the *Four Bells* then.'

***

The sermon seemed to go on even longer than usual and Rosemary found it hard to concentrate on her father's words. She was half wishing she hadn't agreed to meet Floyd in the pub after the service. He had hinted more than once that he was falling for her and, although she enjoyed his company she couldn't take him seriously. Still, she supposed there was no harm in being friendly. Besides, even if he was serious there was no future in it. To her, a serious relationship meant marriage and that would mean going to America when the war ended. An exciting prospect but she would never leave her father.

The thoughts went round and round in her head and she started when the organ suddenly pealed with the opening bars of the closing hymn. She hastily rose to her feet, almost dropping her hymn book.

Jenny had attended the service but sat at the back of the church. Hoping she was forgiven for interfering in her friendship with Will, Rosemary was pleased when her friend whispered, 'I'll wait for you outside.'

She stood in the porch beside her father smiling and shaking hands. When everyone had gone, she turned to him and said, 'I'm going for a walk with Jenny.' She hated lying, but he didn't approve of her going to the pub.

'Don't be too late back then,' he said.

Guiltily, she kissed his cheek and hurried to meet her friend.

'Are we going to the *Four Bells*?' Jenny asked.

Rosemary hesitated then said, 'I promised to meet Floyd.'

'Oh, it's all right for you to be friendly with an American then.'

Rosemary flushed. 'We're just friends.'

'And that's all I am to Will,' Jenny snapped.

'I've said I'm sorry for jumping to conclusions.'

'Well, let's forget it then.'

They walked in silence the short distance to the pub, pausing at the door. Even from outside they could hear the laughter and banter and Rosemary paused. She had planned to have a serious talk with Floyd but it would be impossible in a pub packed with Americans enjoying their off-duty time.

Jenny pulled on her arm. 'Come on then.'

Still Rosemary hesitated.

'Look, I said forget it and I meant it. I know you were looking out for me and mean well.' Jenny gave her arm a little shake. 'Let's just enjoy the rest of the evening.'

Rosemary smiled and accepted the olive branch.

They were greeted with good-natured banter and offers of drinks which the girls accepted. They fought their way through the crowd of airmen and land girls to where Floyd was sitting.

To Rosemary's surprise he was chatting to Percy Fenton and she was reluctant to interrupt their conversation. The blacksmith was staring moodily into his half empty glass and Floyd patted his shoulder, then looked up and saw the girls approaching. He waved to them and fetched another chair so that they could all sit together.

No chance of a serious conversation now, Rosemary thought.

Will appeared with a tray full of glasses and pulled up another chair. 'Evening ladies – been to church then?'

Jenny nodded and laughed. 'We needed a change of scene.'

Rosemary nodded agreement. 'My father's sermons do go on a bit.' She took a sip of her orange juice.

Will looked around. 'No Maggie tonight?'

'She's been called up – gone to work in a factory.'

'I thought she might be missing Hank since he's been posted.' He grinned. 'I don't suppose she'll miss him for long though. Bound to find someone else.'

Jenny slapped his arm making his beer slop over on to the table. 'That's not a nice thing to say.'

'Well, you must admit...'

Before he could continue, Floyd said, 'That's enough, bud. We all know some of the girls have made fools of themselves over our guys – and our guys take advantage.' He turned to Rosemary. 'As I said before, we're not all like that.'

'I accept that. Let's talk about something else.'

Percy drained his pint and grabbed another glass off the tray. He looked as if he'd already had enough and he was obviously upset by them talking about Maggie. He took a swig and slammed the glass down in the table.

'She was *my* girl,' he said, 'before that yank took a shine to her.' His voice was slurred but loud enough to turn heads.

Rosemary put her arm round his shoulders. 'We all know Maggie. She liked a bit of fun but there was no harm in her flirting.' It wasn't the whole truth as she knew but it wouldn't help Percy to hear the truth.

'But she's gone away – I miss her.' He pushed his chair back and shoved his way through the crowd at the bar.

The front door slammed, leaving a shocked silence.

'Poor guy,' Floyd said after a moment. 'He's really smitten.'

The chatter at the bar had broken out once more and Jenny said brightly, 'Will, have you heard from home lately?'

'Had a letter yesterday.' He fumbled in his breast pocket. 'Lyn sent me a photo.' He took it out of the envelope and passed it over. 'Yeah – that's Dex, my youngest and Grant – he's five now,' he said, pointing.

Jenny showed it to Rosemary. 'What a lovely family. Dex looks like you, don't you think?' she asked her friend.

Rosemary smiled and nodded. 'Spitting image.' She nudged Jenny and mouthed 'Sorry.'

'You're forgiven,' Jenny whispered.

The talk turned to the men's families and how much they were missed. Floyd said he was worried about his brother. 'Don't know what he was thinking joining the marines, he's a country boy like me,' he said.

His buddies laughed and made rude remarks about the rival service.

Mostly the conversation stayed cheerful, although there was an undercurrent of sadness. The bomb group had encountered yet more heavy losses on their last mission.

Dot, the landlord's wife, called time and there was a rush to finish their drinks, followed by a scraping of chairs as the patrons poured outside into the still spring night.

Rosemary stood for a moment looking up at the crescent moon and the stars against the velvet sky. The men from the base piled into the truck they had parked across the green but Will insisted on he and Floyd seeing the girls home. His friend agreed and took Rosemary's arm. Jenny lived at the opposite end of the village so Will said he would accompany Jenny, leaving Floyd to walk up to the Rectory with Rosemary.

'Alone at last,' Floyd said with a little laugh, then more seriously, 'This is the first chance we've had to talk for ages. You always seem to so busy with the church and the children.'

'What do you want to talk about?' She'd guessed of course but they couldn't put it off any longer.

'You must know how I feel about you. I've tried to hide it. I didn't want you to think I was like some of my buddies after the girls for all the wrong reasons.'

'I've never thought that,' Rosemary protested. 'I like you, but it's not so simple.'

He stopped walking and turned her to face him, gripping her arms. 'Why? You told me there was no one else - and your father approves of me.' He chuckled. 'I know how important that is to him – and you.'

Before she could say anything, he pulled her towards him and gently touched her lips with his. At first, she didn't respond, then gradually she leaned into him. She had enjoyed kisses before but nothing like this. She didn't want it to end but after a moment he pulled away.

'I'm sorry. I've been wanting to do that ever since we first met.' His voice was husky and a little hesitant. 'Please tell me you feel the same.'

She shook her head. 'I don't know.'

'You don't know? Haven't we known each other long enough?' He spread his hands. 'Rosemary, I love you. I can't say plainer than that.'

A picture of Simon flashed into her mind. They had never kissed, only exchanged a few words but he had stolen her heart – foolish, she knew but...

Floyd stepped away from her. 'I know you like me, think of me as friend but I hoped...' He sighed. 'I can only think there must be someone else despite what you told me.'

Rosemary decided to be honest. 'I don't even know if he's still alive. I haven't heard since he went away – but I keep on hoping.'

'Well, I'll keep hoping too then, although...' It was his turn to sigh. 'I hate the thought of stepping into dead men's shoes.'

Rosemary recoiled at his harsh words. Simon wasn't dead – he must be a prisoner. That was the only explanation she would allow to enter her mind. News of soldiers in captivity in Malaya and Singapore was only just filtering through. She must hear something soon.

Choking back a sob, she muttered, 'sorry,' and rushed away through the dark up the Rectory drive.

Chapter 19

May 1944

The war dragged on with its mixture of good and bad news but Rosemary tried not to listen to the wireless news. It was best to just get on with things, she felt, doing her bit with Red Cross parcels and helping with the evacuee children.

Over the past few weeks there had been a building of anticipation. Rumours of the invasion of the continent were rife. But there had been rumours before and Rosemary tried not to get too excited.

She still hadn't heard from Simon but since hearing that many soldiers of the Royal Norfolk Regiment were prisoners in Singapore, she hoped that soon Simon's father would be informed. She couldn't contemplate hearing worse news.

Since Floyd's declaration of love, she had tried to avoid him, making excuses when Jenny asked her to join her and their American friends at the cinema.

The good news was that no Atlantic conveys had been attacked during the past few weeks and the allies had also invaded Sicily. Did this mean the war might be drawing to a close? But there were still heavy bombing_raids on Germany and it seemed the village would be living with the constant roar of hundreds of B17 and B52 bombers passing overhead for months to come.

Sometimes the ground shook with the noise and one day at lunch, the Rev Turner muttered that it was all too much. 'They drowned out my sermon,' he complained. 'Surely they don't need to fly on a Sunday.'

Rosemary swallowed a retort and made a soothing reply. She sometimes wondered if her father really understood what was going on in the wider world. It was only when he was conducting services and declaiming from the pulpit that he came alive and she could see some of his old personality. Otherwise, he seemed to be in another world, holed up in his study or praying in church. He seldom even went out visiting the sick or lonely parishioners and, when she had time, Rosemary would take his place.

On this fine day, she was in the garden picking the first of the strawberries and currants for Mrs Norton to bake into tarts. She was due at the Manor after lunch to take over from Betty but she was determined to make time to visit Percy's elderly mother later on.

She was licking strawberry juice from her fingers when she saw the postman walking up the path to the back door. Her heart leap as it always did when the post arrived. Today – surely...

She leapt up, almost overturning the bowl of fruit. 'Anything for me?' she called, with no real hope in her voice.

He waved an envelope at her and she hurried over, barely restraining herself from snatching it out of his hand.

Her heart sank when she realised that it was just an ordinary envelope with a local postmark. She recognised the hand-writing though and smiled her thanks at the postman, despite her disappointment, once more telling herself that she hadn't really expected to hear from Simon.

She put the bowl of fruit on the bench beside the back door and sat down to read the letter from Maggie.

'I am very well and despite everything I am happy. I have a beautiful baby daughter and I am determined to keep her. Dad wants me to give her up for adoption but I just can't do it. I will manage somehow. My mum has told everyone I was called up to work in a munitions factory but I am staying with my aunt who

154

is looking after me. She says I can stay with her until the baby's a bit older and then get a job. I am very lucky she's standing by me but I would love to come back home.   I don't think I can though. I dread everyone knowing.

I realise now, I was being silly over Hank, expecting him to stand by me. That was why he asked to be transferred, just to avoid any responsibility.'

Maggie finished by saying, *'I hope you will keep in touch and let me know what's going on in the village.'*

Rosemary folded the sheet of paper and put it in her pocket. She stood up to take the fruit indoors. It was good to know that Maggie was all right but she felt sorry that things had gone so badly for her. She guessed that life would not be easy for her if she managed to keep the baby. Maggie was right in dreading coming back to the village – that's if her parents even welcomed her back. Staying in Ipswich was probably the for the best.

Mrs Norton was in the kitchen making pastry and she said, 'Did I hear the postman?'

'Letter from Maggie.'

Mrs Norton sniffed. 'What's she writing to you for?' Like most of her friends and neighbours, she had her opinion as to why Maggie had been 'called up' so suddenly.

'Just saying how much she's enjoying her job and making friends with the other factory girls. She's missing her friends here and our jaunts to the dance hall and pictures.' Here I go, lying again, Rosemary thought.

'She'll find someone to dance with, I'm sure.' Another sniff and a thump of the rolling pin on the pastry.

Rosemary didn't answer. She excused herself saying she must get ready for her stint at the Manor.

Even with the door and window open it was hot in the manor dining room with the sun pouring in. Good weather for the ripening crops but not so good for packing parcels and humping boxes around, thought Rosemary.

She worked hard though, managing to get most of the goods sorted and packed. The big boxes were stacked by the door when Percy drove up in his van.

He got out and started to load up, scarcely greeting Rosemary and muttering, 'I can manage,' when she offered to help.

Poor Percy. Everyone knew how he felt about Maggie and if he had guessed the reason for her hasty departure, he must be feeling angry – and foolish. Or perhaps he was just missing her, Rosemary thought.

She ignored his snappy reply and carried one of the boxes to the back of the van. 'How's your mother?' she asked.

He sighed and swiped his hand over his sweaty forehead. 'Not too well. Her leg's playing up and this heat doesn't suit her.'

'I thought I'd pop in later on, if that's all right.'

'Mum would love to see you. Cheer her up a bit,' Percy said.

You're the one who needs cheering up, Rosemary thought, but she smiled and said, 'Betty's picking Lily up from school and taking her for tea at the Manor so I'll pop in to see your mum when I finish here.'

As Percy drove away, she wondered whether she should have mentioned the letter from Maggie. Had he guessed about the baby or did he really think she was working in a factory in Ipswich? And what difference would it make? He had to get over her.

The back door to the Fentons' cottage stood open and Rosemary tentatively tapped on it before calling out, 'It's only me, Rosemary. Can I come in?'

'Come in and welcome, my dear,' Mrs Fenton called. 'I'm in the front room. 'It's cooler in here.'

Rosemary stepped across the flagstone kitchen floor and into the tiny front room. The window was open and a breeze flowed through from the open door.

'How are you, Mrs Fenton?'

'Not too bad, considering.'

The old lady sat in an armchair propped up with cushions, a blanket of brightly coloured crocheted squares over her knees in spite of the heat.

Rosemary sat opposite her. 'Percy said your leg's playing up,' she said.

'Oh, that boy. He worries so. It's just the heat. My ankles swell too but nothing to fret about. I'm well enough and the lad looks after me.'

'Can I do anything for you – make some tea or anything.'

'A cup of tea would be nice but Percy will see to my supper when he gets home.'

'He's just off to Felixstowe with the Red Cross parcels so he might be late back. Let me make you something. I've brought some eggs – the hens are laying well at the moment.'

'That's kind, dear. Let's have a cup of tea and you can tell me all the gossip. Then, if you've time perhaps you could do me some scrambled eggs. That would be lovely.'

Rosemary went into the kitchen and put the kettle on. She reached up to the sugar canister on the shelf above. There was only a little in it but she would put one spoonful in Mrs Fenton's cup. She herself had learned to do without since rationing began.

As she scooped some out, the old lady called, 'No sugar for me, dear. I save it for Percy. He needs the energy working as hard as he does.'

She laid a tray and carried it through to the other room, setting it down on a little table between their chairs. As she poured, she said, 'I don't take sugar now either. We use our ration to make fruit pies and cakes.'

'I do miss baking.' Mrs Fenton sighed. 'My poor old legs won't let me stand too long.'

Rosemary commiserated and decided that next time she visited she would bring some of Mrs Norton's home-made buns or tarts.

They chatted about the goings-on in the village, the progress of the war, the Americans and inevitably, Mrs Fenton mentioned Maggie.

'I hear she's working in Ipswich now but you can't believe everything you hear. My Percy's still mooning after her but I said to him, you've got to snap out of it, I said. She's not for you.'

Rosemary decided to mention the letter – and lie again. 'I've just heard from her. She's quite happy working in the factory – doing valuable war work, she said.'

'You do surprise me. If ever anyone was cut out to be a barmaid, it was her.'

'I don't think she ever intended to work in the pub permanently – she was only helping her parents when the barmaid left to join the forces.' Rosemary felt bound to defend her friend. 'Besides, you don't have any choice when you're called up.'

'Perhaps I'm being unfair then. It's just, she's made my boy so unhappy.' The old lady straightened up and said, 'Well, you're all right, dear, doing war work from home. I bet the Reverend's pleased about that. He does depend on you doesn't he.'

Rosemary nodded. 'I'm very lucky.' She gathered up the tea things. 'Now, what about that scrambled egg.'

***

When she got back to the Manor to fetch Lily, she saw the three Rook boys with Brian chasing each other round the kitchen garden. The girls were sitting on a bench looking at a picture book.

She hoped the boys weren't trampling the precious vegetables and she called out to them. Brian ambled over to her, his hands in his pockets. 'We've been good,' he said. 'We helped to tie up the runner beans to the poles and Amos says the peas will be ready soon.'

'What have you done at school today?'

Brian shrugged. 'Nothing much.' He wasn't too keen on schooling. Then his face creased in a big grin. 'Mr Davis had got us doing war work on Saturday.'

'Oh. What about helping Mr Fenton with the horses?'

Mr Davis said the factories need more stuff for the planes and things. So, we're going scrap metal collecting. That's more important than shoeing horses.'

'Maybe. But you can't let Mr Fenton down. The other boys can do the collecting.'

'Don't worry, Miss. I won't let him down. I can do both jobs.'

Rosemary smiled and called to Lily. 'Time to go home, love.'

Lily put down the book, said goodbye to Maisie and ran over to her.

'Have you had your tea?' Rosemary asked.

'Mrs Rook made us sardines on toast – lovely.'

'Ooh you lucky thing. I haven't had sardines for ages.'

'She told us she got the last tin they had in the shop.'

No use me going along there then, Rosemary thought, wondering what she could give her father for supper. It was getting harder to please him these days. He just didn't seem to understand about shortages and rations.

Her worries about food melted away when she entered the Rectory and saw the envelope lying on the hall table. The letter couldn't possibly be from Simon but ...

She snatched it up, her heart racing when she saw the Bury St Edmunds postmark and recognised Dr Spencer's spidery handwriting. She started to rip it open, pausing when she noticed Lily watching her. 'Go and wash your hands, dear,' she said, and continued to tear open the envelope.

The note was short and it confirmed Rosemary's worst fears. Simon was a prisoner of the Japanese.

'I promised my son I would pass on any news although I know he planned to write to you himself so I am writing to you just in case you haven't heard from him. They do not say where exactly he is but it must be either Singapore or Burma. I wish I could give you an address but he gives no real details at all I am sorry to say. I just hope he is being treated well but I have my doubts.

I wish I could give you better news and I promise I will let you know if I hear any more.'

She sank into a chair in the kitchen and read the short note again. Joy and sadness mingled and she gave a half sob. At least she knew something. But he must have been a prisoner for months – even years. Why had it taken so long for news to filter through?

Chapter 20

June 1944

Rosemary switched off the wireless, grabbed Mrs Norton's arms and swung her round the kitchen in an impromptu dance.

'It's happened! It's finally happened.'

Mrs Norton laughed and pushed her away. 'I grant it's good news but don't get carried away. The war isn't over yet.'

The day they had waited so long for had finally come. The Allies had invaded France. 'It can't be long now though. Oh, I must go and tell Jenny.'

'She'll have heard surely. No need to go rushing off.'

'She's at work and I know she doesn't have time to listen to the wireless first thing.'

'Aren't you supposed to be working yourself this morning?'

'Don't worry, I'll do my shift and go up to the school in time to meet her at dinner time.'

***

Rosemary and Betty had packed up the last of the parcels and were drinking tea in the Manor kitchen when Mrs Pargeter bustled in.

She waved a hand at them. 'Don't get up, finish your tea. I can see you've been busy.'

'Percy's coming to pick the crates up later,' Rosemary said.

Mrs Pargeter picked up the teapot and shook it. She got a cup and saucer from the dresser and poured herself a cup, taking a seat at the table.

'Now, ladies, I have some news – good news I think.'

'More news?' Rosemary asked. 'We've heard about the invasion. Our troops have landed in Normandy – it's so exciting.'

Mrs Pargeter smiled. 'Something else - we have heard from the International Red Cross that we can now send parcels to the far east – Singapore, the Philippines.'

'That *is* good news,' Rosemary said. She paused, then said. 'I heard from a friend that letters from there are now getting through.' Of course, Dr. Spencer wasn't really a friend but she couldn't tell anyone who he was. She hadn't confided in anyone about Simon, apart from Jenny.

Mrs Pargeter sighed. 'Who knows if the prisoners will get the parcels? I've heard through the International Red Cross that the POWs are treated very badly by the enemy.'

'I expect this means we'll be busier than ever,' Betty said.

'I'm afraid so. We must still keep sending to Germany and Holland, all over Europe as well. There are so many of these camps.'

'I like to be busy,' Betty said. 'And it feels as if we are doing some good.'

'Me too,' Rosemary agreed. 'What will we send to them out in the far east?' Since hearing that Simon was a prisoner in Singapore, she had looked up her father's encyclopedia and learned about the climate – the heat and humidity. 'They'll probably need different things to what we send to Europe.'

'You're right. It's dreadfully hot all the time – and then there's the monsoons.' Mrs Pargeter gave a little laugh. 'At least they won't need knitted socks and scarves. Headquarters are sending me a list and a new consignment will arrive from Norwich in the next day or two.'

August 1944

The school holidays meant that Rosemary was able to see more of Jenny and, when she wasn't on parcel duty, she was enjoying the long summer days helping with the harvest and taking the evacuee children out on country walks.

Brian and the Rook boys had really taken to scrap metal collecting and the girls were proud of their enthusiasm. Amos had made them a cart from an apple crate and old pram wheels and Percy had allowed them to store their collection in a shed behind the forge.

Rosemary was in the church arranging flowers on the altar and was startled when the west door opened, letting in a flood of sunshine. Thinking it was Jenny come to help, she turned with a smile to see Brian and Ted manoeuvring the cart down the steps into the main aisle.

'What are you doing boys – you can't bring the cart in here,' Rosemary protested.

'We've come for some metal,' Ted said.

'There's nothing for you here.'

'Mr Fenton said there is.' Brian stuck his lip out defiantly.

'Are you sure?' Rosemary thought Brian was pulling her leg.

'Yes, miss. We've been to every house in the village and Mr Fenton's shed's nearly full.'

'We need more if we're going to win the prize for collecting most stuff so we asked him where else we should try,' Ted said.

'He said 'I suppose you even want the candlesticks from the church,' so we've come for them,' Brian said.

Rosemary stifled a laugh. Percy and his jokes! She could understand the boys misunderstanding. 'You can't have the candlesticks – they belong to the church. They're very old and very valuable. The Rector would be most upset if they were melted down for scrap.'

'But Mr Fenton said...'
'Brian, he was joking.'
'You sure, miss?'
Rosemary nodded. 'Yes, I'm sure.'
Brian turned to Ted. 'Looks like we won't get the prize then.'
'After all our hard work.'
Rosemary thought for a minute. 'Did you say you've been to every house in the village?'
The boys nodded vigorously.
'Even the Rectory?'
'The Rector told us to go away and stop disturbing him.'
'We were going back later but we were scared,' Ted muttered, his lip trembling.
'You mustn't be scared of Father. He gets cross when he's busy but he would be very upset if he thought he'd frightened you.'
'Well, I ain't going back there,' Brian declared. 'Come on Ted, let's take the cart back to the forge.'
'Wait boys. I'm going home in a minute. Come with me. I might be able to find something for you.'
They hesitated but Rosemary smiled encouragingly. 'You want to win the prize, don't you?'
'Yeah,' they chorused, wide grins spreading across their faces.
They followed her up to the Rectory pulling the cart and rounded the corner of the house into the kitchen garden where Mrs Norton was picking tomatoes.
'Come to help with the picking, have you boys?' she asked.

'Not today. They're going to help me clear out the shed,' Rosemary said.

Mrs Norton said, 'More exciting for them, I suppose.'

Rosemary pulled the shed door open revealing piles of rusty garden tools and boxes of screws and nails covered in cobwebs. She indicated the bench where seed trays and pots lay and pointed to the shiny spades and forks hanging from nails on the wall. 'Don't touch any of those,' she said, 'Amos is very fussy about his garden tools. But you can fill your cart with all that stuff in the corner.'

The boys set to with a will and she left them to get on with it, deciding to help Mrs Norton with the tomatoes.

'Such a good crop this year. What are we going to with them all?' she asked.

'I'll make chutney and puree from most of them.'

'I love chutney with cheese.'

'It'll help to make our cheese ration go further.' Mrs Norton stripped the last truss off the plant and added it to her full bowl.

Rosemary followed her into the kitchen, placing her own bowl onto the table. 'I must get changed,' she said, brushing at her skirt which was dusty from the shed. Then I must go and finish the church flowers.'

When she got back to the church, she found Jenny sitting on the bench in the porch. 'Where's Lily?'

'Up at the Manor playing with Maisie. Betty Rook is working on the parcels and has promised to keep an eye on them.'

'I came to help with the flowers,' her friend said.

'I made a start but the boys turned up and I had to persuade them not to take the church silver for scrap.'

'Really? Good job you were here to stop them.'

Rosemary explained that Percy had been teasing but Brian had taken him seriously. 'Anyway, I took them up to the Rectory and got them to clear out the old gardener's shed. Some of that stuff has been untouched for years – not since the days when we actually had a gardener.'

'They're doing well with the collecting. It's good they have something to keep them out of mischief in the holidays.'

'Brian is behaving much better since he started helping Percy in the forge. He's growing up.'

'He seems to have taken to country life,' Jenny said 'Most of the evacuees have too, surprisingly. They're all so different now from the frightened children who arrived two years ago.'

Jenny agreed. 'The other Rook boys have been helping at White's farm with some of Mr Davis's class.'

They finished the flowers and tidied up, pausing in the porch to adjust to the bright sunlight after the gloom of the church. Rosemary flinched at the rumble of hundreds of planes taking off and a shadow passed overhead, blocking out the sun.

'We should be used to it by now,' Jenny said, shading her eyes and following them as they disappeared beyond the village.

'I'll never get used to it – I think I'll still be hearing them in my sleep even when the war is over.'

'Do you worry about Floyd? I know he doesn't fly but...'

'I worry about them all – and pray for them. Such brave lads...' Rosemary swallowed. 'So many of them don't come back.'

Jenny sighed. 'I've promised Will I'll write to his family if...'

Rosemary didn't know what to say. She had long accepted that Jenny's friendship with Will was just that

- friendship – and she regretted that her hasty judgment had almost caused a rift between them.

Jenny shrugged. 'Better get off home,' she said.

'Why not come up to the Manor for a cuppa? The girls would love to see you.'

'I think they see enough of me at school.' Jenny laughed. 'All right then.'

Chapter 21

August 1944

It continued hot and dry and many of the villagers rallied round to get the harvest in before the inevitable change in the weather.

Rosemary had finished her morning shift and Betty had taken over for the afternoon, so she decided to take the children for a picnic. She hurried back to the Rectory to prepare sandwiches, thankful they had eggs from their own hens, as well as the meagre remains of the cheese ration and sliced tomatoes from the garden. She filled a bottle of water and added lemonade powder. It would have to do. No one had seen a real lemon for years.

On the way back to the Manor she bumped into Jenny coming out of the shop and asked her to join them. 'It's a bit hot but we can go into the woods where it's shady.'

They collected the girls from the Manor and began the walk to the woods on the other side of the farm. They stopped for a few moments to watch the horses pulling the machines which cut the corn, separating the grains and pouring them into a hopper. The straw was bound into sheaves and tossed out of the back to be picked up and stacked into stooks by the many helpers.

Rosemary spotted Brian running across the field. She wasn't surprised to see him and she waved back when he waved to her. Since he'd starting helping Percy in the forge, he had become fascinated by the big Suffolk punches pulling the harvester.

He ran across to the fence, pointing and shouting, 'I helped to shoe him – the big one. I wasn't scared of him. Mr Fenton said he's gentle as a lamb.'

'Well done, Brian. But hadn't you better get back – can't let your friends do all the work.'

'Some of the yanks are helping too,' he said before running off to join the Rook boys.

Rosemary had already spotted Floyd and some of the off-duty Americans, but she turned away when Jenny pointed him out. She remembered Floyd talking about his home on a farm in Oklahoma and telling her that she would love it there.

She fanned her face with her hat. 'Come on. It's too hot standing around,' she said. 'Let's get to the woods.'

The girls ran ahead and Jenny took the opportunity to ask about her friend's relationship with the American.

'It's not a relationship,' Rosemary protested. 'It's like you and Will – friendship.'

'But he wants more than that doesn't he.'

Rosemary flushed and nodded.

'But you don't?'

'I don't know. It's difficult. I couldn't leave Father...'

'It's not just that though, is it? You're still thinking about the mystery man in the church.'

'I know it's silly but...'

'Not silly at all. We can't help how we feel. But you haven't heard from him. Surely, if he...'

'I had a letter.' Rosemary interrupted.

'Oh, that's wonderful. You've been so worried.'

'Not from Simon – from his father.'

Jenny's face fell. 'Bad news? Oh, Rosie, I'm so sorry.'

Rosemary hastened to reassure her. 'Not bad – but not exactly good.'

'Tell me.'

'He's a prisoner in Malaya or somewhere out there. His father's only just heard.' She clutched Jenny's arm. 'It's almost worse than no news at all. I can't write. Dr

Spencer said they could only write to close family – not even a proper letter, he said, more like a postcard. He said he has written back and spoke as if I am his cousin so that he can write to me as a family member. He'll let me know if he hears anymore.'

The girls had disappeared into the trees and Rosemary suddenly became concerned. She should have been looking after them instead of thinking about her own concerns. She was about to call when Maisie burst out of the wood.

'We've found a good spot for our picnic – and there's a stream.' She grabbed Rosemary's hand. 'Come on.'

'Where's Lily?'

'Don't worry. She's taking her shoes off and going for a paddle.' Maisie smiled up at her. 'We used to paddle in the sea when Mum took us down to Brighton for the day.'

Jenny looked alarmed. 'Show us where she is.'

The little girl led them between the trees until they came to a clearing. 'There she is.' Maisie pointed to where Lily was standing in the shallow stream, bending and splashing her hands in the water, her little face alight with laughter.

Relief flooded Rosemary when she realised the water was only inches deep. She couldn't be cross with Lily while she was having such fun. She put the bag containing the picnic down on the grass and said to Maisie, 'Would you like to take your shoes off too?'

Rosemary and Jenny sat on the grass watching the children happily splashing in the water. '

Jenny returned to the subject of her friend's love life. 'You must impress on Floyd that he's wasting his time – that's if you really think Simon is *the one*'. It's not fair on him.'

'You don't have to tell me. The thing is, I don't really know.' She sighed. 'Oh, Jenny, how can I tell after only two brief meetings? It's just, I can't stop thinking about him. And I like Floyd - I really do'.

'It's complicated, isn't it,' Jenny said.

'Oh, let's not talk about it.' Rosemary pulled the bag towards her and started unpacking the picnic. She spread a tablecloth on the grass. 'Time to eat.' She called to the girls.

Lily and Maisie ran towards them, carrying their shoes. The hems of their dresses were wet but Rosemary didn't comment. They would soon dry in the hot sun.

Jenny had laid the sandwiches out on the cloth – no plates. 'Eat up,' she said. 'No cake till the sandwiches are all gone.'

Maisie, a sandwich halfway to her mouth, gasped, 'We've got cake too?'

'Mrs Norton made it,' Rosemary said, turning to Jenny. 'I don't know how she does it on the rations we get.'

'I like picnics,' Lily declared, her mouth full of egg sandwich.

Rosemary nibbled at a sandwich but she wasn't hungry. However hard she tried, she couldn't get thoughts of Simon out of her head.

The children needed no encouragement to finish the sandwiches and eagerly devoured the fatless sponge Mrs Norton had made using one of the wartime recipes in her weekly magazine.

The shadows under the trees were lengthening and Jenny declared it was time to go despite protests from Maisie and Lily.

As they reached the edge of the wood the sky darkened and the ground trembled. The children covered their ears as the rumble of engines filled the air.

'It's just the squadron coming home,' Rosemary reassured them.

They stood watching in silence as the planes passed overhead making for the airfield. The sound died away and they started down the path towards the Manor. Jenny was quiet, probably worrying about Will and the crew they had become so friendly with over the past months. So many planes had been lost lately. How many wouldn't return this time?

They had reached the Manor gates when another sound drew their eyes skywards. A late returner. Rosemary hoped the crew were safe. But as it passed overhead, she saw plumes of smoke issuing from the rear of the aircraft.

Jenny stopped and grasped her arm, her face white.

Rosemary urged her on. 'Best get the girls inside,' she said urgently.

Jenny nodded, took Maisie's hand and they hurried up the Manor drive.

Mrs Pargeter stood in the porch, shading her eyes against the sun. Her shoulders slumped as an explosion shook the ground and Rosemary clutched Lily's hand.

'Big bang,' the little girl said. But she didn't sound worried, probably unaware of what the noise meant, Rosemary hoped.

Mrs Pargeter beckoned frantically to them, calling, 'Come along in, girls.' But her voice sounded surprisingly steady. 'Did you have a nice picnic, children?' she asked brightly.

'We paddled in the stream,' Lily said and Maisie added, 'We had cake.'

No mention was made of the noisy aircraft and the crash. The children were far too excited about their fun afternoon. They had probably become used to the planes constantly flying over the village.

Mrs Pargeter listened patiently to their chatter, saying quietly to the friends, 'It looks bad but we don't want to upset them,' nodding at the two little girls. 'The Colonel's gone up to the base with some of the Home Guard chaps to see if they need any help. I'll let you know what he says when he gets back.'

Jenny's face was still white with shock but she nodded. Rosemary took her arm. 'Come along, Jen. Better get Lily home and out of that wet dress.'

'And this one needs a bath,' Mrs Pargeter said, taking Maisie's hand.

Neither child protested, both tired out after their walk and paddle. Rosemary said little on the walk back to the Rectory but as they reached the gate, she said, 'Try not to worry, Jenny. We don't know which plane it was.'

'It was Will's, I know it was.'

'You can't know for sure. Anyway, Floyd will tell us.' She tried to put her arm around her friend but Jenny pushed her away and rushed off, choking back tears.

Rosemary stood for a moment gazing after her. So, despite her protests, it seemed Jenny felt more than friendship for Will.

***

The next day Rosemary was helping Mrs Norton in the kitchen before getting ready for work at the Manor when there was a knock at the back door. She answered it, expecting to see Jenny who was still on holiday from the school.

'Sorry to disturb you, Miss Rosemary,' Percy Fenton said. 'I thought you'd like to know...'

'Come in, Percy. What is it?' Her heart sank – she knew he had come to tell her about the plane crash.

'It's about your friend – that yank.'

'Floyd?'

'He's been hurt.'

'He can't be. He's not a flier,' she protested.

'I know, but he rushed over to the burning plane to help. He pulled one of his mates out but he was too late.' Percy paused, running his hand through his hair. 'He was very brave.'

Rosemary swallowed. She'd always thought that Floyd, being ground crew, was safe. 'How bad?' she whispered.

'He was burnt, quite badly. He's in hospital in Norwich.'

'Norwich? Why not the base hospital?' He must be badly hurt then, she thought.

'They couldn't cope with his injuries – dreadful burns I heard.'

Rosemary swallowed. Poor Floyd. She hoped he would recover. Shaking her head, she asked, 'What about the crew?'

'All dead - I'm sorry.' He paused, twisting his cap in his hands. 'It was the *'Oklahoma Belle'*. All those boys, the ones who took you dancing.' Percy hung his head. 'The ones I was so jealous of,' he muttered.

Rosemary felt a stab of compassion. Poor Percy. He hadn't stood a chance with Maggie when the yanks arrived.

Percy's mouth twisted. 'Pity that Hank wasn't on board.'

'Percy! What a thing to say.' Her sympathy evaporated.

'Sorry. I didn't mean it. It's just – I still miss Maggie, you know.'

'Maybe she misses you. I know she's not happy in Ipswich. Why don't you go and see her.'

'She won't want to see me.'

'Why don't you write to her then? You've got her address.' Percy didn't answer and she opened the door to let him out. 'I must go and see Jenny. She'll be devastated about Will.'

'Another yank taking over our girls.'

'You're wrong. Will's a decent chap. Jenny knew he was married. They really were just friends.'

Rosemary could tell he didn't believe her but what did it matter? She went to get ready for work determined to ask Mrs Pargeter for time off to go and see Floyd in hospital. She was worried about Jenny too. Although she and Will had just been friends, despite what others had thought, she would still be devastated by his death, not to mention the other members of the crew who had all been welcomed in the village.

***

There wasn't another bus to Norwich until later that evening – too late to visit the hospital. Rosemary crossed the road to the forge where Percy was just finishing for the day.

'I thought you were going to see Floyd,' he said.

'No bus.'

'I can take you in the van – that's if you don't mind it being a bit dirty.'

Rosemary's face lit up. 'That's so kind, Percy. I don't mind at all. Have you got enough petrol?'

Percy grinned. 'I get extra for delivering the Red Cross stuff.' He brushed the dust off the passenger seat, saying, 'Are you sure it's all right? Maggie hated riding in the van, always fretting about getting dirt on her nice clothes.'

'I'm wearing my work clothes so it doesn't matter. I didn't want to waste time changing.'

The drive to Norwich seemed to take forever, slowing down as they approached the city. Heaps of rubble from the bombing still clogged up many of the roads and they were diverted out of their way. Nearer the hospital Rosemary started to feel nervous, hoping she could cope with whatever injuries Floyd had - that's if she was allowed to see him. Usually, it was family only but surely they'd let her in. She didn't know if his family in America had even been informed.

Percy opted to wait for her outside and she walked into the hospital dragging her feet as she made her way along the corridor to the ward. There were six beds arranged three on each side and at first, she couldn't make out which of the patients was Floyd. But they were all older men and she was about to turn away when there was movement from a bed in the far corner. She could tell who it was from the shock of bright red hair poking up through the bandages, which was all she could see from where she stood.

She rushed over and leaned over the bed. 'Floyd, how are you?' She reached out to take his hand but both arms lay outside the covers swathed in thick dressings from fingertips to elbows and she stepped back.

'I'm Ok' he whispered, his voice hoarse. She leaned closer to hear, gasping as she saw the burns on his face.

'It's not as bad as it looks.' The husky voice again.

'Don't talk if it hurts. I was just so worried about you. Percy told me what happened. I'm so sorry about your friends.' The words stuck in her throat and she just sat, her hand covering the bandages.

'It was good of you to come,' Floyd struggled to speak and his eyes closed.

Rosemary sat for a few more moments but his rasping breaths alarmed her and she called for a nurse.

'The smoke he breathed in has damaged his lungs,' the nurse said.

'Will he get better?' Rosemary asked.

'They got to him in time so he will recover but it will be a long job.'

'I'd better leave him to rest. I'll come back when he's feeling better.'

She staggered outside the ward to find Percy leaning against the corridor wall. He took one look at her and hooked his arm through hers, supporting her until they reached the parked van. She was thankful he didn't ask questions, just said, 'Let's get you home.'

Darkness had fallen while she was in the hospital and she huddled into the corner of the passenger seat, trusting Percy to navigate through the dark lanes to the village.

As they neared the village, Percy said. 'I'm sorry about Floyd. We were getting to be real friends. Why did it have to happen when we're so near the end of the war?'

'I'm not so sure we are near the end,' Rosemary said. 'We thought once we'd invaded, it would all be over quite soon.'

'You're right,' Percy said. 'It seems we've a long way to go yet. The Krauts won't give up so easily.'

They lapsed into silence, Rosemary deep in thought. Never mind about Europe, what about the Far East?

Chapter 22

September 1944
The loss of the *Oklahoma Belle* had an enormous impact on the village. Since throwing the Christmas party for the village children, even those locals resentful of the Americans had become more welcoming and the crew of the *Oklahoma Belle* were especially popular.

There had been so many aircraft losses over the past year but somehow, the crash happening so close to home seemed to affect the village more.

Brian especially, seemed to have lost his enthusiasm for the planes and never went up to the base now. He spent more time in the forge which pleased Percy although he and Rosemary were worried about the lad.

'I tried to reassure him after I visited Floyd,' she told Percy. 'He wanted to come with me to the hospital but they don't allow children in.'

'I'll try to keep hm busy. Take his mind off it,' Percy said.

The first Sunday after the crash, the Rev. Turner held a special service mentioning Floyd Bowman and his brave attempt to rescue the pilot. Rosemary choked back the tears, remembering her visit to the hospital. Since then, she'd visited several times.

She sat by the bed and watched as the nurse undid the bandages. 'Would you like to wait outside?' the nurse said.

Rosemary shook her head. When she saw his hands, she barely restrained herself from recoiling in horror. Floyd hadn't seemed to notice, smiling wryly and saying, 'Not a pretty sight, are they?'

She forced a smile. 'They say they're getting better,' she said.

The next time she came, the nurses were busy and she volunteered to re-dress his hands. They were grateful for her help and each time she came she tended to him and it got easier.

Floyd's burns were healing and his face was barely scarred. But his breathing was strained and his hands, now unbandaged, were irreversibly damaged, his fingers scarred and twisted.

Apart from his hands he was recovering well and hoped to be out of hospital in a few days. Today, his face lit up as she entered the ward and her heart sank. She knew how he felt about her but she could not return his feelings, although she was becoming very fond of him. Perhaps she shouldn't visit so often, she thought, anxious not to give him the wrong impression.

Still, she smiled warmly and reached out to take his hand, stealing herself not to flinch at the feel of the misshapen fingers. He let her hold his hand for a moment but then pulled away.

'I have something to tell you,' he said.

Rosemary bit her lip and clutched his hand more firmly. He may look so much better but there were still underlying problems. Perhaps his lungs were more damaged than he'd let on.

'Are you all right – really all right, I mean?'

He grimaced and pulled his hand away from hers, holding them both up. 'What do you think?' His voice was harsh and he shook his head. 'I'll never be all right.'

'Oh, Floyd, I'm so sorry.'

'It's not just this.' He held his hands up again. 'I can cope with that. It's just...' His head sank onto his chest.

He was quiet for a few moments and Rosemary waited patiently. She knew there was more. She took his hand again.

'They're shipping me home,' he said abruptly.

She forced a smile. 'That's good news, isn't it.'

'How can I go when my buddies will never go home? I thought their bodies would be flown home but I heard there are no planes available. They'll be buried here – in your churchyard.' His voice broke on a sob. 'How can I face their families, people we all grew up with, went to school with...'

Rosemary understood. The crew of '*Oklahoma Belle*' all came from the same farming area of Oklahoma - Okie as the boys called it. They had grown up together and joined the air force together. It was one of the reasons they had settled so well in her little Norfolk village. They felt at home in the rural village with its surrounding farmland.

'People will understand. Besides, your own family will be happy to have you home.'

'I guess,' he said quietly.

She wanted to praise his heroism and assure him of the welcome he was sure to receive back home. But he would dismiss it as he had before. She glanced at her watch. 'I'm sorry, I have to get back to work. I must go if I don't want to miss the bus.'

She leaned over and dropped a light kiss on his scarred cheek. As she hurried down the corridor, she thought she heard him calling her back but she ignored him and carried on.

Perhaps she wouldn't visit again, she thought. Sympathy and caring could be misinterpreted and she didn't want to give him hope. Besides, he was being sent home and she wouldn't be going with him although if things had been different, she acknowledged that she might have been.

As she looked out of the bus window at the harvested fields, the poppies growing in the hedgerows, she pictured a different life away from the confines of her small village, life in another country, a country with wide open spaces golden under the sun, the corn, taller than that which grew in her home county, waving in the breeze.

She shook her head. It was a tempting picture but not for her. However hard she tried she could not forget the tall, brown-eyed, soldier she'd met in the church so long ago, crouched over his sketchpad, his dark hair flopping over his forehead as he drew. Even if they never met again, she would always remember Simon.

***

The postman had been but there was still nothing for her. Stifling her disappointment, Rosemary took the letters into her father's study. He raised his head from his notes, frowning and throwing down his pen.

'Has Michael written?' he asked.

'No. It's been a while. I do hope he's all right.'

Seth ran his hands through his sparse grey hair. 'When will it end?' Despair choked his voice.

'Oh, Father. I'm sure the war can't go on much longer now we've invaded France and Michael will be set free. We *will* see him again one day.' She tried to put her arm around him but he shrugged her off.

'I'm not just thinking about your brother. It's those poor lads up at the air base. So many lost – and now, right on our doorstep.' He groaned. 'It's the funeral in a couple of days. I'm trying to write the eulogy but I just don't know what to say. Those boys came to my church, worshipped with us...' His voice choked on a sob.

Rosemary had never known him to get so stressed over a funeral. In some ways it was almost routine for him, part of his work. She could find no words of comfort. She was struggling herself. But there was something she had to say.

'Father, they're letting Floyd out of hospital tomorrow. He'll be looked after at the base hospital until he can be flown home. He was surprised that the funeral hadn't been held before but he's pleased he'll be able to attend.' She paused and laid a hand on her father's arm. 'Can I ask you, please, Father – don't mention his bravery in your eulogy. He doesn't see

181

himself as a hero and he gets upset when people try to praise him. He got really angry with Percy when we visited him in the hospital.'

'I'm not sure I agree with you, dear. He deserves recognition for what he did.'

'He'll get recognition. Their CO told Jenny that he's in line for a medal. Besides, his colleagues, the villagers - we all know and appreciate what he did.'

Seth nodded reluctantly. 'I feel I should say something but, you may be right. After all, he's your friend, you know him best.'

'Thank you, Father.'

He picked up his pen and started to write again almost instantly becoming absorbed by his words.

Feeling dismissed, Rosemary turned to leave the room but as she reached the door, he raised his head and said, 'This young man – he *is* more than a friend, isn't he?'

She shook her head. 'No, Father, definitely not.'

'I wouldn't stand in your way if he *was*. I would miss you, of course, but you need a life of your own even if...' His voice trailed away.

'Father, stop worrying.' She managed a little laugh. 'I have no intention of leaving you, and certainly no plans to go and live in America.'

The look of relief on his face almost brought a smile. But before he could speak again, she said, 'He's being sent home to convalesce.' That should reassure him, she thought.

*****

The church was packed for the funeral. More people stood outside as the coffins, draped in the Stars and Stripes, were carried in, the pall bearers in full dress uniform. It seemed that all those not on duty or flying had marched down through the village behind their fallen comrades. The villagers not already in

182

church lined the narrow road, doffing their hats as the procession passed by.

Floyd had been discharged from Norwich hospital but was still under the care of the base physician. He'd wanted to march with his comrades but was still not fit enough. One of his friends had driven him to the church and he had taken a pew at the front, sitting between Rosemary and Jenny, with Percy on the end of the row.

The congregation rose as Amos pounded the organ and Rosemary gripped Floyd's hand. She no longer flinched at the feel of the twisted bones and scarred skin. She struggled through the familiar hymns and prayers, then held her breath as her father mounted the pulpit.

To her surprise his voice was strong, his faith shining from his eyes. No longer the depressed, despairing man he had been just a few days ago. She had heard him pacing his room, his anguished muttered prayers. But his prayers had been answered, he had found strength from somewhere.

He didn't mention Floyd by name as she had requested, but he praised the bravery of the strangers in their midst – no longer strangers but friends, the friendly invaders, he called them.

Rosemary glanced around, noting the smiles and nods of their neighbours, many of whom had not been so welcoming when the Americans had arrived just over a year ago. In the rear pews, officers and men of the Oakleigh Bomb Group sat straight-backed, their caps held on their laps. The notes of the last hymn faded away and Amos began playing the US National Anthem softly as the congregation filed out, following the pall bearers down grassy paths to the small plot at the rear of the churchyard which had been set aside for the crew of the *Oklahoma Belle*.

***

It was hard saying goodbye to Floyd. They had already made their private farewells the day before in a secluded corner of the *Four Bells*. He had confessed that before the crash he had determined to ask her to marry him. 'I couldn't imagine going home and leaving you behind,' he'd said.

She had let him down gently, feeling guilty for using her father's health as a reason for not wanting to go and live so far away.

He said he understood. 'Besides, what use would I be to anyone – a cripple, unable to work...' He had covered his face with his useless hands.

Rosemary fought back tears and in a choked voice said, 'It wouldn't make any difference if...'

'If you loved me,' he muttered bitterly. He stood abruptly and pushed his chair back. 'I know you've never led me on, always said we were just friends. I have to accept that.'

He turned and strode out of the pub, leaving Rosemary with tears running down her cheeks. It was true. If she'd loved him, she would have gone anywhere, coped with his disability, nurtured him. If only she had never met Simon Spencer and fallen in love.

Now, she stood by the gate to the airbase, gazing across the runway at the aircraft which would soon be winging its way across the Atlantic, taking Floyd out of her life forever. A group of men stood beside the big plane, too far away to make out individual features. But she spotted Floyd – his flaming red hair a beacon in the August sunshine. She was tempted to ask the guard to let her in – he knew her and would understand her need to say goodbye. But it was too late. He was climbing the steps into the plane and in seconds he was lost to sight. He didn't see her final wave of farewell and she turned away determined not to cry.

Chapter 23

September 1944

In Oakleigh St James life slowly returned to normal – or what passed for normal in wartime. The bombers continued to roar over the village, many not returning from their missions, rationing got more stringent and housewives found ever more creative ways to eke out the food they were allowed. And the land girls continued to meet the Americans in the *Four Bells*, to the scandalised comments of the older villagers.

On top of that was the threat from the German rockets which the locals called 'doodlebugs'. Although they were aimed at London, many went off course and landed in the Norfolk countryside with horrendous loss of life. Now there was a new more powerful type called V2s which couldn't be shot down. Bombers were taking off from Oakleigh Air Base at all hours as they attempted to wipe out the launch sites.

Rosemary's optimism that the war would soon end had faded in the light of these new threats. She understood her father's worry over Michael's fate and there was little she could say to cheer him up.

Since the tragedy of the *Oklahoma Belle,* Brian's enthusiasm for the American bombers had faded somewhat and he no longer took every opportunity to run up to the base. Now, he spent most of his time when not in school helping in the forge, declaring that he wanted to be a blacksmith when he grew up like Mr Fenton.

Percy too was missing Floyd. He remembered when the Americans had first arrived and his resentment at them appearing to take over the pub. But Floyd had been interested in his work, visiting the forge and talking about his life back home in Oklahoma. They'd ended up being good mates. He admired the American too, not just his bravery in trying to rescue the pilot of the crashed plane. It was the way he had coped with his injuries, his acceptance that he could no longer carry out his duties. He was different from most of the others, especially that Hank who had taken Maggie from him.

Percy still hadn't got over Maggie although he doubted if she would ever take him seriously. She'd probably found someone else already.

Rosemary had given him her address and urged him to write to her. Perhaps he would – as a friend. After all, they'd been playmates as children. He made up his mind and that evening after work he settled at the kitchen table and started to write.

He had cleared away their evening meal and settled his mother in her favourite chair with her knitting and a library book. He didn't tell her who he was writing to. He knew her views on that 'flighty barmaid' and hoped to avoid her caustic comments.

At first, he didn't know what to say to Maggie and he spent some minutes chewing the end of his pen. He glanced across at his mother who seemed immersed in her book but he smiled as he noticed her glasses had slipped down and her eyes were closed.

He began to write, anxious to get the letter written before she woke up. He started by asking how she had settled in Ipswich and if she was liking the factory work and hoped she was making friends. Then he went on to describe what had been happening in the village, glossing over the tragedy of the crashed bomber.

'We are all so proud of young Brian and his friend Ted. They've been collecting scrap metal – doing their bit for the war effort as Brian said. They won a prize for the most scrap collected in the surrounding villages. Col and Mrs Pargeter drove them to Norwich

to be presented with their award, a silver plaque and a big bar of chocolate each. I took Rosemary and Jenny in the van and several others villagers were there too.'

Percy paused for a moment, chewed his pen again and took the plunge.

'I do wish you could have been there too. I miss you. The Four Bells isn't the same without you there. Let's hope the war will be over soon and you will be back.'

He almost crossed out the last few lines but decided to leave them. She knew how he felt. He sighed. She probably wouldn't write back anyway.

A few days later, he had to go to Ipswich to collect some coke for the forge. His usual supplier had run out and had advised him where he might find some. As he drove into the town centre he thought of Maggie – truthfully, she was never far from his mind. He had heard the rumours of why she had left the village. But he didn't care. That Hank had probably led her on.

When he had completed his business, on impulse he turned away from the main road out of town and entered the little huddle of Victorian terraces where Maggie's aunt lived. He had to stop several times to ask for directions but he wasn't going to give up now he was near.

October 1944

'Come ye thankful people come, raise the song of harvest home...' The sound of many cheerful voices rose up to the rafters of the little church. Rosemary smiled across at the children all singing lustily. The evacuees, most of whom had never been to church before coming here, followed the words in their hymn books, struggling to keep up but determined to join in. Harvest was Rosemary's favourite of the church festivals apart from Christmas, the hymns so joyful, the church so beautifully decorated. And despite the awful events of the past year there was much to be thankful

for. The harvest had been the best for some years and there was a new mood of optimism about the progress of the war. It couldn't go on for much longer, surely.

Best of all for Rosemary was the improvement in her father's health. He had been mired in grief and depression for so long in the years after her mother's death but now seemed to have come to terms with his loss.

The hymn came to an end and he mounted the pulpit for his sermon. As he began to speak, Rosemary smiled again as he spoke, his theme echoing her thoughts and the words of the hymn – praise and thankfulness.

Outside in the mellow autumn sunshine, the children ran about as if released from prison, shouting and laughing.

Mrs Pargeter called them to order, but for once the Rev. Turner did not join her in telling them off. 'Let them enjoy the sunshine while they can,' he said. 'Who knows what tomorrow will bring.'

Jenny standing behind her, stifled a giggle and Rosemary nudged her to be quiet. She was so pleased to see her father back to his old self. He had always been strict, especially in church, but he always acknowledged that children needed to time to be free, to laugh and play. She and Michael had enjoyed such a happy childhood but that had all changed with her mother's long illness and subsequent death. Father had carried on with his ministry but she knew his faith had suffered over the years.

Impulsively she kissed her father's cheek and to her delight he accepted the caress. 'I'm going to take the children up to the Manor', she said. 'Betty's cooking a meal for us. Mrs Pargeter would like you to join us.'

Expecting a refusal, she was about to try and persuade him but to her delight he accepted straight away. 'I'll be there soon,' he said and turned to greet one of his parishioners.

As she and Jenny accompanied the children up the lane, Rosemary pondered the change in her father. It occurred to her that it had begun after their conversation about Floyd Bowman. He had obviously thought their friendship was serious and had been dreading her telling hm that she wanted to marry him and accompany him back to America after the war.

Thank goodness he had accepted her reassurance. Whatever happened in the future she vowed she would never leave him – or the village.

***

Percy parked his van in a side street and walked up to the door of number twenty. He didn't know Ipswich very well and it had taken him a while to navigate the warren of terraced streets behind the railway station. Heaps of rubble clogged the streets after a recent bombing raid. The docks had been the enemy's target but inevitably the civilian population had suffered as they had in Norwich.

Percy gazed around at the devastation, muttering a prayer of thankfulness that Maggie's aunt's house had been spared. The door opened and his heartbeat quickened in anticipation of seeing the girl he loved.

An older woman wearing a wraparound pinafore, her hair confined in a pink turban, confronted him. 'Yes?' she snapped.

'I've come to see Maggie,' he stammered.

'And who are you?' She peered at him. 'If you're that yank, you can buzz off. She doesn't want to see you.'

Percy's spirits rose. So, she wasn't still hankering after him. He took a deep breath. 'I'm a friend from Oakleigh. I had some business in Ipswich and thought I'd look her up, pass on some news of home.' The woman was still staring at him suspiciously and he paused, shuffling his feet. This was harder than he'd anticipated.

189

'Is she at work then?' he asked, thinking it best to maintain the story that she had been called up. 'I didn't know which factory she was in – that's why I called here first.'

'What's your name then?'

'I'm Percy Fenton, the local blacksmith. We were in the same class at school.'

'I'm Maggie's Aunt Alice.' She stepped back, holding the door open. 'You'd better come in – that's if you really are a friend.'

He followed her along the narrow passage into a small room overlooking the back yard. Through the window he could see Maggie hanging washing on the line. It took him a moment to realise that the white objects flapping in the breeze were baby's nappies.

So, the rumours *were* true then. Rosemary had tried to prepare him but it was still a blow. He almost turned away but at that moment she looked up and saw him, her face white with shock.

She had changed a bit - no lipstick, no bottle-blonde curls. But with her blue eyes, her naturally fair waves, she was still his beautiful Maggie. His face creased in a wide smile and he stepped towards the back door as it opened and she rushed inside.

'What are you doing here? Come to gloat, have you?' she screamed.

'Oh, Maggie, love. How can you think that? I just wanted to make sure you were all right.' He seized her hands. 'Your friends have been worried about you.'

'What friends?' She shook him off. 'No one in that village likes me. They'll probably be gossiping about me more than usual once you tell them my news.'

Before Percy could speak, Alice stepped in. 'Give the lad a chance, Mags. He didn't have to come.' She turned to Percy. 'You didn't really think she was working in a factory, did you?'

Percy shook his head. 'Rosemary told me to come. She said Maggie needed a friend.'

Alice nodded. 'Rosemary, the Rector's daughter. She's the one been writing to you?'

Maggie nodded. 'She promised not to talk about...'

'She didn't, but there was gossip – there always is in a small village like Oakleigh as you know.' Percy said.

'So - everyone knows.' She turned to her aunt. 'I wanted to go back, but you do see that I can't – not that Dad would have me.'

'Your mum misses you,' Percy said.

A sob caught in Maggie's throat. 'I've really messed up, haven't I. I can't stay here forever and I can't go home...'

'I can't leave you like this,' Percy said. 'Can we go somewhere and talk. There's so much I want to say.'

'Take him in the front room, Mags. I'll make some tea.' Aunt Alice filled the kettle from the tap over the sink.

'What's to talk about?' Maggie snapped but, after a brief hesitation, she led him along the passage to the front room. She threw open the door, pointing to the cot under the window. 'Now you see why I can't go home,' she said, choking past the lump in her throat.

The baby was fast asleep, a thumb in her mouth, a fluffy pink banket tucked around her. Wordless, Percy stared down at her, a strange feeling stirring in his chest. She was the image of Maggie, peaches and cream complexion, a wisp of golden hair visible at the edge of the knitted bonnet she wore. Percy had the feeling that when she opened her eyes, they would be as blue as the sky, just like Maggie's.

'What's her name?' he asked.

'Daisy.'

'Sweet,' He bent down and gently touched the smooth cheek. 'She's beautiful,' he murmured. 'Just like her mother.'

Maggie sighed. 'They want me to give her away,' she said. 'But I can't.' A sob caught in her throat.

'I understand. How could anyone give their child away?'

'I may have to.' Her voice broke. 'But how can I...?'

His arms came round her and he stroked her hair. 'Oh, Maggie, love. Don't cry.'

He led her to an armchair and pulled her onto his lap, soothing and murmuring until her sobs died away. Deep in his heart he knew the answer to her dilemma but did he dare to voice it? Could he find the courage to declare his love?

Chapter 24

November 1944

Rosemary placed a small tablet of soap and a packet of razor blades in the box she was packing. This consignment was going to Singapore and, as she had when she was working on parcels for Germany, she tried to imagine who might receive it. Maybe Simon would open it and, with this reminder of home, might remember his visits to Oakleigh and their conversations. Did he ever think of her, she wondered. Was she wrong to have imagined a connection between them? If only she could get a letter. After all, he had promised to keep in touch.

She picked up the bar of soap and sniffed it but it had no real smell. Like everything nowadays, it was just plain, unscented, the same as what they had in the village shop. Soap had been rationed for over a year but the last time she had tried to buy some they had sold out. She remembered back to the days before the war when she had thought nothing of spending all her money on a tablet of Yardley's roses soap.

'Hey, wake up, Rosie.' Betty's voice shook her out of her day dream.

She rubbed her eyes and put the bar of soap into the parcel. 'Sorry. I can't help thinking of those poor lads and hoping these parcels get to the people they're meant for. How do we know if they even get there?'

'No use brooding. We just have to hope. It is worrying though. Mrs P said so many ships have been sunk out in the Pacific.'

Rosemary shuddered. 'Don't, please. As if we haven't got enough to worry about.' In the months since the invasion, hopes of a quick end to the war had faded as news reached them of the Royal Norfolk's tremendous losses at Arnhem, followed by more setbacks.

'We need some good news,' Betty said.

Rosemary agreed but she was reluctant to share what she had heard from Percy the other day. She knew not many would agree with her but as far as she was concerned, the news that Maggie had a daughter was the best news, especially as her friend was planning to keep the baby.

She had promised to keep Maggie's secret and wondered how her parents felt about it, remembering Ron Newman's anger the last time she had spoken to her friend. Would they ever accept their grandchild?

As they worked Betty chattered on about the boys and their progress at school but Rosemary scarcely listened.

She couldn't stop thinking about Maggie and wished she could go and see her – and little Daisy. Perhaps she would ask for an afternoon off and ask Percy to take her.

The next day she was passing the forge and spotted Percy talking to Farmer White. The farmer was leading a big Suffolk Punch who seemed to be limping. Percy took over the reins and tied the horse to the post outside the forge.

He waved to Rosemary and carried on dealing with the horse. She walked on towards the shop. He was obviously busy and probably wouldn't have time to talk to her.

As she waited in the queue, she saw Farmer White leading the horse, which seemed to be walking normally now, up the lane. After doing her shopping, she hurried over to the forge, hoping Percy hadn't started on another job.

He came out wiping his hands on a dirty rag. 'Can I do anything for you?' he asked after greeting her.

'Not a blacksmithing job,' she said with a grin. 'And I won't bother you if you're busy.'

'Never too busy for you,' he said smiling.

She returned his smile and said, 'I wondered if you might be visiting Maggie again. If you are, could you take me with you please? I'd love to see her – and the baby.'

'I'd like to but I have a lot of work on at the moment. But next time I go, I'll gladly let you tag along.'

'Thank you. I hope she'll be pleased to see me – we've been writing to each other so...'

'Of course she'll be pleased. You've been a good friend to her – not like some in this village.'

Rosemary bit her lip, embarrassed. 'I'd better get this shopping home,' she said and hurried away.

***

The weather had changed from mild misty mornings to strong winds and constant rain. Sudden heavy downpours filled the little stream that ran behind the forge and the cottages where Mrs Norton lived. The culvert under the road became blocked with fallen leaves and the water rose, spilling over the back step into Mrs Norton's kitchen.

She and Rosemary were preparing vegetables in the Rectory kitchen when Amos knocked on the back door to tell them what had happened.

'Just when I was fixing to go back home,' Mrs Norton groaned. 'I've taken advantage of your hospitality for far too long, Rosemary.'

'Nonsense, we've been happy to have you,' Rosemary protested. 'You can't possibly go back until it's dried out.' Truthfully, Rosemary had become used to having the housekeeper there, taking some of the burden of looking after the household from her and giving her more time for her Red Cross work.

The bomb damage to Mrs Norton's cottage had only recently been completed, a shortage of manpower and materials had meant that temporary repairs had made the place weatherproof but, until now it had still not been safe for her to live in.

'Well, I must admit I've been happy staying here as well as helping out at the Manor. It's good to feel useful. I don't think I'm cut out for retirement.'

Rosemary laughed. 'You're right. I don't know where you get your energy from.'

'I like to be busy,' she declared and as if to prove her words, she reached a big pan down from the shelf over the stove. 'Time to get started on that soup.'

'I'll just go and tell Father about the flooding,' Rosemary said.

'I hope he's not too upset that I'm staying longer.'

'He'll be delighted. He likes your cooking.'

'Get away.' Mrs Norton flapped a hand and shook her head but Rosemary could tell she was pleased.

A few days later, the boys helped with clearing the culvert and the stream returned to its usual level but the damp grey weather continued and the house still smelled musty. To Rosemary's pleasure, Mrs Norton had a good excuse to stay on at the Rectory.

***

Simon and Ron lifted the heavy wooden sleeper and staggered over to the railway line, dropping it heavily into place. Simon straightened and took a deep breath – almost impossible in the humid air. Ron tugged at his arm as one of the guards shouted and waved his sword threateningly. 'Chin up, mate,' he whispered.

Simon managed to stay on his feet and stumbled over to the pile of sleepers. One more, he thought, then surely it would be time for their ten-minute break. He glanced down the length of the railway line, the rails dazzling them as the sun glanced off them. How he would welcome even the monsoon rains now, but they were months off.

He wiped a hand across his forehead, then bent to pick up his end of the sleeper. At the other end Ron stumbled and the heavy block of wood slipped and fell. Simon tried to grab it but it hit the ground, bouncing a little and landing on his hand. He tried to stifle his cry of pain and Ron rushed to help lift it off. But a guard had seen what had happened and he beat Ron out of the way.

As Simon tried to free his trapped fingers, the guard stamped down on them. Other guards had heard the commotion and hurried over. They dragged Simon away and threw him down on the side of the track.

He lay there for hours, cradling his wounded hand against his chest and trying not to cry out. As work came to an end for the day, Simon watched as the men were lined up for the march back to their hut. They were going to leave him here along with the others who had fallen, succumbing to heat and disease.

He closed his eyes, resigned to his fate, only to open them as hands dragged him to his feet. Hugh and Ron took an arm each, forcing him to into the long line of prisoners stumbling back to their quarters.

In the hut, Hugh tore a strip off the bottom of his singlet and bound Simon's injured hand, trying to straighten the broken fingers. 'Try to rest,' he said. 'I'll try and scrounge some painkillers.'

Simon worked on, helped by his friends, but he was in constant pain. Unable to hold his pencil he almost gave up on his sketches. But he persevered with his left hand, determined to carry on keeping a record.

***

They had been working on the railway for months and Simon had no idea how many miles of rail they had completed. His broken bones had healed after a fashion, fused into twisted shapes, and he was in constant pain. He still tried to make little sketches but often had to give up. But keep a note of the date in his sketchbook which he was careful to keep hidden. One of his fellow prisoners had kept a diary and a few days ago it had been discovered. The prisoner had been forced to burn it, the guard holding his hand over the fire until it was ashes. Simon and his fellow POWs had been forced to watch, then threatened with worse if any other forbidden writings were found.

'Be careful, Si,' Hugh warned.

'I will,' Simon assured him.

'Get rid of it,' Ron urged.

'I can't. It's not much but it's the only record we have of what's been happening here. The people at home must be told.'

Hugh scoffed. 'Who knows if we'll ever get home. For all we know the war's already over. These madmen will fight on to the death.'

'We mustn't think like that. We must keep on hoping and praying.'

Now, Simon wondered if his friends were right. The guards shouted at them to stop work and they fell in at the side of the track, relishing the ten minutes respite and the chance to take a drink from their water bottles.

He didn't agree with Hugh – if the war was really over, they would have heard via the secret wireless – that's if it hadn't been discovered. Besides, the Japs would surely have been celebrating their victory. Simon refused to contemplate such an ending. The allies must win. He must get home, back to Rosemary, the girl he could not forget. It was thoughts of her that kept him going when he was so weary and in such pain that it was tempting to give up.

The guards were shouting and chivvying them back to work and Simon helped Ron up. The back-breaking work began again.

Simon kept his head down, concentrating on staying on his feet. If he fell and couldn't get up, he would be left to die at the side of the track. Ron was worse off than he was, the sores on his arms and legs, badly infected. His friend could not last much longer.

Occasionally Simon glanced surreptitiously along the line, noting how many of his fellow prisoners had succumbed to the heat and disease. He gritted his teeth. It would not happen to him, he vowed.

***

A few days later news spread along the line that the Italians were out of the war and Simon and his friends felt renewed hope.

'I heard it on the wireless in the next hut,' Ron said. 'The Japs are going mad trying to find it.'

'They'll be searching here next. Better make sure your notebook is well hidden,' Hugh said.

'Don't worry – they won't find it.'

The wireless wasn't found and their captors were extra vigilant for the next few weeks but eventually conceded that there was no wireless. Instead, they patrolled the perimeter of the railway line accosting and beating any natives who dared to speak to the prisoners.

Even so, a little news of the war's progress filtered through and when they'd heard of the D-Day landings in France, Simon and his friends had begun to feel that their optimism wasn't misplaced. But months had passed and there was little news of the Allies' progress,

The Japs remained determined that the railway would be finished. And finished it was – eventually – four hundred miles from Bangkok to Rangoon.

'At the cost of how many lives? Simon asked bitterly.

'I estimate one death for every sleeper we laid,' Hugh said.

'And the rest,' Ron muttered. 'At least half of our blokes.'

Simon looked around at the exhausted and dying men around him. They were hardly recognisable as men, naked, gaunt and covered in sores, their limbs swollen with beri-beri. He sighed. Even if the war ended today, how many of them would survive to get home? He was beginning to have doubts that he would be among them and, although he still hung on, Ron was in an even worse state.

He shook his water bottle. There was a little left. He crawled over to his friend and held it to his lips. Not that it would do much good, he thought. He doubted Ron would still be with them by the following morning.

Hugh grabbed his arm. 'Save it for yourself,' he said quietly. 'It won't do him much good.'

Simon ignored him. Ron would do the same for him if their positions were reversed.

'I wonder what's going to happen to us now the railway's finished,' Hugh said.

The answer came the next day when the survivors were loaded onto trains and taken down to Kamburi, stopping on the way to bury the dead, Ron among them.

They stayed there for weeks.

'It's as if they don't know what to do with us,' Hugh said.

There was no further news of the war's progress as day followed day. The men were still gaunt and hollow-eyed, still covered in festering sores, still barely surviving on one meagre bowl of rice each day but something was happening to them. Freed from the unremitting back-breaking toil of the railway they remained physically weak but their spirits rose.

The best news was when they heard that the Burma railway had been bombed.

'What a shame – after all our hard work,' Hugh said, with an ironic grin, then joined Simon and their hut mates in resounding cheers.

A few days later they were assembled on the parade ground and the camp commandant announced, 'All men go to Singapore.'

They were loaded on to trains and after five days they were escorted to a new camp.

It felt like coming home and, as Simon said, 'Nothing will ever be as bad as those months in Burma.'

Then came the best news of all – letters from home, sixteen months late but 'God bless the Red Cross,' Hugh declared as he and Simon were both handed their mail. There was no sign of the hoped-for parcels but getting mail was the next best thing.

Simon's letter was from his father – he really hadn't expected anything from Rosemary. But he tore it open and devoured the heavily censored words, tears streaming down his face.

Dr Spencer hoped they were treating him well and that they had received the Red Cross parcels. The words brought a sarcastic laugh. He knew parcels had arrived but the prisoners had seen nothing of them. His father ended by saying, *I have been in touch with your cousin Rosemary and she sends her best wishes and looks forward to seeing you when this is all over. Do write to her when you are able.*

Hugh's letter was from his sister and he read bits out to his friend. Then he said, 'What about you, mate? No word from the lovely vicar's daughter?'

'Rector,' Simon corrected. 'Her father is the Rector. Don't ask me what the difference is. Anyway, these letters are more than a year old so she probably didn't know where I was.' His face fell. Did she not know or didn't she care?' Was he just dreaming?

He read his father's letter again and smiled. 'Cousin Rosemary!' He didn't have any cousins but he remembered that they had only been permitted to contact close family. His father's words must be a sort of code. She wanted him to write. Perhaps he was reading too much into it but the thought cheered him. He would write straight away and he would enclose one of his drawings if he could get away with it.

Chapter 25

December 1944

All too soon it was time to start planning for Christmas again – the sixth one of the war. The Rev Turner closeted himself in his study, worrying over his sermons for the special services. Unusually, he sought Rosemary's advice on the hymns.

'How can we expect people to sing *'Joyful and triumphant'*? Where is the joy? How can I preach *'Peace on Earth'* with what's going on in the world? '

Rosemary tried to be positive but she feared her father was once again experiencing doubts about his faith. He had seemed so much better recently, even resuming his sick visits, and his sermons had become more cheerful.

'Father, we must pray that better times will come. The war can't go on much longer. Surely it is better to give people hope and optimism. As for the carols – we have sung these songs every year ever since I can remember and they are so uplifting. Our church members leave the service feeling warmth in their hearts.'

Seth sighed. 'You're right, my dear. I must put these gloomy thoughts aside.'

'For the children too. Jenny is teaching them a new song which they will sing at the Christmas Day morning service. I'm sure that will lift your spirits.'

'Thank you, my dear. I feel better already. I must write my notes while your words are fresh in my mind.'

'Well, don't get so absorbed you forget to come down for your lunch. Mrs Norton is making a pie.'

That brought a smile to Father's face and Rosemary hurried along to the kitchen, thankful she had escaped before he sunk into gloom again. She had dreaded him asking if there had been a letter from Michael and she too was beginning to be worried about her brother as they hadn't heard from him for several months.

***

Rosemary was determined to make this Christmas a more joyful celebration this year. They had done their best in previous years but no one had expected the war to go on so long. But, despite the increase in rationing and the shortage of anything to brighten up their lives, everyone in the village had vowed to make it as happy as possible, especially for the children.

She and Jenny were sitting at the Rectory dining table helping the girls to make Christmas decorations from cut up newspapers and magazines.

Maisie was getting quite adept at twisting the strips of paper and gluing them into circles but Lily wasn't quite so competent.

'Here's a damp cloth,' Jenny said. 'Wipe your fingers before starting on the next one, otherwise you'll get the paste everywhere.'

'She's doing very well though,' Rosemary said encouragingly. She showed them how to link the circles together to make chains but Lily couldn't get the hang of it.

'Never mind you can colour in the holly pictures and tree shapes.' Rosemary helped the little girl to clean the paste off her hands and gave her the crayons which she had found upstairs in the Manor nursery.

Once the girls were happily engrossed in their tasks, Jenny leaned towards her friend and said, 'Come on, let's hear your news. I know something's up. You've been dying to say something all morning.'

204

Rosemary blushed and lowered her voice, glancing at the children before saying, 'I've had a letter.'

Jenny grinned. 'I don't need to ask who from,' she said. 'Are you going to let me read it?'

'Certainly not.' Rosemary's face became an even deeper crimson.

'Well, tell me what he says.'

'They're not allowed to say much. He tells me he's well but I'm not so sure. Mrs Pargeter hears a lot through the Red Cross and she says the Japanese treat their prisoners very badly. I can't imagine what Simon's been going through.' She pulled the envelope from her apron pocket and took out several sheets of paper. She smoothed one out and showed it to her friend.

Jenny gasped. 'Oh, my gosh – is that a picture of the prison camp?'

'I don't know how he got away with sending it.'

Jenny turned the paper over but Rosemary snatched it away. 'You can't read what's on the back,' she said. She clutched the page to her breast and smiled. 'I thought he'd forgotten me but he says he's thought of me every day and can't wait to get home.'

'Is that all? Not very romantic, is it.'

'Well, he has to pretend I'm his cousin. The Japs read everything and they're only allowed to write to close family. His father told me to write as if we're related.'

'I'm pleased you've heard from him though. At least you know he's OK.' Jenny sighed. 'Let's hope it won't be long before they're all home.'

'It could be months yet. I've stopped listening to the news – it's so gloomy.'

They had been talking in low voices, not wanting to disturb the children who seemed quite happy with their Christmas preparations. Now, Rosemary stood up and said, 'Let's clear away this mess and have some tea.' She picked up one of the paper chains Maisie had finished.

'Look at this, Jenny. And look at Lily's colouring. Well done both of you.'

'Can we do some more after tea?' Maisie asked.

As she buttered bread for fish paste sandwiches, Rosemary couldn't stop thinking about Simon's letter. Maybe she was reading too much into it but the fact that he had written at all and remembered their meetings in the church was enough for now. She couldn't wait for the children's meal to be finished and Lily safely in bed. Then she would sit down and reply to him.

She wrote a few lines sticking to neutral language, although she wanted to convey how much his letter meant to her and how she longed to see him again. From writing to her brother, she knew that letters were censored and she had to be careful not to give away too much news. She said how much she looked forward to the Christmas service in 'our lovely little church' as a reminder of their meetings there. Mrs Pargeter had warned her not to mention the Red Cross parcels when she wrote to Michael so she left that out.

She finished: *I hope it won't be too long before you are home with us. Your loving cousin, Rosemary.'*

She sighed as she sealed the envelope and said a silent prayer that it would reach him.

***

There was no party for the village children at the base this year. So many of the young men who had befriended the village children had been lost on missions overseas and their replacements, although friendly enough, had not entered into village life in the same way.

Rosemary didn't mind too much— there would be too many reminders of happy times up at the base, the parties and visits from the school children. She stifled the sad thoughts and smiled when Jenny spoke up.

'We'll give them a party in the school rooms instead,' Jenny said. 'Mr Davis suggested we put on another magic lantern show.'

'Will they enjoy it though?' Rosemary asked. 'The boys are growing up. They won't be interested in anything they think is childish.'

'I think they'll be all right. It's still a novelty for them. Besides, the little ones haven't seen it – I suggest we ask Mr Davis what to do about the boys.'

Rosemary agreed and they set about organising what other entertainments they could put on. 'And what about food?' she asked with a worried frown.

'We'll ask people to contribute – not just the parents – I'm sure everyone will help.'

For the next few days Rosemary was busy making lists and canvassing the villagers for contributions to the children's party. Farmer White donated a box of eggs which Mrs Norton received joyfully.

'It's so good to be able to make some proper cakes,' she said with a beaming smile.

Best of all was when Mrs Pargeter and her husband came in while Rosemary and Maggie were packing up parcels.

'The Colonel has some good news,' she said. 'He's been talking to the Base Commander about the children's party.'

The Colonel stepped forward. 'He's so sorry they can't entertain the children this year. As you no doubt realise, things are hotting up and they are running constant missions.' A shadow crossed his face and Rosemary saw how the continuing loss of aircraft was affecting him. As Colonel of the Home Guard he had become very involved with the personnel at the airbase.

He straightened his shoulders and smiled. 'However, I'm pleased to tell you that Colonel Hamilton has offered to supply the food for the party.'

Betty gave a small cheer and said, 'That will please my boys. They do love their grub.'

The colonel and his wife both laughed. 'Colonel Hamilton has assured me there will be plenty of grub,' he said with a grin.

They turned to go but Colonel Pargeter paused at the door. 'You're doing a grand job, ladies. Keep up the good work.' He saluted and then they were gone.

Betty burst out laughing. 'I nearly saluted him back.'

With the worry over feeding a horde of hungry children on wartime rations relieved, Rosemary joined in the laughter.

***

The party was held on the last day of the school term a few days before Christmas and the mothers had helped Jenny and Rosemary to decorate the big classroom. Percy and a couple of men from the base had moved the school desks and set up trestle tables for the food

'You've done wonders, ladies,' Mr Davis said looking around the room with a smile of approval.

The tables were laden with an abundance of food, some of it cooked and prepared by the villagers, but true to his promise, Colonel Hamilton had sent two of his men with crates of American cookies and pastries and a huge metal tub of ice cream. There was also another crate full of small bottles of Coca Cola, enough for the children to have one bottle each.

Once they were settled in their seats, Mr Davis said Grace and then there was silence except for the sound of munching and slurping.

In no time the plates and dishes were empty and the headmaster announced it was time for the magic lantern show. He ushered them all into the classroom where he had set up the apparatus.

Brian groaned. 'Seen it before,' he said. 'It ain't like the real pictures.'

Ted Rook, who had not seen the earlier showing asked, 'What's it like then?'

Brian tried to explain but shrugged and gave up. 'You'll see,' he said.

Rosemary, who had heard the exchange said, 'Never mind, Brian. The war will soon be over and you can go home to London – proper cinemas there.'

'I s'pose I'll go home to see me mum but I like the country. I'd like to live here even if there ain't no picture houses.'

'We'll see. Now, settle down. Mr Davis wants to start the show.'

The younger children who hadn't experienced the magic lantern before, sat rapt as the pictures were shown, unfolding colourful stories.

Even the older ones, who like Brian had seen the show before, watched with interest, although a few of them, seated at the back, whispered and fidgeted throughout.

When the lights went on at the end, Rosemary said, 'It went well. Now to get the little ones into their coats. The parents will be here soon to pick them up.'

Ted tugged on Jenny's arm. 'My mum said I can walk home on my own but I've got to look after my little brothers.'

'Make sure you keep an eye on them then. No getting into mischief on the way.'

'Yes, miss.' He turned to his friend. 'Come on, Brian, you can walk with us.'

Rosemary held Maisie and Lily's hands. 'Don't worry, Jenny, I'll look out for them.' They said goodbye and started off down the dark lane, guided by a tiny glimmer from Rosemary's torch. Over the past few years, they had got used to walking around in the dark. There had never been any street lights in the village but there had always been lamplight spilling out from the pub and the cottages lining the street.

Now that there was no longer a threat of invasion, Rosemary was looking forward to the blackout restrictions being lifted but that wouldn't be for some time, she thought. She left the Rook children and Maisie at the Manor gates and stumbled on to the Rectory, clinging tightly to Lily's hand.

'Did you have fun tonight?' she asked.

'Nice pictures,' Lily said, rubbing her eyes sleepily.

'Let's get you indoors in the warm. Time for bed.'

Once Lily was tucked up in bed, Rosemary looked in on her father who was in his study reading. He looked up briefly and she said goodnight and went to her own room. She was tired but not too tired to reach into her bedside drawer for Simon's letter.

She read it again, smiling, although by now she knew the words off by heart. She smoothed out the little drawing, frowning. Was this really what it was like in the prison camp? She guessed he had taken quite a risk sending it. His captors wouldn't be pleased that outsiders had even got a glimpse of that was going on over there.

Chapter 26

January 1945
The new year dawned with heavy snowfalls and icy roads. Coal was almost unobtainable and there were frequent electricity cuts. Few of the cottages had electricity and relied on oil lamps but they were no better off as oil was in short supply too.

Mrs Norton had planned to go back to her cottage after Christmas but Rosemary persuaded her to stay at the Rectory until the thaw.

'I shall worry about you,' she said, sighing. 'I worry about everybody. There's old Mrs Fenton on her own, and so many others.'

'Percy looks after his mum though. She'll be all right.'

Rosemary thought about the letter she'd received from Maggie a couple of weeks ago. She'd been thrilled at the news that her friend was getting married. Percy had promised to bring little Daisy up as his own but they were waiting until the deed was done before breaking the news to his mother. Rosemary had promised not to tell anyone yet.

'Yes, he's a good son,' she said now.

Lily was sitting at the kitchen table drawing a picture. She had begged to go outside to play in the snow but Rosemary had persuaded her to stay indoors till it stopped.

Mrs Norton looked out of the kitchen window where the snow was still falling. She shivered. 'I'd like to stoke the range up to start on the dinner, but we're getting low on coal. Mustn't grumble - we're all in the same boat.'

'There's a pile of wood in the garden. I'll get Amos to chop it and bring some in. That will help.'

Mrs Norton turned from the stove. 'I've just had a thought. My cottage has been empty for ages but I'm sure there was some coal in the shed. Do you think Amos could fetch it in the barrow?'

'We can't ask Amos to plough through the snow to your cottage – it's too far. I'll go. I'll get young Brian and Ted to help me. They've still got the barrow they made for their scrap collecting.'

'I don't think you should be doing it,' Mrs Norton said.

'Why not? I'm younger and fitter than poor old Amos. I'll let him deal with the wood.'

She went into her father's study where he sat at his desk with a knitted shawl round his shoulders.

His face and hands looked pinched with the cold and she said, 'Oh, there you are, dear. Could you make the fire up. It's freezing in here.'

'We don't have enough coal, Father. You'd better come and sit in the kitchen where it's reasonably warm. Amos is bringing in some wood to eke out the coal so we can keep the range going.'

'I can't work in the kitchen with Mrs Norton clattering about and that child chattering on.'

Rosemary swallowed her impatience. 'You can't stay in here, Father. You'll freeze. Come and have a cup of hot cocoa to warm up, then we'll see what the fuel situation is.'

He agreed reluctantly and followed her down the passage. She didn't tell him where she was going but went to get her boots, then wrapped up warmly with a knitted scarf and wooly hat. Pulling on her gloves, she said, 'I won't be long.'

She plodded though the snow up to the Manor, sure that she would find Ted and Brian playing outside. She heard their shouts of delight before she saw them. They were throwing snowballs at each other but stopped when they saw her.

'What you doing 'ere, miss?' Brian tossed the snowball from hand to hand, grinning as he pretended to throw it at her.

She laughed. 'Got a job for you lads,' she said and explained what she wanted. They hauled the cart out of the shed and trudged off down the drive. The main village street had been cleared of snow although it was fast being covered again by the relentless new fall.

As they passed the forge, they saw Percy standing in the doorway, looking up at the sky. He shouted a greeting as they passed, asking where they were off to.

Rosemary explained their mission and then asked, 'How is your mother coping?'

'I took her some of my coke. It burns all right if you mix it with the coal, makes it go further.'

'Is she well?'

'I suppose, but she's not happy with me. She knows I've been seeing Maggie.' He shrugged and grimaced. 'She'll have to put up with it when we're married,' he added quietly, glancing at the boys who had started making snow balls.

'She'll have to know some time. When are you going to tell her?'

'As soon as it's done. We've booked the Ipswich register office.' He sighed. 'I always dreamed of getting married in our church but this is the best way.'

'Can I be a witness?' Rosemary asked.

'Of course. Maggie would like that.'

The boys started throwing the snowballs so Rosemary called to them and said, 'We'd better get on with the job. I'll speak to you soon, Percy.'

'Is he your feller, miss?' Ted asked.

Brian laughed. 'Mr Fenton's too old.'

'No, he's not, but no, Ted, he's not my feller. I haven't got a feller.'

She marched off towards Mrs Norton's cottage and the boys followed, pulling the cart and laughing and pushing each other.

Cheeky lads, Rosemary thought. But she couldn't help smiling. They *were* cheeky and full of mischief but they were helpful and willing when needed. Brian worked hard when helping in the forge and they had made a grand job of their scrap metal collecting. And as they went round the back of the cottage to the shed and started shoveling the coal, she watched with pride as they filled the cart up and hauled it out into the street.

The snow was deeper by now and she had to help pull the cart up the slope towards the Rectory. They arrived at the kitchen door hot and breathless and Mrs Norton bustled out and said, 'Leave it out there for a bit. Come in and get warm.'

'We're already warm,' Brian said, puffing out his cheeks.

'Well, come in and have a drink – and one of my scones.'

The boys didn't need telling twice and they kicked their boots off and followed her into the kitchen.

Rosemary was pleased to see the Rector still sitting by the fire, the shawl over his knees. He seemed to be dozing but he started up when he heard the boys.

'What's all the noise?' he asked.

'We've got some coal,' Brian announced.

'So we can light the fire in your study if you want to carry on with your work,' Rosemary said.

To her surprise, he said, 'No, no. I'm quite comfortable here. I can finish my sermon tomorrow.'

'Where's Lily?' she asked.

'Mrs Pargeter called while you were out,' Mrs Norton said. 'She's taken her back to the Manor to play with Maisie. She said you wouldn't mind and she'll bring her back later, when she's had her tea.'

'Of course, I don't mind. Lily gets bored on her own and she misses Maisie.'

'She said Maisie asked for her. She finds living with those noisy boys a bit much.'

'How did Mrs P get here?' Rosemary asked.

'She managed to drive the car down in spite of the snow. She said the van managed to get through with more goods for the Red Cross parcels and could you go up to the Manor tomorrow and help Mrs Rook with the packing.'

'I'll be there.' Rosemary turned to the boys who were drinking their cocoa and munching on warm scones. 'You'd better finish up and start back,' she said. 'It'll soon be dark.'

'Can't we wait and get a ride with Mrs P?' Brian asked.

'Certainly not. Look at the state of you both – coal dust all over. You can't go messing up the lady's car.'

Brian stuffed the rest of his scone into his mouth and mumbled. 'Come on then, Ted.'

At the door they turned and thanked Mrs Norton for the cocoa and scones.

'And thank you for the help with the coal,' Rosemary said, waving them off. They might be cheeky and mischievous but during their time in Oakleigh their manners had improved a lot. She smiled fondly and closed the door.

***

During the next few days, the weather brightened up but it remained bitterly cold and the snow still lay in frozen piles at the sides of the roads and some of the narrower lanes leading up to the farms were impassable for several weeks. Rosemary walked up to the Manor every day to work on the parcels with Betty Rook.

Some days she felt too exhausted to carry on but the thought of one of the parcels one day reaching Simon or Michael kept her going. A lot of love went into each lovingly packed parcel as she day-dreamed the time away.

She longed for another letter from Simon but was just as thrilled when they heard from Michael at last. It

215

had taken months to get here but the letter, addressed to both her and their father, carried a note of optimism.

'We can hear the rumble of tanks and the sound of gunfire but they still sound very far away. It can't be long now. Dare I hope that I'll be home with you both by the spring. The good news is that the Red Cross parcels which we know had been stored for weeks in the Commandant's office, were finally distributed. What joy it was to see those familiar reminders of home. I bless those responsible for getting them out to us.'

Rosemary swallowed the lump in her throat. If only she could tell him that she was one of those Red Cross workers.

March 1945
When she heard on the wireless that the Royal Norfolks had entered Germany. Rosemary ran up to the school, skidding on the icy patches which still lingered in the lane. She had to share the news with her friend.

Jenny was in the playground supervising the little ones. Despite the bad weather she and Mr Davis both agreed it was good for the children to get out in the fresh air for a little while provided they were wrapped up warmly.

Rosemary waved to her and called, 'Have you heard? Our boys are in Germany – it can't be long now.' She threw her arms round her friend and they did a little jig, much to the amusement of the children.

At the sound of the bell, they broke apart and Jenny ushered the children indoors. 'I'll pop round after school,' she said.

As Rosemary reached the Rectory, she saw Percy standing by the front door. 'Is everything all right?' she asked.

'Couldn't be better,' he said with a grin. 'Are you free on Saturday? You did volunteer to be a witness at the wedding, didn't you.'

'Wonderful. Of course I'm free. I can't wait.' She paused with a hand to her mouth. 'Oh, goodness, what shall I wear?'

'Anything you like – we just want you to be there.'

'But – it's a wedding,' she protested, 'and I haven't got anything decent and no clothing coupons either.' She had passed hers on to Betty Rook to buy new shirts for the boys, who were fast growing out of everything.

'Never mind – that dress you wear to church and the hat with the flowers on it will be fine,' he said.

'I didn't think men noticed things like that,' she said.

He grinned. 'I don't usually. Maggie suggested it. She knew you'd be worrying.'

'All right. That's me sorted.' She paused for a moment, then said, 'Do Maggie's parents know, have you invited them?'

'We're hoping they'll turn up.'

'And your mum?' Rosemary knew that old Mrs Fenton had no time for 'that barmaid' as she still called Maggie.

'We haven't told her. I'm hoping once we come back to the village and she sees the baby, she'll change her tune.' Percy shuffled his feet.

'So, are you coming back after the wedding?'

Percy shook his head. 'We'll stay with Aunt Alice for the time being.'

'I know Maggie was nervous about returning to the village but what about the forge?'

'I'll close it up. Bill Hubbard over Palburgh way can take on any shoeing, I've told him I won't be around for a while.'

You'll miss the forge,' Rosemary said.

Percy shrugged. 'I'll get a job in Ipswich easy. They're still crying out for factory workers.'

Rosemary didn't know what to say. Blacksmithing was Percy's life. He'd done nothing else since he was a lad apprenticed to the old smith, who'd died a few years before the war. 'Well, I hope you'll both be happy,' she said.

'We will.' Percy sounded confident but Rosemary wasn't sure. Giving up his business and leaving the village he'd grown up in was a big step. Percy seemed to sense her feelings. 'I love her. I'd do anything to make her happy,' he said.

As he said goodbye and walked away, Rosemary watched him go, praying that everything would work out for him and her friend. Percy was such a good man – he deserved to be happy.

If only Mrs Fenton would change her attitude towards Maggie. She wasn't getting any younger and would soon need someone to look after her. How would she cope with her only son living miles away in Ipswich?

***

Percy stopped the van outside Alice's front door and sounded the horn. The front door opened immediately and he threw open the van door and stepped out. Maggie stood in the doorway dressed in a pale blue summer dress, despite the chill March wind. She carried a small posy of primroses and, to Percy. she looked more beautiful than ever. He stood for a moment drinking in her lovely face, before rushing forward and taking her in his arms.

'I wasn't entirely sure you'd keep your word,' he whispered.

A little cough behind them forced them apart and he turned to see Alice holding Daisy in her arms. He leaned over and stroked the baby's soft cheek. 'My little Daisy' he breathed.

Rosemary had got out of the van and heard. He really has accepted the child as his own, she thought - the power of love. She hoped that seeing the little family would put a final end to the unkind gossip when they finally returned to the village.

218

'Time to go,' Aunt Alice said. She closed the front door and, accompanied by Rosemary, followed the couple up the street.

It was only a short walk to the register office but as they drew near, Maggie's steps faltered. She glanced round wildly. 'I thought Mum and Dad would be here.'

'They're definitely coming,' Alice said. 'Perhaps they're already inside.'

'I'll go and look,' Rosemary offered. But in seconds she re-appeared, shaking her head.

Maggie's eyes welled with tears. 'They promised,' she said.

Alice put an arm round Maggie's shoulder. 'Come on, love. You mustn't keep the registrar waiting. Besides, baby's getting cold. We'd better go inside.'

The registrar's assistant came out of the nearby room, saying that they were ready.

Still, Maggie hesitated but, as they entered the room, main doors opened and Dot and Ron hurried in.

'Thank goodness we're in time,' Dot gasped. 'The train was late and it was quite a walk from the station.'

There was no time for proper greetings as the assistant ushered them into the wedding room. Maggie and Percy were told where to stand and the family were shown to the row of chairs in front of the desk where the registrar sat.

'Let me see the baby,' Dot whispered and Alice handed her over. Tears filled Dot's eyes and she hugged the child to her breast. 'My granddaughter,' she whispered. '*Our* grandchild.' She nudged Ron's arm, but he barely glanced at the baby.

Rosemary caught Alice's eye and shrugged. She hoped there wouldn't be any awkwardness. Still, he was here and that must mean something.

The ceremony was brief and they were soon standing outside, huddled against the chill wind.

'Come on, let's get out of the cold,' Alice urged. 'There's a pub round the corner. The landlord has opened specially for us and laid on some food.'

Rosemary was hesitant about taking baby Daisy into a pub but she needn't have worried. The landlady showed them into a back room where there was a cheerful fire and a table laden with sandwiches and slices of pork pie.

When they were all seated, Maggie took Daisy from her mother and Alice produced a bottle wrapped in a towel to keep it warm. Percy leaned over and said, 'Let me feed her, love.' He gently held her and offered her the bottle, grinning round at everybody when she started sucking greedily.

Ron pulled a face and Dot laughed. 'Remember how you used to feed Maggie when she was a wee mite when I was busy in the bar.' But he didn't smile.

When the bottle was empty, Daisy fell asleep and Percy handed her back to her mother who tucked her up in her shawl and laid her on a sofa in the corner, placing cushions around her to prevent her rolling off.

Gradually, as they ate and drank, the rather sombre atmosphere lightened, and Alice said, 'We should toast the bride and groom.' She nudged Ron. 'Come on brother-in-law, say something – welcome Percy to the family.'

Ron finished his beer and plonked the glass down on the table. He stood up and looked down at his daughter. After a few moments, he coughed and said, 'Well, this isn't how I pictured my only daughter's wedding but I must admit she couldn't have found a better man to take her on after...' His voice stumbled to a stop, his cheeks flushing and Dot gave him a nudge. He coughed again and went on, 'Well, let's drink to them and wish them well.' Someone had re-filled his glass and they all stood and drank to murmurs of 'Long life and happiness,' 'Here's to the happy couple.'

Rosemary had never drunk a toast in lemonade before but she added her good wishes to the others and went round the table to give Maggie and then Percy a kiss.

At that moment little Daisy woke up and let out a loud cry. Rosemary hurried over and picked her up, loving the warm baby smell and stroking the soft down on her head. She had never thought of having her own child, accepting that it was her lot in life to care for her father after the death of her mother. That was, until she met Simon. And now, she occasionally let herself daydream. She hastily handed the baby to Maggie.

Ron laughed. 'See what you've let yourself in for, lad?' But the words were said in a friendly manner and Rosemary smiled. Perhaps he was beginning to accept the idea of becoming a grandfather, even if the circumstances were not ideal.

Just as the party was breaking up, Rosemary had a chance to speak to Maggie. 'Have you decided where you're going to live?' she asked.

'We're going to stay at Alice's for a while but I'm coming round to the idea of returning to the village.' She held her hand up, displaying the gold ring on her finger. 'After all, now I'm a married woman, what can they say?'

'You're not planning on moving in with Mrs Fenton though, are you?' Rosemary couldn't imagine the two women getting on, even if Percy's mother accepted her son's choice of wife.

Maggie shook her head vigorously. 'Not on your life. The old bat never liked me. We'll try and find somewhere in or near the village. We need to come back so Percy can open up the forge. He says he's happy to stay in Ipswich but....' She smiled. 'He would do that for me but I know he's missing his work - especially the horses.'

Rosemary tucked a fold of shawl around Daisy and touched her cheek. 'I'm so pleased things have worked out for you,' she said.

'I can't believe how lucky I am – I don't know why I didn't see it before. I don't deserve Percy. I'm really going to try and make him happy.'

'I'm sure you will.' Rosemary paused. 'Did you invite Percy's mother to the wedding?'

'I wanted to but Percy said not to bother as she wouldn't come anyway. He didn't even tell her he was getting married.'

'Oh, Maggie – she knows. She heard me talking to your mum.'

'Oh, heck. Was she upset?'

'She must have been - she just hurried off without a word.'

'Come on girls,' Percy interrupted. 'They want to clear up ready for opening time. I'm taking your mum and dad and Rosemary to the station but I'll be back in no time.' He kissed Maggie's cheek. 'Sure you'll be OK walking back to Alice's?'

Maggie kissed him back. 'Don't be too long though. I can't wait for us to be alone together.' She gave a cheeky wink and Rosemary was amused to see his face redden.

He bent and kissed Daisy and hurried outside to get the van.

Chapter 27

April 1945

On a bright spring morning with primroses and violets blossoming in the grass verges and the hawthorn hedges sprouting their fresh green leaves, Maggie and Percy with baby Daisy drove in to the village and stopped outside the *Four Bells*.

Dot hurried out and opened the passenger door before Percy could do it. She leaned in and threw her arms around Maggie, almost squashing the baby.

'You're here! I'm so happy you agreed to come,' she cried, then lowering her voice, 'I know it will be hard for you being back but you'll be all right. You know who your real friends are.'

She helped Maggie out of the van and took the baby from her while Percy helped with the luggage.

'Thanks for putting us up. It won't be for long,' Percy said.

'It's your home now – yours and Maggie's,' Dot said.

'Just till we find our own place, Mum,' Maggie said.

'I've scrounged a cot for Daisy – it's in your room,' Dot said. 'And just for now, she can sleep down here in the big drawer from my wardrobe.'

Maggie followed her mother into the pub and watched her tenderly placing Daisy in the drawer which was well padded with cushions and blankets. 'Mrs Rook says you can have her old pram now her youngest doesn't need it any more. It needs a good clean as the boys have been using to collect the scrap.'

'I thought they had the old barrow,' Rosemary said.

'The wheel fell off.'

Maggie laughed. 'I hope the boys don't mind us taking their pram.' She followed Rosemary into the kitchen, where her friend went to the sink to fill the kettle.

'I couldn't wait to see you and the baby. I've got a morning off from the Manor so I popped round but I can't stay long,' Rosemary said, setting cups and saucers out on the table. She got the big teapot down from the shelf over the sink.

'You seem to know your way around our kitchen,' Maggie said.

'Rosemary's been helping us out – the girl we had after you left home decided she could earn more money in Norwich,' Dot said.

'What does your dad think of you working in the pub?' Maggie asked.

'He's all right with it – accepts we all have to help each other during these dreadful times. He's changed a lot over the past few years.'

'We've all changed.'

Percy came in with the luggage. 'Where shall I put these?' he asked.

'Come and say hello to Rosemary and sit down for a cuppa. Plenty of time for unpacking.'

'I was going over to the forge, must check everything's in order,' he said.

'Plenty of time for that too.' Maggie said, pushing him into a chair and leaning over to give him a kiss. 'We're still on our honeymoon, don't forget.'

Percy blushed and picked up the cup she had put in front of him.

Chapter 28

April 1945

Rosemary had been looking out for the postman but without much hope. She realised how difficult it must be for the prisoners in Singapore to write, let alone for letters to reach home. When there was no sign of him at his usual time, she busied herself in the kitchen. There was plenty to do as Mrs Norton had not been feeling well and Rosemary had persuaded her to rest. She kept insisting that she could go home now that her cottage was habitable once more but Rosemary and her father had persuaded her to stay.

'She's really not herself,' Rosemary said when her father came into the kitchen asking how Mrs Norton was. 'I forget that she's getting older – she's always been so energetic but just lately...'

'I fear the past winter has taken its toll on her health.' The Rector paused. 'I'm worried about you too. It's all too much for you – your Red Cross work, the housekeeping and looking after our little evacuee.'

'Nonsense, Father – you know I like to be busy. And I'm not neglecting my church duties.'

'Of course you aren't dear. I wasn't suggesting...'

At that moment Rosemary heard the rattle of the letter box and she hurriedly dried her hands and rushed out to the hall. Her heart leapt when she saw not one, but two, envelopes on the mat. She snatched them up, her hands trembling.

She was tempted to tear open the one from Singapore immediately, but her father was standing behind her and he whispered, 'Michael?'

'Yes, Father – at last. Shall I open it?'

He nodded and she took out the closely-written sheet of paper.

'Read it to me,' he said.

'Dear Father and Sis,' she read. *'I'm sorry it has been so long since my last letter. There has been much unrest in the camp since our captors realised that the Allies are getting nearer and they have forbidden us to write. We hope for liberation any day now and long to be home with our families. Please God it will be soon. Some of us are hoping to smuggle these letters out and I pray this reaches you.'*

Rosemary's voice faltered as she read the last line and she handed the letter to her father.

'I'll leave you to read your other letter in peace,' he said. 'I take it, it's from your artist friend.'

Rosemary nodded and her father turned and went into his study. She returned to the kitchen and sat at the big scrubbed table, pushing aside the heap of vegetables Amos had brought in from the garden.

She looked closely at the envelope, hesitating before opening it. She didn't recognise the handwriting and she took a deep breath. Was he alright? Had one of his fellow prisoners written to give her bad news? She had to know and, swallowing her anxiety, she tore the envelope open.

A sigh of relief escaped her as she turned to the signature at the bottom of the page. 'Simon, thank God,' she breathed and began to read. He began by apologising for his 'dreadful scrawl.'

'They have been working us half to death and my hands are suffering for it. I can scarcely grasp a pencil but the camp doctor assures me that in time they will heal. I have had to stop drawing for fear of making things worse which you may imagine, I am finding very hard. I do hope the doctor is right as it has been my hope, ever since visiting your lovely little church, to get permission to restore the wall painting. We get very little news in camp of the war's progress but rumours abound and we are hopeful that it will soon

come to an end. I cannot wait to get home to you. There is so much I want to say which I can't do in a letter. I know we only met twice so long ago now, but I have never forgotten you and long to see you again. Your loving friend, Simon.'

Rosemary leaned back in the chair, clasping the precious letter to her breast. He hadn't forgotten her. So often in the long months with no news, she had told herself she was chasing a dream. How could she have fallen in love on such brief acquaintance – but she had. And now she had grounds for hope.

Ignoring the heap of vegetables waiting to be made into soup for their dinner, she ran upstairs and knocked on Mrs Norton's door. She had to tell someone. The old lady was lying on her bed on top of the covers, still fully dressed. She sat up when Rosemary burst into the room.

'What is it?' she asked, a worried frown on her face. 'Not one of those awful doodlebugs again?'

Rosemary hastened to reassure her. 'It's good news, Mrs N. Two letters – from Michael and Simon.'

Mrs Norton sat up and swung her legs over the side of the bed. 'And Michael is safe?' she asked.

Rosemary nodded.

Mrs Norton smiled. 'The Reverend will be so happy.'

'He is. And Michael is feeling optimistic. He can hear the guns and thinks the allies will be at the gates before too long.'

'Praise the Lord – and your friend?'

Rosemary frowned. 'Of course, I'm happy to hear from him and to know he is still alive. But the letter must have taken months to get here. I can't help worrying – it sounds as if he isn't in the best of health.' She shook her head. 'Mrs Pargeter gets news via the Red Cross and she hears that the prisoners there are treated quite badly. The Japanese don't seem to recognise the Genevea Convention. She doesn't even know if the parcels we send out ever get to the prisoners.'

Mrs Norton stood up and slipped her feet into her shoes. 'I'd better come down and get that soup on,' she said.

'I'll do it. You're supposed to be resting.'

'I'm fine. Did Amos dig the carrots?' She patted Rosemary's shoulder and went downstairs.

Rosemary followed, feeling a bit guilty for letting Mrs Norton take over in the kitchen. Besides, she needed to be doing something, not sit brooding over Simon's letter or worrying about her brother. She went along to her father's study and knocked, entering the room at his call.

'Wonderful to hear from Michael,' he said with a smile. 'And how is your friend?'

Rosemary told him about the injuries to Simon's hands and his difficulty in writing. The more personal parts of the letter she kept to herself.

***

Percy had re-opened the forge and was kept busy catching up with the work he had neglected for the past few months. He and Maggie were still staying at the pub but he longed for them to have their own place. Although Dot had accepted him and had forgiven her daughter for her fall from grace, Percy still felt uncomfortable in Ron's presence. His offers to help in the pub had been brusquely rejected and, in the long evenings when Daisy was asleep and Maggie was helping behind the bar, he felt very awkward.

Maggie encouraged him to come down and have a drink while she was working. But he still wasn't keen on the Americans who still thronged the bar every evening. Since the loss of the 'Oklahoma Belle', he had avoided becoming too pally with the other crews, especially as so many of them never returned from their missions. He still missed Floyd most of all, and he

228

couldn't go through all that again. Then there were the regulars with whom he had always enjoyed a drink and a laugh, but he was convinced they were talking about him behind his back. He'd been told several times by people he thought of as friends that he was a fool for taking on another man's child.

He wasn't a fool. He'd loved Maggie since they were kids at the village school and couldn't believe his luck that she was finally his. As for little Daisy, he adored her and thought of her as his own child.

If only he could mend his relationship with his mother. She had grudgingly accepted his marriage and was even fairly civil to Maggie when Percy took her and the baby to visit her. But there was no warmth and she still hadn't accepted Daisy as her grandchild. Percy hoped she would mellow in time. Who could fail to be captivated by the beautiful child and her lovely smile?

'Would you like to hold Daisy while I make the tea?' Maggie asked one day when she had reluctantly accompanied Percy to visit his mother.

Reluctantly, Mrs Fenton took the baby and balanced her on her lap. She didn't coo and fuss over her as most people did, exclaiming over her pale blonde curls and bright blue eyes, the gummy smile. Instead, she constantly glanced towards the kitchen, pursing her lips at the thought of 'that barmaid' in her kitchen.

Percy leaned over and stroked Daisy's head. 'Isn't she lovely Ma?'

Mrs Fenton gave a non-committal grunt.

Percy chucked the baby under her chin, eliciting a wet gurgle and chuckle. He laughed. 'Now then, Daisy love, no dribbling down Granny's front.'

The old lady held the child out. 'Take her Perce. I'm not her granny.'

'Mum, please. It's my name on the birth certificate. She's legally a Fenton.'

'Maybe but I...' Percy's mother faltered. 'Give me time, son.'

Maggie came in with a tray of tea and set in down on the little table beside her mother-in-law. 'Would you like me to pour?' she asked.

'If you like.'

Maggie glanced at Percy with raised eyebrows. At one time she would have fired off a hasty retort. But she had promised Percy she would be polite and try to win his mothers' approval. She had heard Mrs Fenton's remark and knew she had a long hard battle. But she would persevere.

She poured the tea and handed a cup to her mother-in-law, receiving a muttered thank you. She then took Daisy from her husband and concentrated on soothing and rocking the child who had become a bit restless.

'Better put her back in her pram,' Percy said.

They drank their tea in almost silence and then Percy announced that they must be going. 'We'll come and see you again soon,' he said, bending to kiss his mother's cheek.

'I can't get used to you living in the pub,' she said.

'Well, I pop up every day to make sure you're all right,' Percy protested.

'If you can spare the time,' his mother snapped.

As they opened the back door and prepared to lift the pram down the step,' Mrs Fenton said, 'I'll admit she makes a good cup of tea.'

'Thank you,' Maggie said, forcing a smile.

As they set off down the lane, she dissolved into giggles. 'I think she's beginning to accept me,' she said.

'Yes, hopefully, the thaw's setting in.'

***

Percy had confided to Rosemary that his mother still hadn't forgiven his choice of wife. 'Maggie understands but I think it upsets her.'

'Father was asking about the christening,' Rosemary said.

'We talked about it but I'd like to wait. Mum ought to be there. I know she says Daisy isn't really her grandchild but she's *my* daughter in every way that matters. I'm trying to persuade her and she does seem to be coming round.'

Knowing Mrs Fenton, Rosemary thought he was fighting a losing battle. 'Well, let Father know when you've decided,' she said.

'And don't forget, we want you to be Godmother,' Percy said.

Rosemary hurried away, wishing she could help in some way. Perhaps she would go and see the old lady, take her some of Mrs Norton's scones and a jar of the plum jam. They
still had a few jars left.

A few days later, Rosemary dropped Lily off at school and walked up the lane to the Fentons' cottage. She wasn't sure what she could say to Percy's mother to change her mind about Maggie but if she could just get her to accept that Percy really thought of Daisy as his own child, it might help.

She didn't hold out much hope but she had to try. She didn't like her friends to be unhappy and, although Maggie tried to pretend that she didn't care, Rosemary knew she was deeply hurt, more on Percy's behalf than her own. She knocked on the cottage door and opened it, calling out, 'It's me, Rosemary.'

'Come in, love. It's good to see you.'

Rosemary put her basket down on the table and went to sit beside Mrs Fenton who, as usual, was swathed in a knitted shawl with a crochet blanket over her knees. 'You're looking well,' she said.

"Not doing too badly. Better now the weather's warming up. I was getting fed up with all that wind and rain.'

"I've brought you some of Mrs Norton's scones. We managed to get hold of some currants this time. The shop soon ran out once the word got around.

'I don't know how we manage on these rations. My Percy says there's not much in the shop these days. He's a good boy though. He still looks after me even now he's a married man with other responsibilities.'

'I know he's very busy now he's started up the forge again.' Rosemary hesitated. 'Couldn't Maggie do your shopping for you?'

'I doubt it. She's too busy with that by-blow of hers and working in the pub. I don't think she's changed that much despite hooking my son.' Mrs Fenton's voice was bitter.

'Have you seen the baby?'

'They brought her to see me the other day.'

'She's such a sweet little thing don't you think?' Rosemary held her breath for the reply.

'Very pretty, like her mother at that age - but who knows what she'll grow up like.'

'With your Percy for a father, she'll be perfect.'

' To Rosemary's surprise the old lady's eyes filled with tears. 'But he's not her father, is he? Oh, how could he do this to me – everybody knows it was that Yank.'

'He told me he's her father in every way that matters and to see the way he is with her you'd never think any different. You should be proud of him, Mrs Fenton. He's always loved Maggie and he's done what he considers is the right thing.' She reached out and touched the woman's hand. 'It doesn't matter what the gossips say. The main thing is that your son is happy and you have a beautiful granddaughter.' She held her breath, waiting for the denial but Mrs Fenton gave a deep shuddering sigh.

'You're right, dear. My Percy's happiness is the important thing. I'll think on it.' She wiped her eyes and smiled. 'Now, come on, girl where 's that cup of tea you were going to make.'

' Rosemary busied herself in the kitchen, relieved that her interference had been accepted. She buttered the scones and poured the tea and they spent a pleasant half hour catching up with village news.

' Mrs Fenton was delighted that she'd heard from Michael and talk turned to the hoped for ending to the war and how life had changed in the village over the past six years.

Just as she was about to leave, Rosemary said, 'My father is arranging Daisy's christening' She hesitated, then said, 'You will be there, won't you. It would mean such a lot to Percy.'

'I'll see how I feel on the day,' Mrs Fenton said.

Rosemary left well satisfied, certain that Percy's mother would be there. She seemed to have slightly softened in her attitude, if not to Maggie, at least to the innocent little child.

Chapter 29

May 1945

When Rosemary went into the village shop for their weekly rations, the whole place was abuzz with gossip and speculation.

'Is it really over?' one woman asked.

'We haven't been told officially. I expect Mr Churchill will make an announcement soon.'

'But the Americans are still flying - it can't be over or they would have stopped their bombing raids.'

'I heard Hitler was dead.'

The noise increased as each customer tried to make their opinion heard. Finally, Moira rapped on the counter. 'Ladies, please, I'm trying to serve here. Why don't we wait until there's an official announcement.'

'But my Harry's in the Home Guard and he should know. He said...'

The woman was drowned out by a chorus of competing voices but Rosemary managed to make herself heard. 'Moira's right. Let's wait for the official news.'

She was just as excited as everyone else. The thought that it might all be over was almost too much to bear. She would see her beloved brother once more as well as the handsome soldier she had fallen love with five years ago.

Several days later it was official. Hitler was dead and the war was over. At least the war in Europe was over. To Rosemary's despair, it was announced that Japan refused to surrender even when it was announced that Rangoon had been re-captured.

She was cheered a little when they heard that the RAF was bringing prisoners of war home. Soon she would see her beloved Michael again.

Amid the general rejoicing, flags hung from every post and window sill, plans were hurriedly made for victory parties and hoarded tins of fruit and other delicacies were brought out to swell the party goodies. The school children drew pictures which were displayed around the village. But although Rosemary joined in the celebrations, she found it hard to feel the same elation that her friends and neighbours did. Her thoughts were constantly with Simon as stories began to emerge of the horrific treatment those prisoners in Singapore and Burma had endured – were still enduring.

She began to despair that she would ever see Simon again. She said as much to Jenny when her friend came to the Rectory after school to discuss the victory party.

Jenny was still mourning Will, who she had confided had been more than a friend as Rosemary had suspected.

'But I'm getting over it,' she said. 'And of course, I knew nothing would ever come of it. I just pray that your story has a happy ending.'

'I won't give up hope,' Rosemary said. 'Meantime we've heard that some of the German prison camps have been liberated so Michael should be home soon.'

'That's good news. I expect your father is happy.'

'Yes, his sermon on Sunday will be full of hope and optimism.'

'Good news too that the most of the evacuees are going home. It will be strange for them back in London though.'

'But they'll be with their families. Lily's mother is coming up at the weekend to take her home.' Rosemary had to be happy for Lily although she would miss her dreadfully – the Rectory wouldn't be the same without her childish laughter about the place. Even the Recor had admitted that he would miss her.

'The village will seem very quiet when they've gone,' Jenny said.

'But some them are staying. The Rook boys of course, now their mother isn't likely to go back to Norwich. Young Ted leaves school soon and has got a job at White's farm. And Brian too. He leaves school at the end of the summer term and Percy is taking him on as an apprentice.'

'What do his parents think about that?'

'Mr Cox has been invalided out of the army and is delighted that Brian will have a job. The family will miss him of course but they are very proud of him. And they'll still have Maisie.'

'Did you say the Rooks aren't going back to Norwich?'

'Mrs Pargeter has asked Betty to stay on at the Manor as housekeeper. I think she would like to – after all, they have no home since their house was bombed in the blitz. But she has to consult with her husband who is now in a convalescent home in Norwich. Poor Betty. She confided to me that at one time she had thought he would never come home.'

'What will happen when he's well enough to leave the home if Betty is still living at the Manor?'

The Pargeters have agreed that she and her family can have the old gardener's cottage. It's been empty for years but I'm sure they can soon get it shipshape.'

'The Pargeters have been very good to them.'

'Mrs P has been wonderful through the whole war – she works so hard and she's been so good to the children. I can't believe I used to be in awe of her.'

'Yes, she's seems to have mellowed a bit.'

'So, despite the changes over the years, some have been for the better,' Rosemary said with a smile.

'I suppose so.' Jenny sighed. 'Everything's changing. I know the village is no longer the place I came to when I got the job at the school but we can't expect it to go back how it was. It'll be strange having so few children to teach. I've got used to the big classes and become very fond of the London children. I'll be sorry to see them go.'

'I'll miss Lily dreadfully. Her mother has promised to keep in touch.'

'I suppose we'll adapt, as we have over the past few years.' Jenny stood up. 'I must go. I've promised to help Robert to re-arrange the school rooms now we have fewer children.'

'Robert? When did you start calling the headmaster by his Christian name?'

'Jenny blushed. 'We've become more than colleagues recently.'

'Really?' Rosemary laughed. 'I suppose I should have guessed. You *have* been spending a lot of time at the school. But why didn't you tell me? I didn't think we had any secrets."

'Robert wanted us to keep it quiet for a while. So much happening at the moment. It didn't seem right to announce our engagement while there is still so much uncertainty in the world.'

'I won't say anything – you can trust me.'

'I know. I hated keeping it from you but Robert insisted.'

'Is he worried what people will think?'

'Of course not. His wife died years ago – before the war. He might be concerned about the age difference though, but it doesn't bother me.'

'Well, I'm pleased for you – I was quite worried about you at one time.' She didn't elaborate, knowing Jenny realised what she meant.

'I understand. But it wasn't just losing Will – it was the whole crew. The war – and being so close to what was happening. I'm sure people in London and Norwich and the big cities think we in the country had it easy.'

Rosemary patted Jenny's hand. 'Well, it's all over now – or nearly. And I wish you and Mr Davis – Robert – every happiness.'

'I feel mean now, knowing how worried you are about Simon. That's another reason why I didn't tell you about me and Robert. I was waiting till you got some news.'

When Jenny had left, Rosemary went along to her father's study. He looked up from his desk with a smile and put his fountain pen down.

'I'm planning my sermon for the service of thanksgiving. It's wonderful to be able to write something so uplifting.'

'Yes. We have much to be thankful for but...' Rosemary hesitated, then said, 'It's not quite over for some though, is it?'

'I'm sorry, dear. You're thinking of your friend. But it can't be long now, surely.' He reached out a hand to her. 'I'm sure he'll be home soon – and so will Michael.'

'Of course, you're right. I should be happy.'

'So, Rosemary dear, will you help me choose some uplifting hymns for the service?'

It was hard to concentrate and she did her best but she couldn't stop thinking about Simon. What if he never came home? Worse still, what if he returned and didn't feel the same way about her as she did about him? She tried not to think about the future, dreading that she might have to face it without him.

***

Simon and Hugh with several of their hut mates crouched round the forbidden radio. It was tuned to its lowest volume and they strained to hear.

'   Hope flowered in Simon's breast at the announcement of Hitler's death and the surrender of the German army. No more fear of bombs dropping on his loved ones. Prisoners of war would be released and at last, he would see his lovely Rosemary again.

But, amid the cheers there was a sombre note from some of his fellows.

' Hugh's voice was loudest. 'What about us though? The Germans may have surrendered but not these bastards. They'll fight on to the bitter end.'

'Do you think so?' a lone voice said.

' Simon knew Hugh was right. 'I do. And what will happen to us? '

'But they must give in eventually, surely.' Another spoke up.

'And what if they do? They're not going to waste time and energy on us,' Simon said. 'They'll kill us all,'

'We won't wait for that. I say we try to escape,' Hugh said.

It was a good plan in theory but most of them were too weak to even try. Simon's legs were so swollen with beri-beri that he could scarcely walk, as well as being weak from malnutrition.

Every evening they crouched round the radio, praying it wouldn't be discovered and praying even harder for better news. But the Japanese continued to hold out.

Chapter 30

July 1945

Shockwaves went through the village when the result of the General Election came over the wireless. Rosemary, in common with her friends and neighbours, had been convinced that Mr Churchill would be justly rewarded for seeing them through the war.

'What a blow it must be for him,' Rosemary said as she switched the wireless off.

Mrs Norton sighed. 'I can understand it though. The poor man's getting old. Maybe people thought he needed a rest.'

'I suppose you're right. We must give this man Attlee a chance. There's a lot to do to get the country back on its feet.'

'Yes, and the war's not completely over yet.'

Rosemary didn't need reminding. The nightly news found her glued to the wireless hoping for news of Japan's surrender. But she couldn't see an end to it all.

So much was happening here at home and, in some ways, it helped to take her mind off Simon's plight. It was only in her bed at night that she allowed herself to give in to negative thoughts. She re-read his few short letters over and over and gazed at the little drawings he'd sent, trying to picture his life in the prison camp and falling asleep with the pages in her hand.

During the day she stayed cheerful, filling the long hours with work. With no further need to send Red Cross parcels to the camps, instead they were now sending much-needed food parcels to those European countries where, after years of occupation, the people were near to starvation.

When Victory in Europe had been announced, Mrs Rook had said, 'So, it'll be goodbye to the yanks soon then.'

'Not at all,' Mrs Pargeter said. 'They're still flying over Holland and Belgium, but it's food, not bombs they're dropping. Our work is still important.'

***

August 1945

The Americans in the Pacific were still bombarding the Japanese-occupied islands and now began bombing Japan but there was still no surrender.

'Will there ever be an end to it?' Rosemary wailed, switching off the wireless and throwing herself into a chair. Only her closest friends and family knew of her concern for the young soldier she had met all those years ago.

She wiped her face and sat up. Keeping busy was the only solution. And busy she was nowadays. Mrs Norton was leaving them, but not to go back to her own cottage. Rosemary had been concerned for the older woman's health for some time but she had finally admitted that she couldn't carry on. She had already given up helping out at the Manor and Betty Rook had taken on the role of housekeeper full time.

Now, in addition to her household tasks, Rosemary looked after Mrs Norton, who scarcely left her room, unless it was to sit in the garden on fine days.

She was out there now enjoying the summer sunshine. But she wasn't dozing or sitting idle. She had a bowl of peas on her lap and was shelling them slowly, her arthritic fingers hardly able to cope. But she had insisted on having something to do while she waited for her son to drive down from Norwich to take her back with him.

'I can't abide being idle,' she'd said. 'I told my daughter-in-law that if I'm going to live with them, they must let me make myself useful while I still can.'

Rosemary sympathized and admired Mrs Norton's attitude. She just hoped that living with family would work for her.

***

Rosemary and Jenny had taken Maisie and Lily for a walk along a path beside the woods. It was a hot sultry day but that didn't stop the children running about excitedly looking for the blackberries which grew profusely in the hedgerows.

It was much too early but that didn't stop them from picking some that looked almost ripe.

'Don't eat those,' Jenny exclaimed as Maisie plucked a red one and put it in her mouth.

The little girl spat it out, her face screwed up in disgust. 'Nasty,' she said.

'They're not ripe, lovie. Wait till they're black and juicy – a couple more weeks if the weather stays fine.'

'We won't be here then.' Maisie sounded disappointed.

'But you'll be back with your mum,' Rosemary said. 'Won't it be lovely to be home again?'

'I wish I was staying here like Brian. Why can't I?'

Rosemary was at a loss to explain and Jenny said. 'Aren't you looking forward to seeing your mother? She'll be pleased to have you back home. Besides, Brian has a job now, he has to stay.'

Lily ran back to them, a spray of leaves in her hand. 'I can't wait to go. Mum's coming to fetch me tomorrow. These are for her.'

Rosemary smiled although she was holding back tears. It would be a huge wrench to say goodbye to the child who had become almost like her own during the five years she had been with the Turners. She smoothed

242

Lily's curls. 'You're looking so grown-up. Your mum will hardly recognise you,' she said.

They walked on to where the path ran alongside White's farm. They leaned on the fence watching two of the land girls stacking up the straw. Pigeons flew overhead, the clatter of their wings breaking the rare moment of peaceful silence.

All too soon, the roar of returning bombers broke in, bringing back the reality of war. It might be over but there was still plenty for the aircrews to do. Now, they were taking food and other essentials to the formerly occupied countries. But the sound of those aircraft could still send a shiver down Rosemary's back and she could tell Jenny felt the same.

'Come on girls, it's getting late. Let's get you home,' she said.

It was a mutual decision not to talk about the war, especially the fact that the Royal Norfolks were still fighting in Asia and there was still no news of a Japanese surrender.

On the way home, Rosemary started a game with the children and the friends couldn't help laughing at their attempts to hop, skip and jump along the rutted lane.

Simon's possible fate was always on her mind but concentrating on the children helped a little.

When they got back to the Rectory, she invited Jenny and Maisie in to tea.

'Thank you, that will be nice.'

'I'd better telephone Mrs P and let her know. You know what she's like for regular meal times.'

'I'll do it,' Jenny said.

Rosemary sat the children at the table and poured them glasses of milk, before cracking eggs into a china bowl and whisking them, adding a little milk. She lit the grill and placed slices of bread for toasting on the rack.

How lucky we are to have hens, she thought, wondering how the children would fare back in London with its strict rationing. Despite the war ending it seemed that rationing would go on for some time.

As she stirred the eggs in the pan Jenny came back saying, 'All OK. Mrs P is happy for us to give Maisie her tea. Betty is still working and also has her hands full with the boys. I think she misses Mrs Norton too.'

'I do too. I do hope she's happy with her son.' She checked the toast and gave the eggs a final stir. 'I noticed her cottage is still empty. It was never let again after the repairs to the roof were done. I think once it had dried out after the flooding, the landlord hoped she would return.'

'It's a shame when so many are homeless after the bombing,' Jenny said.

'It occurred to me that it would be ideal for Maggie and Percy. The pub's not really the best place to bring up a baby and it would be nice for them to have their own place.'

'Convenient too, being so close to the forge.'

'Should I approach the landlord do you think?' Rosemary asked.

Jenny shook her head. 'Perhaps it would be better...'

'You're right,' Rosemary interrupted. 'I don't want them to think I'm sticking my nose in.'

'A quiet word to Maggie or her mum would be best.'

'I'll talk to Dot,' Rosemary said.

Jenny went over to the wireless in the corner. 'Do you mind if I switch on. It's almost time for the news.'

'Oh, please don't. I've been avoiding it. I keep telling myself no news is good news.'

'Oh, Rosie. If we don't listen, we might miss something important.'

'All right then.' Rosemary took the pan off the stove, giving the eggs a final stir, then pulled the grill pan out to check the toast.

She had started to butter the toast – just a thin scraping to eke out the ration – when the voice of the announcer had her gasping, the butter knife poised in her hand.

'Three days after the atomic bomb which fell on the Japanese city of Hiroshima, a second bomb has been dropped on the Japanese city of Nagasaki, causing even more devastation than the first. Both cities have been razed to the ground with untold loss of life. A statement from the United States ambassador in London stated that, the first bomb having failed to bring about a Japanese surrender, it was deemed necessary to send a further warning.'

Rosemary dropped the knife and the friends stared at each other in shocked silence, broken only by Maisie's shout. 'Miss Turner – the eggs.'

Rosemary snatched up the saucepan but it was too late. The gluey blackened mess was firmly stuck to the bottom. She just stood there, staring at it, her mind a jumble of confused thoughts.

The BBC announcer was still talking and his words gradually penetrated her consciousness. They'd all heard rumours of the secret bomb being developed by the Americans as well as the Germans, but it was a secret no longer. More devastating than anything used by the British and Americans over Europe during the past years - if what they were saying was true.

'I can't believe they actually used it,' Rosemary whispered.

Jenny recovered first. She gently took the pan from Rosemary's hand and made her sit down. She scraped the mess into the pig bin under the sink and filled the pan with cold water then turned to the children. Forcing a bright smile, she said, 'Well, girls it looks like it'll be beans on toast today.'

She opened a tin and put the beans on the hob to warm, then put the kettle on for tea.

Rosemary hadn't moved, her face a white mask of shock. 'How could they do that?' she asked faintly. 'Two cities, razed to the ground.'

'We've had our share of that over the past few years, 'Jenny said.

It was true and, if this drastic action brought an end to it all, Rosemary couldn't condemn it, especially if it meant that all those hundreds of prisoners still out there could come home at last. She prayed it would not be too late for them – especially Simon.

***

August 1945

The bombing of the Japanese cities was the only topic of conversation in the *Four Bells* that evening. Opinion was divided but most agreed that the 'bastards' deserved everything they got. A few refused to believe these new bombs were quite as horrific as they'd been portrayed. But then one of the Land Girls who had just returned from the cinema in Norwich described with horror the graphic newsreel pictures of the stricken cities taken from the air.

'It's unbelievable,' she said, choking back a sob.

'They deserved it,' one of the Home Guard said.

The Americans in their corner did not join in and they didn't stay long, although the Home Guard group bought them a round of drinks.

'At least it now means it's really all over,' Ron said, pulling a pint for Percy who had come downstairs to help clear up. He rang the bell over the bar calling 'Time'.

'Yes, but the effects will be felt for a long time. I read in the paper that stocks of food here are so low that rationing might last a bit longer,' one of the regulars said.

'There's a shortage of petrol too,' Ron said. 'If it carries on, my beer deliveries will have to be made by horse and cart like the old days.'

'That's if there's any beer to deliver,' Percy said with a laugh.

The two men finished tidying up in companionable silence. As they went upstairs, Percy said, 'Are you and Moira still happy to have us here for a bit longer?'

'Stay as long as you like. Dot loves having Maggie and the baby here.'

'We need to find our own place though. I'll put a notice up in the shop.'

Ron nodded. 'I understand, son.' He remembered what it had been like all those years ago living with the in-laws when he and Dot were first married. They'd been so lucky to get the tenancy of the *Four Bells*.

September 1945

Many of the prison camps had been liberated and hundreds of prisoners, Michael among them, were on their way home. Rosemary couldn't wait to see her brother and as soon as she got the news, she set about getting his room ready and planning a welcome home party. She still missed Lily but planning for her brother's return helped. With clean bedding and newly-washed curtains it was hard to believe a little girl had grown up here.

She still worked at the Manor, although Red Cross parcels were no longer needed, but there was still a desperate need for aid for the starving people of Holland and Belgium.

On this misty autumnal day, she was counting tins of food ready to be packed into crates. She worked quickly as an American jeep was due to arrive that afternoon. The huge B 17s would be loaded up with a much friendlier cargo now.

She finished her work and stretched. She didn't mind working alone but she missed the companionship of the other women. Maggie was busy with the baby and helping in the pub, and today Betty had gone in to Norwich to visit her husband in the nursing home. She hoped that he would soon be allowed home she had told Rosemary, saying how grateful she was to the

Pargeters for letting them have the old gardener's cottage

Their chatter had served to take her mind off her constant worry over Simon. If only she could get some news. When she'd heard about Japan's surrender on the wireless, she had daringly telephoned Dr Spencer to ask if he had heard anything of the POWs. But he could tell her nothing definite.

'I'll telephone as soon as I hear,' he'd promised.

She stood up and went to the window and, as usual, her thoughts turned to Simon and what was happening out in the far east. Such news as filtered through was not encouraging –the horrific tales of the prisoners' ill treatment terrified her and she tried to close her mind to them. Simon was all right she told herself. He had to be. Hadn't he promised to come back and restore the church wall paintings?

She could not stop the tears that welled up and she brushed her hand across her eyes, just as Mrs Pargeter opened the door.

'All done?' she asked.

Rosemary nodded.

'Come and have some lunch then. Betty made soup before she went to Norwich – vegetable, of course. Luckily, we still have plenty.'

'I'm not really hungry,' Rosemary said.

'Nonsense, you must eat.' Her voice softened. 'Look, dear, I know you're worrying about that young man of yours but making yourself ill won't help when he does come home – as I'm sure he will.'

Rosemary was surprised at the concern in the older woman's voice. She had thought only her close friends knew of her feelings for Simon.

'How can you be sure?' she asked.

'Of course, I can't. But I've been hearing from the Red Cross HQ that some of the prisoners have been liberated...'

'Thank God.' Rosemary sank into a chair.

'Don't get too excited. We don't know any details. But my understanding is that the desperately ill and injured are being released first. At the moment a hospital ship is on its way here.' She patted Rosemary's shoulder, a gesture of comfort quite alien to her usual brisk no nonsense demeanor.

Rosemary's thoughts were in turmoil. How she longed for Simon to be in one of the first ships to arrive, but she chided herself for her selfish thought. The longer she had to wait, the more likely it was that he would be in good health and fit to make the journey to Oakleigh St James. She just had to be patient.

***

The motion of the ship was soothing Simon thought, although for the first few days he had thought he was hallucinating. The doctors on board had dosed him up with painkillers which had kept him sedated.

Now, he woke up to see a Red Cross nurse bending over the bunk. She was swabbing his leg with some foul-smelling concoction and he gasped as he inhaled it. The nurse looked up and smiled.

'Good to see you back with us,' she said. and carried on with her work.

'I'm not dreaming, am I? Or dead? Are you an angel?'

'Certainly not. You're very much alive and I'm not an angel, just a nurse trying to make sure you stay that way. I'm Nurse Janman.' She put the swab into a tray and washed her hands, then set about removing the dressings from his hands. He still wasn't sure if he was dreaming. He had very little recollection of being taken from the camp and carried on to the ship. In the weeks since the news of Japan's surrender the men in the camp had waited for liberation, most too weak to take matters into their own hands.

Simon's health, precarious at the best of times, had deteriorated and he was in terrible pain. The sores on his hands were healing, but the damage to his right hand from handling the rocks was worse. Hugh was not much better but did his best to help his friend. At last, the liberators arrived, just in time for most of them.

Now, he struggled to sit up. 'Hugh – my friend – is he...?' He sank back on to the pillow.

'You mean Lieutenant Wilson? He's fine, making a good recovery. He's been asking about you.'

'Can I see him?'

'Later, Lieutenant. You're still very weak. You must get your strength up. We want you to be much improved by the time the ship docks.'

'I will be.' Simon's voice was stronger now, determined. He'd survived this far. 'How long till we dock?' he asked.

'A few days. Until then, you must rest.' She adjusted his pillow and smoothed the sheet.

He didn't feel like resting, his mind busy making plans. He'd go and see Dad first, of course, but then he'd be on his way to Oakleigh – and Rosemary. His eyes closed and he drifted off into a deep, dreamless sleep, proper sleep - the first he'd had since landing in Malaya all those years ago.

Chapter 31

September 1945

Simon often woke in pain but Nurse Janman was there with her pills and her swabs and gradually his strength returned. The swelling in his legs went down – a little. But the sores refused to heal. His hands were the main concern. The left one still bore the scars of years of ill treatment but was improving. But the broken fingers of the right had not healed properly. He had tried flexing his fingers, wincing at the agony which brought tears to his eyes. Each day he set about exercising them, determined that he would eventually be able to hold a pencil, a paintbrush, despite the misshapen crooked fingers.

Soon, he was able to get out of bed, crossing the cabin on unsteady legs, then later, walking out on deck relishing the cool air and the vastness of the ocean.

Hugh joined him and they strolled on deck, holding each other up and pushing themselves to stay up longer.

And then, one day – land.

'Nearly home,' Simon whispered.

'Nearly but....' Hugh paused. 'They won't let us go home until we're really fit. The state we're in - they think it'll be too much of a shock for our families to see us like this.'

'My father's a doctor. He'll be able to cope.'

'Good for you,' Hugh replied.

Simon didn't reply. But would Rosemary cope? How would she react to his scars, his misshapen hands? Could he expect her to accept him as he now was – no longer the upright handsome soldier she had met in the churchyard so long ago but a crippled skeletal figure.

There was a sudden bustle on board ship, orders shouted, deckhands rushing around and an air of excitement among the former prisoners.

Ambulances lined the quayside and the worst affected were loaded first. Simon and Hugh were among the last to disembark, proudly managing to walk unaided down to the waiting ambulance, albeit in a slow shuffle.

***

Simon lay in his bed at the far end of the ward looking out of the window, scarcely able to believe that he was home at last. Well, not quite home, he thought, but at least he was on British soil. He could just catch a glimpse of sea in the distance, grey and stormy, matching the sky. Autumn – his favourite season – more so since those years in the torrid humid atmosphere of Malaya and Burma.

He was still a long way from home but the doctors had told him he was making good progress, His hands lay outside the covers, the wounds healing but his fingers still stiff and painful. He tried to clench his fists, wincing at the stab of pain. Undaunted he flexed his fingers. He would persevere though. He had to be able to hold a pencil, a paintbrush.

One of the nurses had written on his behalf to his father. 'Is there anyone else you would like to contact?' she'd asked.

He'd shaken his head. He wasn't ready to write to Rosemary - what could he say? He'd promised to come back to St James's church and restore *the Doom* but would he ever be fit enough to keep that promise? He clenched his fists again, fighting the pain.

When he was completely fit, then he would go back. He held his hands up to his face, grimacing at the sight of his twisted, scarred fingers. He couldn't bear for her to see him like this. It wasn't just his hands. His legs and feet were in no better shape. He sometimes wondered how the nurses who looked after him could bear to look, much less touch them. At least his body was filling out after the years of starvation and he was finally able to eat fairly normally.

He heard someone enter the ward and kept his gaze on the window. More medication, more exercises.

A cough, and he turned his head, struggling to sit up. 'Dad!'

'Hello son, how are you?' Dr Spencer pulled a chair up, sat and leaned over to grasp Simon's hand, pulling back at the last minute. 'Sorry – they look painful.'

'Getting better though,' Simon said. 'I didn't think you'd come – Southampton's a long way from Suffolk.'

'I got the train. Driving's a nightmare these days, not to mention the shortage of petrol.' Dr Spencer ran a hand though his hair. 'Well, son, you're looking a lot better than I anticipated. The pictures on the newsreels are quite horrific. I didn't know what to expect.'

'The doctors and nurses have been wonderful – here and on the ship. I'm glad you didn't see me when we were first liberated. I've still got a long way to go though.'

'I spoke to the doctor in charge. He said you're almost ready to go home. I think me being a doctor and able to look after you, they will release you sooner.'

Simon didn't reply. He longed to be home but the thought of facing everybody terrified him – the pitying looks, the insensitive questions.

'It will be so good to have you home,' Dr Spencer said. 'I'm sure you're longing to catch up with friends.' He paused. 'I had a letter from that young lady – the Rector's daughter. She asked if you were on your way home. She wants to see you.'

Simon's heart leapt. It was so long since he'd heard from her that he wondered if he was foolish to hold on to the memory of their short acquaintance. It was good to hear that she wanted to see him. It was no good

though. He looked down again at his useless hands –
ugly, grotesque. He shook his head.

'I can't see her,' he said, lifting his hands from the
counterpane. 'Not like this.'

'If she's the sort of girl I think she is, from her
letters to me, your injuries won't make any difference.
At least give her a chance.'

'No Dad. I'm an artist – I was going to paint her
portrait, restore the wall painting in the church. It was
what I dreamt of in the camp. These hands are useless.
I won't even attempt to see her until I can pick up a
paint brush again.'

Dr Spencer gave up trying to persuade him and
turned the conversation to plans for his return home,
his rehabilitation.

Chapter 32

October 1945

Rosemary was in the hall checking for the post – nothing as usual. She turned to go into the kitchen just as the front door flew open and she was pulled into a hug. She gasped, almost uttered 'Simon' and stopped as a voice came in her ear. 'Aren't you going to say hello to your brother then?'

She wriggled out of his arms and turned to face him. 'Michael – is it really you? Why didn't you let us know you were coming?'

'No time. I managed to hitch a lift on one of those American lorries.' He grabbed her again, staring into her eyes. 'It's so good to see you, Sis.'

'When did you get back?' She shook her head. 'No, wait. You must see Father first – you can tell us all about it together.'

She dragged him long the passage to the Rector's study, throwing open the door and shouting, 'Surprise.'

Her father looked up from his book, blinking through his glasses. He stood up and came round the desk, pumping his son's hand and saying, 'Welcome home, son, welcome.'

'Let's go into the other room,' Rosemary said. 'More comfortable. We can have a drink, toast the prodigal son.'

They settled into the sitting room and Rosemary poured drinks. 'Sorry,' she said as she handed them round. 'You must be hungry – I'll get something...'

'Don't worry. The yanks fed me. Perhaps later. I need to get all your news and tell you mine.' Michael leaned back in the armchair and took a sip of his whisky, sighing with content. 'It's good to be home.'

With some coaxing he told them he had landed in Dover a few days ago and together with some men from his old unit had been taken to the barracks up near the castle. 'We all thought we would be on the first train home but we had to be de-briefed. Then there were medicals before we were sent to our old garrison just outside Norwich. Finally, we were given leave – only a short one, I'm afraid.' He sighed. 'I have to be back in two days' time.'

'So soon?' Rosemary interrupted. 'Surely they could have given you longer.'

'I was pronounced fit so have to go back – there's still a lot to be done over there.'

Rosemary had to admit he did look fairly fit. She didn't dare hope that Simon would be in a similar state – a forlorn hope from what Mrs Pargeter had told her.

'I was planning a welcome home party,' she said.

'We'll have a proper shindig when I get my discharge,' Michael said.

'Are you not planning to stay in the army then?' the Rector asked.

'I've had enough, Father. Don't worry, I'll find a job. I've even thought of teacher training.'

Rosemary wondered if his friendship with Jenny had influenced him. They had been quite close before the war. She'd better tell him about her friend's engagement to Robert Davis and hoped he wouldn't be upset.

He was delighted however and wished them well. He went on to ask about his other village friends so she told him that Percy and Maggie were married and had a little daughter – no need to tell him the details. He would hear about that soon enough from the village gossips when he finally returned to Oakleigh.

Now the three of them chatted animatedly about how they had coped during the long war years. Rosemary told him about the Red Cross parcels and how she had day-dreamed of him receiving one that she'd packed.

'I wish I'd known –that would have meant so much to me,' Michael said.

'We weren't allowed to put notes in the parcels or to mention our work with the Red Cross in our letters,' she said.

Her father had been very quiet and Rosemary noticed that his head was nodding, worn out by the emotion of his son's unexpected return. 'Come along to the kitchen,' she whispered to her brother. 'I'll fix you something to eat.'

'No Mrs Norton?' he asked.

She explained that the housekeeper had gone to live with her son in Norwich. 'She worked so hard, helping with the evacuees up at the manor as well as keeping house for us.'

'I suppose I'll have to get used to the changes,' he said. 'But it's so good to be home, even for such a short time.' He glanced at his father who was now dozing in the chair. 'Is he all right?' he asked.

'He gets tired but there's nothing really wrong. Let him rest.'

Michael followed her along the passage and offered to help prepare the food. 'We got quite domesticated in the camp,' he said with a laugh.

She refused his help and managed to put a meal together with the meagre contents of the larder. 'We thought rationing would stop when the war was over but things seem to be worse than ever,' she said.

'This is fine, Sis.' He scraped the remains off his plate and chewed appreciatively.

'Not exactly the fatted calf,' Rosemary said. 'But tomorrow we'll have a proper Sunday roast. We've killed one of the chickens – well, Amos did the deed. And we have plenty of vegetables from the garden.'

'I'll come to church in the morning – that'll please Father and then, after lunch I'll have to make tracks.'

'How will you get back? There's no buses on a Sunday.'

'I'll cadge a lift. People are always willing to pick up anyone in uniform.'

'No need. I'll ask Percy. He's still got the van and he seems to have plenty of petrol.'

'Fine. I'll pop over and have a word. I want to congratulate him on his marriage.'

'If he's not at the forge, he'll be in the pub,' Rosemary said.

Michael grinned. 'Maggie driven him to drink already?'

Rosemary slapped his arm. 'No, silly. He lives there - but they'll be moving in to Mrs Norton's old cottage soon.'

At church the following morning Rosemary could sense that Michael was embarrassed when their father publicly welcomed his son home and said a prayer of thanks. He did, however, include those yet to return in his prayers.

As the organ played the introduction to the last hymn, Rosemary whispered to her brother that she had to leave to see to the meal and she slipped out quietly.

She had left the chicken in the oven and only had to cook the vegetables. She guessed that Michael and her father would be detained by the villagers, many of whom had known her brother since he was a boy, all welcoming him home.

If only he didn't have to go back so soon.

***

Rosemary didn't know what to do with herself when Michael had left. It had been a hectic couple of days which had passed all too soon. Father was happy though and kept going over their conversations and speculating as to when they'd see him again.

All she could think about was Simon and wondering if she would ever see him again. His father had sent her a brief note saying that he was still very weak but getting better but she had heard nothing since then. She couldn't hep worrying that even now with the best doctors he might have succumbed to his various illnesses. But surely Dr Spencer write again.

A few days after Michel had left, she rushed to the door when she heard the letter fall onto the mat.

She gasped when she saw the Bury St Edmunds postmark. At last! She snatched the letter off the hall table, her spirits plummeting when she recognised Dr Spencer's handwriting. So, Simon wasn't home from the hospital yet.

Her hand shook as she tore open the envelope. It must be good news though, she told herself. She read quickly, smiling as the doctor told her Simon had been discharged from hospital and had returned home a couple of days ago. He was still weak and needed a long spell of convalescence at home.

Wonderful! She would check the buses and arrange to visit him. Her face fell at the next sentence. *I am sorry to say that Simon doesn't wish to see any of his friends at present. As you know, the POWs in the far east were very badly treated, no medical care at all. Simon's injuries are horrific – and permanent, although we are hoping for improvement over time. He feels that to see him like this would be too distressing for you and hopes you will understand.*

I don't care. I love him. I must see him, she thought. The twice weekly bus was due this afternoon. She would excuse herself from parcel duty and could be in Bury St Edmunds in a couple of hours.

She was still standing in the hall, the letter clasped in her hand when her father called from his study.

'Was that the post, Rosemary?'

She shook herself and managed to call. 'Nothing for you, Father.'

'I hoped to hear from Michael. It was madness to send him back to his unit so soon even if he was declared fit. He should have been given a longer leave.'

Rosemary walked up the passage feeling guilty that she hadn't given a thought to her brother, her mind so full of Simon. 'I've heard from Dr Spencer,' she said, showing him the letter.

'News of your artist friend?' he asked.

Rosemary told him about Simon's injuries and his reluctance for her to see him.

'Understandable,' the Rector said.

'But Father, when Master Sergeant Bowman was so badly burnt it didn't worry me. I helped change his dressings when the nurses were busy. I'm sure I could cope with whatever has happened to Simon.'

'But Simon doesn't know that, does he? Is he even aware of your friendship with the American?'

Rosemary shook her head. If she told him about Floyd he might get the wrong idea. 'I was thinking of going to see him anyway.'

'I don't think you should,' her father said gently. 'Why don't you reply to Dr Spencer - tell him about the crash and how you helped your friend? He might be able to change Simon's mind.'

'You're right. Thank you.' She smiled, thankful for her father's sensible advice and glad that she hadn't acted on her impulse to jump on a bus and visit Simon. 'I'll go and write that letter now,' she said.

***

Two weeks later Rosemary still hadn't been to see Simon. She was getting impatient but deep down she had a feeling he had another reason for putting her off. After all, they didn't really know each other and it had been years. They had both changed of course but even so, she could not forget that instant attraction at their first meeting and then, when she had seen him again, the confirmation that it had indeed been love at first sight. He had felt the same, she was sure of it.

260

She had written and told him about her care for the injured American, saying she had discovered a flair for nursing.

He had answered a week later and it was obvious from the painful scrawl that it had been difficult for him. He had said that he was determined to wait until he was completely fit before coming to see her. Perhaps she was being unreasonable but surely if he felt the same about her, he would want to see her as soon as possible.

She decided to meet Jenny from school and talk things over with her friend. She walked through the village, smiling and waving to the children who poured out of the school gate on their way home. The playground was empty by the time she arrived but the main door was still open.

She went in, calling out to her friend. 'It's only me. Hope you've got time for a chat.'

The office door opened and Robert Davis came out, straightening his tie and running his hands though his hair.

'Is Jenny still here?' Rosemary asked.

As she spoke Jenny appeared, looking a little flushed. 'Rosemary, good to see you,' she said. 'Come in. Robert and I have been discussing wedding plans.'

Rosemary felt a little embarrassed. They didn't look as if wedding plans had been the main thing on their minds. 'I don't want to interrupt. Perhaps you could call at the Rectory later on,' she said.

Jenny glanced at Robert and he said, 'Come in and sit down. You are included in our plans after all.'

Rosemary followed them into the office and Jenny, her face flushed with excitement, said, 'We want to get married at Christmas. We don't want a big fuss though.'

'You'll have to speak to my father about dates.'

'We will. But I want you to be bridesmaid.'

'Of course – I was counting on you asking me. I'm looking forward to it.' Rosemary tried to sound enthusiastic but she had hoped that her wedding to

Simon would be the first in St James's church since before the war. A foolish dream when he was still refusing to see her. She tried to concentrate on her friend as she spoke of dresses and flowers and bridesmaids.

Jenny seemed to sense Rosemary's inattention and she said, 'Forgive me for going on about my plans. It's just that I'm so happy – I can't think of anything else at the moment.' She reached out and took Rosemary's hand. 'I should have asked how you were and if there's any further news...'

Rosemary's smile was tearful and she shook her head. 'He doesn't want to see me.'

'Oh, Rosie -why?'

'His father explained.' She turned to Robert. 'I told you about his injuries, how hard he's finding it.'

Robert nodded. 'I understand. I would probably feel the same in his shoes. He fears being a burden to you.'

'Never! Never a burden.' The tears began to fall and Jenny did her best to comfort her.

Robert stood up and went into the little kitchen at the side of his office. Rosemary was grateful for his tact but she made an effort to dry her eyes. 'I'm being silly,' she said with a sniff. 'But it's this uncertainty that's killing me. His few letters were so sweet. He never actually said...' She paused and wiped her eyes again. 'But the tone of them - I was sure he felt the same way as me.'

'I don't know what to say, Rosie. Your situation is so complicated.'

'I shouldn't be burdening you with my problems. You've found your love and you're happy – and I'm happy for you.'

'It took long enough,' Jenny said with a laugh. 'It kind of crept up on us.'

Robert came back holding a tray with cups and saucers. 'Tea – the universal cure for all ills,' he said.

They all laughed and Rosemary wiped her eyes for a final time, grateful for her friends. As she left them and started back to the Rectory, she made up her mind. She wouldn't wait for an invitation. He would catch the early bus to Bury tomorrow and insist on seeing Simon.

***

Rosemary woke to a dull and windy autumn day. Most of the leaves had been stripped from the trees and lay in gold and red drifts across the garden. She didn't care about the weather and she wanted to look her best for Simon so she decided to wear the blue summer dress she'd had on the first time she saw him. She brushed her curls until they shone and applied a smidgen of pink lipstick. That would do. She didn't want to overdo it.

A patterned silk headscarf would keep her curls tidy when she went out into the wind and the navy-blue costume jacket would keep the chill off. Satisfied, she stepped outside, calling a goodbye to her father who, as usual, was closeted in his study.

There was plenty of time before the bus was due and she decided to pop into the church for a quick prayer.

She opened the door and stepped down into the main aisle. On a sunny day the stained-glass windows threw multi-coloured patterns onto the floor. But today the church was in shadow, almost too dark to see her way to the altar.

Halfway down the aisle she saw movement and she paused, not expecting to see anyone. Perhaps Amos had come in to replenish the candles. She almost called out but she didn't want to disturb him so she turned to go.

Something stopped her – a shadow, a noise? She took two more steps, gasping as she spotted a figure seated on the end of the front pew. Her heart began to beat faster and she held her breath. Could it be?

He was sitting where he'd been all those years ago, pencil in hand, sketchbook on his knee. He hadn't really changed, a few streaks of grey in the dark hair, a few lines in his face and so thin.

'Simon,' she breathed, and ran towards him.

He heard her and stood up, the sketchbook falling to the floor.

'Rosemary, darling.' His voice was husky and he reached for the walking stick leaning against the pew before stumbling towards her.

'Simon, is it really you?' Rosemary, tears pouring down her cheeks, reached for him. He dropped the stick and his arms came round her.

'I've waited so long for this moment,' he murmured.

The kiss was sweet and tender, deepening to scarcely controlled passion. It seemed aeons before he let her go.

He laughed shakily. 'Sorry, darling. I have to sit down. The poor old legs...'

Rosemary helped him to a seat and sat beside him. 'I thought it was your hands that were hurt,' she said.

'Hands, feet, legs – you name it.' He laughed shakily. 'You see before you the ghost of a man.' He coughed and muttered hoarsely, 'Scarcely a man at all.'

'Simon, my love. You are all the man I want.' She took his hand, biting her lip to suppress the gasp at the sight of the scarred and misshapen fingers. She held his hand to her lips recalling Floyd's blistered hands and how she had managed to disguise her horror at the sight. She'd done it before, she could do it again – this time with love.

'Can you bear it, darling?' he asked.

She nodded.

'You haven't seen the worst of it,' he said. 'I wanted to ask you to marry me – but I can't. I need to get fit first.'

Rosemary was about to protest but she had to find the right words to convince hm.

'Simon, listen to me. Suppose we'd been married before you went abroad? In sickness and in health is the vow we'd have made. There must be hundreds of women welcoming their husbands home – many in a worse state than you. Are they going to abandon the men they love?'

Simon was silent for a moment then, with a sigh, he bent and picked up the fallen sketchpad. 'At least I can hold a pencil now,' he said, showing her the drawing he'd started. 'Not bad for a first attempt. A long way to go yet.'

'You'll get there, my love.' She looked at her watch. 'Looks like I've missed my bus.'

'Were you going somewhere?' he asked.

'Bury St Edmunds,' she said with a grin. 'I wasn't prepared to give up on you.'

'And I won't give up either. I'll keep exercising, do what the doctor ordered and one day...'

'One day soon,' Rosemary interrupted. 'I can't wait.'

He drew her into his arms again and she gave herself up to his embrace.

As they drew apart a ray of sunshine pierced the east window and flooded the church with light. Rosemary handed Simon his stick and arms entwined, they walked towards the door.

It was almost a repeat of their first meeting but this time it was so much more.

'The next time we walk down this aisle together it will be as man and wife – and without this,' he said, waving the walking stick. 'But first I have to go and see your father.'

December 1945

The Rev. Seth Turner had no hesitation in approving his beloved daughter's marriage to Simon Spencer. But theirs was not the first post-war wedding to be held in Oakleigh St James's church. She was a little disappointed but at the same time delighted that she would be bridesmaid at her best friend's wedding. Jenny and Robert were to be married a few days before Christmas.

'You do understand why I want to wait, don't you darling?' Simon said, after his talk with her father. 'I am just as impatient as you are but I am determined to walk up the aisle without this.' He banged his walking stick on the ground. 'And I want to be sure that when I put the ring on your finger I don't fumble and drop the blessed thing.'

Rosemary kissed his cheek. 'I do understand,' she had assured him. Truthfully, she couldn't wait, but her sensible head said it was probably for the best. They would have more time to get to know each other properly and to plan their future. She would be happy with a spring wedding.

It had been a wonderful couple of months as, careless of the winter weather, they took long walks in the woods, talking endlessly about the future. On really cold wet days, Rosemary would sit in the church watching as Simon made endless sketches. His hands were improving daily and she was thrilled when one day he showed her a meticulous drawing of the decorated stonework around one of the pillars.

'It's wonderful,' she said. 'You must be pleased with that one.'

'An artist is never entirely satisfied with his work but – yes, I admit, I'm pleased.' He took a deep breath. 'I think I'm ready.'

Rosemary quelled the little skip of her heart. He wasn't talking about the wedding. She glanced up at the *'The Doom.'* Since Simon's first glimpse of the wall painting so long ago, time and weather had caused more deterioration.

'You still want to do it?' she asked.

'It's what I dreamt of while I was in the camp.'

Simon rarely mentioned his wartime experiences, although he kept in touch with Hugh and was delighted when his friend reported that he was sure to be fit enough by then to travel to Oakleigh and take his place as Simon's best man in the spring.

Chapter 33

December 1945

After weeks of ceaseless rain, the day of Jenny's wedding dawned frosty and bright. Her parents had travelled from Somerset so that her father could give her away and had stayed overnight at the *Four Bells*.

A proper wedding dress was out of the question as clothing was still rationed, and Jenny had prettied up a light summer frock with a lace collar and cuffs, and made a head dress of artificial flowers. It was a cold day but Betty Rook had lent her a little silver-grey faux fur jacket which perfectly set off the dress.

'You look lovely,' Rosemary said as she helped her friend to get ready.

'Good job I'm good at needlework,' Jenny said with a little laugh.

Rosemary agreed. 'You'll have to help me with mine,' she said.

Jenny's father knocked on the door and cautiously opened it. 'It's time, love,' he said.

It was a short walk to the church where Robert Davis and his brother were waiting. As Rosemary followed her friend down the aisle her eyes sought for Simon and her heart leapt as she saw him at the back leaning on his stick beside his father. Thank goodness he hadn't had to get the bus from Bury St Edmunds. Dr Spencer had promised that if he was free, he would drive Simon to her friend's wedding. She was pleased that hospital and surgery duties hadn't stopped them from coming.

As the service progressed, Rosemary's mind wandered and she pictured herself standing there at Simon's side.

The service ended and bride and groom, together with friends and well-wishers, gathered outside for photographs.

Maggie nudged Rosemary. 'I've got to go and help Mum with the food. She's probably struggling, especially having to keep an eye on Daisy.'

'I'll tell Jenny.' Photographs done, the party made their way across to the *Four Bells* where soon everyone was laughing and talking and enjoying the buffet lunch prepared by Maggie and her mother.

'Your turn next,' Jenny said, clinking glasses with Rosemary.

'We haven't even set a date yet.' Jenny knew why. She looked across at Simon who was chatting to the Rector. 'He's looking so much better. He won't keep you waiting long.'

'I hope so. He's just so determined to walk up the aisle without that stick.'

At that moment Dr Spencer joined them. 'You look lovely, Miss Blackwell – sorry, Mrs Davis.'

They all laughed. 'I expect it will take some getting used to especially for the school children,' said Jenny. She looked across at Simon. 'Your son's looking well.'

'Yes, he's done amazingly. When you think what he's gone through...' He smiled and turned to Rosemary. 'I'm surprised he's not bitter but I think it's all down to you. He wants to put the past behind him.'

'I'm so proud of him. He's been so brave,' Rosemary said.

'Has he told you?' Dr Spencer asked.

She shook her head. 'Told me what?'

'He doesn't need the walking stick anymore.'

'But he...' She nodded to where he stood, leaning heavily on the stick.

'He brought it today as he knew he'd be standing a lot and he still gets very tired. But he's been walking every day, mostly in the abbey grounds. He was so determined to get well.'

Rosemary, put her drink down and gave the doctor a hug. 'I'm so pleased – and relieved. And I had nothing to do with it. I'm sure it's down to your excellent care. Thank you.'

The doctor pushed her gently away. 'Go and talk to him. I have a feeling I know what he's discussing with your father.'

They set the date for the second week in February. 'Get Christmas and new year over first,' the Rector said.

'Yes, and hopefully the rationing situation will have eased a bit and you can have a proper cake,' Jenny said. 'I'm grateful for the spread Maggie and her family have managed for us but you deserve a proper wedding breakfast.'

Chapter 34

February 1946

The new year had come in with bitter cold and strong winds but by February, although it had become milder, there was incessant rain.

'I do hope it improves by next week,' Rosemary said, looking out of the kitchen window. 'Perhaps we should have waited till spring.'

'It doesn't matter what the weather's like. It will be a beautiful day.' Jenny, who had popped in after school to help Rosemary with the trimmings on her dress, said cheerfully.

'It's all right for you,' Rosemary said. 'It was a lovely day for you and Robert.'

'And it will be for you too, I promise.'

Rosemary grinned. 'Have you had a word with Him, then?' she asked, pointing heavenwards. Truthfully, she wasn't worried about the weather. Although it was only a short walk from the Rectory to the church, Dr Spencer had promised to drive her in his Wolesley. As a doctor, he was never short of petrol which was still rationed. And anyway, what was a little rain so long as he and Simon were together at last?

Food for their guests was another worry though as, despite the end of the war, more goods were coming on ration. Rosemary hadn't been unduly concerned as she and Simon had agreed that it would be just a small affair with close friends as neither of them had big families. Besides, it would be hard for him as, although he was gradually putting on weight and no longer relying on the walking stick, he was still not back to full fitness and he was still sensitive about people seeing him. She no longer even noticed his deformed fingers which were much improved since he had got home from Singapore. As long as he could hold a pencil and paintbrush, he was happy and that made her happy too.

Her friends had talked her out of having a small affair and even Mrs Pargeter insisted she should have a grand wedding. She offered the Manor for the reception and had invited Simon and his father to stay there the day before to save them a long drive from Bury on the day. 'And don't you worry about a thing,' she'd said. 'All your friends and neighbours will rally round. It's all organised.'

Rosemary could only thank her and be grateful that Mrs P was such a good organiser as she had proved over the past few years.

On the day, Rosemary woke with butterflies in her stomach. The door opened and Betty Rook came in carrying a cup of tea. 'Here, Rosie dear. Sit up and drink this, and I'll run you a bath. I've made sure there's plenty of hot water.'

Rosemary rubbed her eyes. 'What are you doing here?' she asked.

'Mrs P's given me the day off to lend a hand. Can't expect you to make breakfast for you and your dad on your wedding day and Jenny will be here soon too. Lots to do before we leave for church.' She crossed the room and drew back the curtains. 'Well, can you believe it, the rain's stopped.' She turned a smiling face to Rosemary. 'And I do believe I caught a little glimpse of blue sky.'

Rosemary finished her tea and swung her legs out of bed. 'It's good of you to help, Betty.'

'We – all your friends – just want to make this the best day for you.'

'I appreciate it. Oh, dear, I don't know where to start.' She looked at the dress hanging on the outside of the wardrobe – not a proper wedding dress, of course. They had got used to making do over the past years but it would have been nice to have something new. She shook her head. It didn't matter. By the end of the day, she would be Simon's wife – a dream come true.

Jenny arrived just as Rosemary finished her bath, and Betty went downstairs to start on breakfast. Rosemary, in her dressing gown, declared she couldn't eat a thing but managed a small piece of toast. Her father also seemed to be having difficulty. He kept looking at his daughter, a big smile on his face.

'I am so happy for you, my dear,' he said. 'Simon is a fine young man.'

He put his cup down and stood up, coming around the table and leaning down to kiss her cheek. 'I'm going over to the church now to put my vestments on. You won't be late will you, dear,' he said with a twinkle in his eye.

Jenny laughed. 'As if...'

Rosemary grinned. 'Father's looking so much more his old self these days.'

'How nice for you to have him take the service. I thought he would give you away.'

'No. He insisted that he officiate. He would have had to get a curate from Norwich but he didn't like the idea of someone I didn't know doing the service.'

'So, Percy's going to give you away then?' Jenny frowned. 'I know he's an old friend but...'

'Well, we were hoping Michael would get leave.'

'I don't understand him going back to his regiment after all those years as a POW.'

'He had no choice – he's still in the Army and they passed him fit so...' Rosemary was still disappointed. When she'd heard that her brother would not be able to get home for the wedding, she had tried to persuade her father to get another priest to perform the ceremony. She had always dreamed of walking down the aisle on her father's arm.

But the Rector had said, 'There's no time. Besides, I still hope that Michael might be able to get here.'

Rosemary looked at the clock. No chance of him turning up now. She sighed. 'Better start getting ready,' she said.

Leaving Betty to clear away the breakfast things, the friends went upstairs.

Jenny had done Rosemary's hair, twisting up into a coronet and leaving little curls to fall down either side of her face. Setting the head dress of artificial roses in place, Jenny said, 'Oh, Rosie that looks lovely. Now for your make-up.'

'Don't overdo it, please. Just a little powder and lipstick. I want Simon to see the real me.'

She was just putting on the dress when there was a knock at the door and Betty called. 'Are you decent? There's someone to see you.'

'No – not Simon. He mustn't see me,' Rosemary cried, snatching up a towel.

'Don't worry, love. I think you'll want to see this young man. I'll let him in, shall I?'

The door opened and Rosemary let out a squeal. 'Michael. You made it.' She threw herself into her brother's arms, hugging as if she would never let him go. 'I'm so pleased you're here.'

'I nearly didn't get here on time but...' He glanced at his watch.

'Loads of time. Besides, I'm nearly ready.'

'I'll wait downstairs,' he said.

'I do hope Percy's not upset that he's been done out of a job,' Rosemary said, smoothing down her dress and picking up the bouquet of roses Mrs Pargeter had sent from the Manor hothouse.

'He'll be fine. Don't worry.' Jenny reassured her.

Michael, tall and handsome in his army uniform, waited at the foot of the stairs. The front door was open and Rosemary could hear the church bells pealing. Amos was in his element, she thought. Dr Spencer's Wolseley waited in the drive and the doctor opened the passenger door and handed her in.

Michael climbed in beside her. 'It will be good to see my old friend today – especially as he's marrying my sister. I never dreamt when you wrote to me that you had met him all those years ago.'

'I hardly dare dream of it myself,' Rosemary said.

The car stopped and Dr Spencer got out, holding the door open for them. Michael took Rosemary's arm and they started up the path.

'I'll follow you in.' He smiled. 'Don't worry – he's here. I dropped him off a few minutes ago,' the doctor said.

Percy was standing in the porch, looking very smart in the suit he had worn for his marriage to Maggie. Rosemary whispered a 'sorry' but he shook his head. 'I'm right pleased made it.'

The organ started up and the choir began to sing and Rosemary, clutching Michael's arm, walked up the aisle towards the altar, her heart overflowing with happiness at the sight of Simon, standing without the aid of a walking sick. Best man Hugh was at his side, and her father in his robes, smiled widely as he spoke the familiar words. 'Dearly beloved, we are gathered here...'

The ring slid on to her finger perfectly with no fumbling, despite Simon's distorted fingers. Rosemary gave him a radiant smile. She knew he had been nervous of dropping it.

The rest of the service passed in a blur and before she knew it, they were standing in the porch greeting the many friends from the village who waited outside. The bells rang out once more, the children from Jenny's school threw home-made confetti. And churchgoers and pub regulars joined in calling good wishes to the happy couple. There were even a few Americans from the base among the crowd.

Back at the Manor, Rosemary was properly introduced to Hugh, whom she had met for the first time today. As she shook hands with him, she became aware of the scars which told her he had suffered as much as his friend, as all who had been in that dreadful place had suffered. She shook the thought away, determined to let nothing spoil this special day. But deep down she knew that the mental scars would take much longer to fade and she determined that she would do her best to help Simon overcome them.

Epilogue

Eighteen months later

Rosemary walked down the lane to the village shop, her steps slower than usual as she felt the movement of the baby who was due in a couple of months. She tenderly caressed the bump. She was so happy. Her only worry now was the health of her father. The Rev Turner was becoming increasingly frail, although he continued to hold services and visit the sick and poor of the village. She and Simon had agreed that they would stay on at the Rectory to look after him.

Simon's health had improved too. He had sold a few of his paintings and now was happy to be able to call himself an artist. He had added to the collection of sketches made during his incarceration in Changi and while working on the Burma railway. Rosemary, despite his protests had shown them to Colonel Pargeter and his wife and both had been very impressed.

'They should have a wider audience,' the Colonel had said. 'Perhaps you could publish them in a book.'

'I don't think they're good enough. Some of these were done when I could hardly hold a pencil,' Simon protested.

Hugh, who had joined the couple for dinner at the Manor, over-rode his protestations. 'I seem to remember you saying that the world should know what went on out there.' He turned to the Colonel. 'Simon risked a lot to hide his sketchbook and to make sure he brought it home.'

Simon finally gave in and Hugh was now negotiating with a local publisher. The book was due out in a few weeks and Rosemary was so proud. She was happier than she had ever been and today, with the sun shining and the fields around the village heavy with golden grain, she felt the need to say a prayer of thanksgiving.

She pushed open the church door and stepped down into the nave. Sunshine flooded the interior, the stained glass throwing multi-coloured patterns onto the floor. Blinking against the brightness, Rosemary gazed around, catching her breath as she saw a figure atop a ladder in the side aisle.

'Simon – what are you up to?' she called.

He turned towards her, a paintbrush in his hand. 'What does it look like?' he said with a grin. 'I got the commission.'

'The commission - really? Why didn't you tell me?'

'I didn't think I'd get it.' He flexed the hand holding the brush. 'The powers that be weren't sure I was up to it.'

'Did Father know?'

'Of course. He spoke up for me with the church people.'

'He didn't tell me.'

'I asked him to keep it quiet – just in case. Didn't want you to be disappointed.' He balanced the brush on the ladder and stepped down. 'Come and have a look. There's a long way to go but I've made a start.' He put his arms around her and she lifted her face for a kiss.

'Oh, Simon. I'm so proud of you.' She looked up at the *'Doom'*. 'It's going to look wonderful.'

They stood together, arms entwined looking up at the medieval painting, picturing how it would be, restored to its original colours, the lettering readable once more.

Rosemary gave a contented sigh. Who would have dreamt on that spring day so long ago when she had first caught sight of the man she had fallen in love with, that after all they had gone through, they would now be standing here in the church where it all began - husband and wife with a little one on the way?

The End

After 22 years of handling other people's books while working as a library assistant Roberta Grieve decided it was time to fulfil a long-held ambition and start writing her own books. Her first novel was published in 2008 and since then she has had 19 novels and 6 novellas published. The Rector's Daughter is her 16th novel for Books We Love.

Roberta moved to a small village in Norfolk three years ago and became involved in the local history group. This has provided inspiration and an exciting new setting for her latest books.

Facebook page: RobertaGrievewriter

Roberta Grieve books also published by BWL Publishing

Abigail's Secret
On Wings of Song
Threads of Silk
Full Circle
Song of Memories
Divided Loyalty
Farewell Innocence
More Precious than Jewels
Madeleine's Enterprise
Daisy's War
Sylvia's Secret
Bishops' Peace
Finding Katy
Flora's Flight
A Place to Call Home
The Rector's Daughter